FIVE SOUTH

A DR. STUART MYSTERY

STEVE SKINNER

Five South

ISBN: 978-1-09832-697-5

ISBN eBook: 978-1-0983-269-2

To Marilyn
My editor, my critic, my Bunches

ACKNOWLEDGEMENTS

Without James Gaynor, poet laureate of the Skinner family and still my best man, this would never have come to fruition. Jim has been my coach, my teacher, my editor, and my support. So many thanks for your help and your patience. Marilyn, my wife, has been so incredibly patient and helpful during the preparation of this book. We've had fun on the ride. Special thanks to Ellen Young for her expert help on all things Filipino.

PREFACE

When I started medical school, most of my classmates had idealistic concepts of the health care system. It was all about taking care of people. We saw doctors and nurses as unselfish warriors in the battle against disease and death. Even now, most of those on the front lines of health care delivery still maintain that focus on the health and welfare of the patient.

Modern medicine is big business, very big business. As such, professionals trained in management and finance are required to direct the apparatus of the health care business behemoth.

Curiously, the clinical side and the business side of the health care system exist in parallel with very little cross-over. Each has its own priorities, its own measures of success or failure, its own ethics and standards. The reality of the two parallel worlds provides fertile ground where mischief can grow. The health care system is the real villain in this book.

This is a work of fiction. One character is clearly inspired by the scrappy little nurse to whom I have been married for half a century. All of the other characters exist only in my imagination. They are not intended to be nor do they resemble any real persons.

ONE

THE OPERATING ROOM always felt cold at 2 A.M. Keith Grant couldn't count the number of times he had been in the surgical suite at that hour. It didn't matter if it was February in Boston or September in San Francisco. It always felt cold in the operating room at 2 A.M.

The rest of the hospital was asleep. Patients were tucked into bed and nurses sat at desks catching up on records. The floors were all shined and supplies stored away. Even the chaos in the emergency room had subsided by then. Only the lights of a single operating room shined.

Surgery at 2 A.M., like all the others that Keith had experienced from medical school to his last year as chief resident in orthopedics, meant that something terrible had happened to someone. Usually it had been a trauma, a car accident or a shooting. Something that couldn't wait. A situation where life or limb depended upon emergency surgery.

The staff was used to this. Surgical nurses and operating room technicians knew what to do. Young surgical residents were toughened by nights like this. Everyone knew his or her job and could perform it with skill. Yet nobody was happy. And everyone felt cold.

Tonight it was a young woman who had undergone elective knee surgery four days earlier. She appeared in the emergency room at eleven at night with a high fever and a knee hot and swollen with infection. The infection had to be cleaned up immediately.

"Damn, damn, damn, damn," said the junior resident when Keith made the incision into the knee.

A torrent of yellow pus poured out onto the operating table.

The junior resident stood back in disgust. "Damn."

Keith reached for a surgical sponge and mopped up the mess. "Quit swearing and start sucking, Mike."

Mike grabbed a stout tube and began to suck up the pus that poured out of the knee.

"Jesus, Keith, you're the chief resident and you're still up all night cleaning up somebody else's messes. I'm only a third year and I was hoping that life would get easier by the time I was chief."

Keith ignored Mike and continued to work on the knee. He enlarged the incision, removed large clots of thick pus and bits of cartilage.

"And where the hell is the hotshot professor, the famous sports medicine surgeon who created this calamity?" Mike continued. "Home in bed, blissfully unaware that his operation has turned to shit in the middle of the night."

"Shut up, Mike, and keep sucking," Keith said. "And let's get the saline irrigation up now. I want at least six liters to start."

The surgical technician and the circulating nurse handed Keith a mechanical pulse irrigation machine, a kind of high powered surgical squirt gun to clean out the loose pus and debris.

Before he began to wash out the joint, Keith asked "Did we get the cultures sent off to the lab?"

"Oh yeah," replied the nurse, "great gobs of pus full of bugs are on their way."

"This knee is ruined, man," Mike said. "Just look at the mess that used to be a joint. We're gonna be up all night working on this damn thing and it's still gonna turn out lousy."

Keith did his best, but the knee was destroyed, that was certain. But Keith couldn't just look at the knee. The young patient's life had just taken a major turn for the worse.

♠ ♠ ♠

"Wee-oo-weet! Wee-oo-weet!"

The gentle, insistent chirp of a small bird broke the morning silence in the apartment.

Not already, Keith thought. He rolled over in his bed.

"Wee-oo-weet! Wee-oo-weet!"

It can't be time yet.

"Wee-oo-weet! Wee-oo-weet!"

She's just not going to let me sleep. If Baby had a bigger brain, he was sure that she would be more understanding.

Wearily, Dr. Keith Grant tossed aside the covers and got out of bed.

"Okay, Baby, you win," said Keith. He stretched his arms, trunk and legs to his full six feet, rubbed his grey eyes, then removed the colorful blanket from the birdcage. Baby, a cheerful yellow parakeet, hopped from her swing to a perch.

"Wee-oo-weet," chirped Baby.

"Wee-oo-weet," whistled Keith in reply. He pressed his nose between the rungs of the cage and Baby pecked gently with her beak.

"Bird kisses to start the morning. Not bad."

Keith opened the cage door and Baby flew out, finding a familiar perch on the curtain rod. The view out the window was not a particularly inspiring, even for a parakeet. Through the overcast, cold San Francisco morning, the window faced only other houses in the outer Sunset district, lots of squarish stucco houses and apartments painted in pastels. One could see neither the sunset nor the ocean from his apartment.

Wearily he put on a pot of coffee, then started on cleaning the birdcage. Clean paper towels. Get the poop off the perches and swings. Fresh seed and water. Going through the motions of the morning bird routine. Every muscle ached and he yearned to go back to sleep. He felt like he had played every down of a football game the night before.

Keith and Baby were the only tenants in the apartment. They were like family, the closest friends each had in the world. They conversed comfortably, although he was pretty sure that neither quite understood what the other was saying.

He wiped the cage with a paper towel. "God, Baby, that poor woman's knee was a mess, I'll tell you. Full of pus and debris. And all from a routine arthroscopic procedure. A routine operation. Done by an excellent surgeon. It just doesn't make sense."

"Wee-oo-weet," chirped Baby from the curtain rod.

"Yeah, well, that young lady may well have run her last marathon," he continued. "And to think that this was the third infected arthroscopic operation in a month. I don't understand what is going on."

"Wee-oo-weet."

He poured his second cup of coffee dressed only in a towel after his shower. He was tall and muscular and looked every bit the former college football player. His light brown hair was disheveled from the shower. Baby had flown back into her cage and was happily munching birdseed.

"You know," he said, "if it wasn't for little nurse Mary DeGuzman, I'd probably skip Mass and go back to bed. It's my day off, you know. I haven't met too many girls as a resident, with all the hours I have to work, but there is something very special about this little Filipino pixie."

Baby continued to pick through seeds. Keith wondered briefly if the bird could actually distinguish one seed from another.

"Yeah, I can tell you're interested," he said. "Well, you seem to like her well enough."

♦ ♦ ♦

Keith saw Mary from half a block away. Something in his chest tightened a little, gently, like a hug around his heart. It was a good feeling. She was waiting on the steps outside St. Anne's when Keith drove up on his Harley Davidson Heritage Softail. He was able to squeeze into a partial parking place right in front of the church, one of the many advantages of riding a motorcycle in San Francisco. Removing his helmet, Keith rubbed his sleeve over a barely discernable smudge on the crimson and cream bike, a gesture of love for a cherished possession.

"For a guy who spends all his time fixing broken bones, one would think you'd have more sense than to ride a motorcycle," said Mary, a tiny Filipino girl with long black hair and a mischievous bright smile.

"For a nurse who is not much bigger than her pediatric patients, one would think that you'd be more respectful to the doctors," he replied.

"I respect the doctors who are smart enough to drive cars instead of motorcycles," Mary said.

"But you never meet those doctors because they can't find a place to park in this city," he said. "And besides, everybody knows that men who ride motorcycles are sexier."

"Is that so?"

"Seems to work for me when it comes to you."

"Maybe I'm just good at overlooking your faults."

Mary gave him a hug and a quick peck of a kiss when he put his arm around her. Keith thought that she was a good fit in his arm and didn't care that he was a full foot taller than she. He took a deep breath, reveling in the smell of her long black hair. He knew that he would probably be paying more attention to her than to the priest for the next hour. The sight and sound of Mary would keep him awake and alert.

As was their custom, Keith and Mary went to a small restaurant not far from Ocean Beach for brunch after Mass. The Sunday treat was Belgian waffles. Keith ordered another cup of coffee, his third that morning.

"Tough night on call?" Mary asked.

"Yeah, awful thing," Keith said. "A young woman, marathon runner, with a horribly infected knee after surgery four days ago. We were up pretty much all night. I got about two hours of sleep."

"Don't they do most of those surgeries with the arthroscope?" asked Mary. "I thought that infections were pretty rare when you do the surgery that way."

"They're supposed to be so rare as to be negligible, like less than one percent." He felt the warmth of the coffee cup in his hands. "There aren't big incisions with arthroscopy, just a couple of little cuts, like little stab wounds. Patients are supposed to recover quickly."

"What happened?"

"The infection in her knee was so bad that we had to make a great big incision to clean out all the pus and junk. She had infection in every corner of the joint. We actually left a big drain in the knee with another tube to run antibiotic solution into the joint."

"That poor woman."

"My heart goes out to her. She's never going to have a good knee again."

"Why did she get infected?" Mary asked.

"I have no idea," said Keith. "But this is the third infected joint after arthroscopic surgery this month. The other two were with MRSA."

Mary set her fork down on the table. "Methicillin Resistant Staph Aureus? The original superbug?"

"Yep."

"Doesn't that mean the she got infected in the hospital?"

"Yep again."

"Who did the original surgery? Not you, I hope."

Keith smiled. As the chief resident in orthopedics at Sutro State University Hospital, he had his own clinic and patients. He had learned by now that in medicine things don't always go according to plan. And if you did surgery, you would get at least some complications. When things went wrong with his own operations, he felt terrible.

"No, I didn't do the original surgery."

"That's good. The other time that one of your operations didn't do well, you beat yourself up with guilt."

"I just, well, feel bad for this young woman," he said. "She went into surgery with high expectations of a return to a happy and vigorous life. Now she's going to have a lifetime of misery with this knee. Her whole life changed and nobody saw it coming."

"I'm glad you care. That's one of the things I like best about you," she said. "Whose case was this?"

"The woman from last night and both of the other infected arthroscopies patients were operated on by the famous and distinguished Dr. Alexander Warren."

"Not so famous. I never heard of him."

"He doesn't take care of kids, so you don't know him. He's head of sports medicine and vice chairman of our department. He's pretty famous as an expert in sports injuries. He was the team doctor for a bunch of professional teams."

"Maybe he should do a better job of washing his hands."

"Actually, he's a very meticulous surgeon. His skills in the operating room are exceptional. And he knows it."

"You mean he's one of those surgeons who thinks he's God? I'm familiar with that sort of surgeon."

"Dr. Warren doesn't think he's God. God doesn't have as skilled hands as Warren."

"Will he be as upset about this complication as you were with yours?"

"I doubt it," he said.

"Will he be as bothered by the future outlook for this woman as you are right now?"

"Let's just say that Dr. Warren will probably be more upset with the damage to his reputation than the damage to this woman's knee."

"Will he blame this on the residents? Will he blame you?"

"He can't blame me. I wasn't there when the original operation was done. I just tried to salvage something last night. He may try to blame the residents who assisted him. I don't know."

Keith took another sip of coffee and savored a bite of waffle. One of the benefits of Sunday brunch with Mary was that he could relax and enjoy his food. Normally, like most residents he rushed through meals without tasting much of anything, never knowing when he would be interrupted. He just wanted to relax, forget the horrors of the last night and look at Mary's sparkling black eyes.

Keith was relieved when she changed the subject.

"You have the whole day off," she said. "How about if we go down near Half Moon Bay and play in the tide pools? I checked and there is a great low tide this afternoon."

He laughed. "That sounds like a great way to escape from work. We can pet some starfish and freeze our asses off by the waters of the Pacific."

"And, when I get cold you can hug me and warm me up."

"So that's your plan," he said. "A scheme to get more hugs."

"And a cup of hot cocoa at that little place near the docks where the fishing boats come in."

"And maybe dinner at the Moss Beach Distillery?"

"If you insist," she said, "but we're dropping your motorcycle off at your apartment. I'm not riding down the coast on that damn thing. We'll take my car."

◆ ◆ ◆

As usual, traffic on the Golden Gate Bridge was complete gridlock. Dr. Richard Phillips pounded the steering wheel and cursed. It's just not fair, he thought. He had been the smartest student in medical school, had acquired the most academic honors. He selected the most noble specialty, internal medicine. As a reward, here he was, stuck with this hellish commute across this horrible bridge. Meanwhile the jocks and the dummies from medical school went into surgery. They lived comfortably in fancy houses in the City, houses he could not afford. The surgeons got all the money in health care, not the true doctors, the smart ones like him. And they got the nice houses and the nice cars. Phillips ground his teeth and struck the dashboard of his Buick, angry that he was not driving a Mercedes Benz. The commute to and from work every day was the same.

Dr. Phillips was highly respected in internal medicine. He was the chief of the medical staff at Sutro State University Medical Center, one of America's most prestigious hospitals. He should be proud of his achievements.

But Dr. Phillips was never really happy.

TWO

A **DOCTOR IN** a white lab coat entered the pediatric unit. Mary had worked with Dr. Raymond Stuart before.

He was about fifty, with salt and pepper hair cut neatly, almost military style. He was obviously very fit and walked with a casual, but purposeful stride. He had a warm and friendly smile. Mary thought Stuart was the best doctor she had ever met. He was absolutely brilliant, but truly modest. He treated all people with respect, from working class families to millionaires. He had a wonderful way of explaining things to families without a lot of technical jargon, using words that they could understand. And he was amazing with children.

She knew that his right eye did not move when he gazed to his left. She had heard about the horrible auto accident a few years earlier. So, she was aware that she was looking at a glass eye when she worked with him. Trying always to be respectful, she tried not to stare.

"Good morning, Dr. Stuart."

"And good morning to you, Ms. DeGuzman," said Stuart.

Stuart was something of a legend at the Sutro State University Hospital. He was the senior pediatric orthopedic surgeon on the faculty. When he recovered from the injuries in the auto accident, he returned to work, but never again performed surgery. No one knew exactly why he refused to operate and no one dared ask him. If he missed the glory of the operating room, he never talked about it. Instead of surgery, he did research in his laboratory, supervised the pediatric clinic in the outpatient department, and provided consultations for difficult cases in the hospital. He was known as one of the most brilliant diagnosticians on the medical school faculty, an unusual accolade for a surgeon of any type. Stuart seemed to be at peace with his new role.

"Are you here to see Joey Gordon?" asked Mary.

"Yes, I am," replied Stuart. "Is Joey your patient?"

"He is. I'll show you to his room."

"Is the resident taking care of Joey around? I'd like to examine the child with the resident."

"Sorry, sir. The residents are all in a conference. I can tell you about Joey."

"OK, tell me about Joey."

"Joey is a six year old boy from Milbrae. He's been healthy until the last six months. Then he started stumbling and falling. He can't run as fast as he used to and he keeps getting cuts on his feet. This is his first time in the hospital. The residents admitted him from clinic to get some tests and consultations. The family is pretty stressed financially and it would be hard to bring him back and forth for testing and clinics. You're being asked to evaluate his gait."

"How old was he when he started to walk?"

"Eleven months."

"Birth history?"

"Firstborn. Full term, uncomplicated pregnancy. Delivered vaginally without any complications. Home with mother and father the next day. Has had regular pediatric clinic visits, never missed an appointment. Right in the 50th percentile for height and weight. Immunizations up to date. No serious illnesses, just colds and sore throats and earaches."

"Family history?"

"Nobody in the family with anything like this. No ataxia or muscular dystrophy or other neuromuscular diseases. The paternal grandmother has Type II diabetes. That's about it."

"On any medications?"

"Nothing. And no medication allergies."

Stuart thought for a moment. "Very well. Bring the chart and let's go see this lad."

Joey was sitting atop his bed, bulldozing the pillow with a toy truck.

"Hi, Joey," said Mary with a smile. "This is my friend, Dr. Stuart."

"Hi," replied Joey, eying Stuart suspiciously.

"Nice truck," said Stuart. "Where'd you get it?"

"Found it in the playroom."

Stuart reached into his pocket and removed a small plastic tiger.

"What's this?" Stuart asked.

"Tiger."

"Wanna pet it?"

"Does it bite?"

"It only bites bad guys. It likes kids."

Joey stuck out a finger and stroked the plastic toy.

"Let's play a game with the tiger," said Stuart. "Come on, swing your feet over the side of the bed."

Joey complied, bare feet with multiple scratches and healed cuts hung over the side. Stuart knelt on one knee and, with the toy tiger, gently scratched the space between the right first and second toes.

"Does that tickle?" Stuart asked.

"Y-yes," giggled Joey.

Stuart scratched the outside of the left foot.

"How 'bout here?"

"Nope."

"Can you feel the tiger scratching you here?" asked Stuart.

"Nope."

Stuart used the tiger to test the feeling over both of Joey's feet. Mary was astonished that there were spots where Joey could not feel anything at all.

"This tiger says it wants to stay with you," said Stuart, handing the toy to Joey. "Would you like to take it home?"

"Yes!" grinned the little boy.

While Joey played with the toy, Stuart took his left long finger and tapped the tendon just below the kneecap. The leg extended quickly.

"Ha ha!" said Stuart.

"That's funny," said Joey.

"Would you like a reflex hammer, sir?" asked Mary.

"No, my fingers will do just fine."

He tapped Joey's other knee and got a brisk reflex. Stuart and Joey shared a laugh. Then Stuart tapped the Achilles tendons on both legs. No response at all. Stuart moved the ankles up and down, then flexed and extended the knees. He asked Joey to lie on the bed and checked the motion of his hips, telling the boy that this was the wiggling test. Joey giggled while the doctor moved his legs "dis way" and "dat way."

"Come on down here with me," Stuart invited. Joey hopped onto the floor.

Stuart proceeded to do little tests on Joey without the boy knowing that he was actually being examined. In fact, Stuart was testing the strength of the muscles in Joey's legs. Joey could not stand on one foot and rise onto his tiptoes

Stuart turned the boy around and looked at his back.

"Bend forward and touch your toes," he said. Seeing a patch of fine black hair in the middle of the boy's back atop a little soft mound of fat, Stuart pressed gently. "Does this tickle?"

"Nope."

"Let's go into the hall," suggested Stuart.

Stuart took Joey's hand and led the way. Mary followed, thinking that this was the most unorthodox medical consultation she had ever seen.

"Do you see that nurse down the hall with the green scrubs?" Stuart asked, pointing to one of the staff nurses who was casually watching him.

"Yep," said Joey.

"Walk down there and give her a hug."

Joey happily strode down the hall, plastic tiger clenched in his hand and embraced the surprised nurse around both legs.

"Now," said Stuart, "run back very fast."

Joey raced down the hall. Stuart caught him in a bear hug and lifted the laughing boy up off the floor, carrying him back into his room and depositing him right back in bed.

"Good job, Joey. You run very fast. Now, see if that tiger will fit into your truck."

Stuart and Mary walked back to the nurses' station.

"Was he ever toilet trained, Ms. DeGuzman?"

"Yes, and you can call me Mary."

"What happened?" asked Stuart, "Joey has a diaper on now."

"He's been having bowel and bladder accidents," she said.

"For the last six months," Stuart said.

"Yes." She looked at him curiously. "Do you know what's wrong with Joey?"

"Joey has a tethered spinal cord," he said. "The little patch of fine black hair on his back is growing out of a lipoma, a benign tumor made of fat. That innocuous looking bump has a stalk that goes right inside his spinal canal, where it's wrapped around the nerves that come out of the tip of the spinal cord.

The fat anchors the spinal chord, not allowing it to move up and down as Joey moves. Normally, our spinal cords move a few millimeters as we flex and extend and move our trunks. The fatty tumor prevents that in Joey. So the nerves get stretched and don't work very well. It's the lowest nerves coming out of the spinal cord that are affected the most."

"I've never even heard of this," she said. Mary resolved to spend her lunch break in the library reading about tethered cords and lipomas.

Stuart took the chart and began to write his consultation note. "It's a little esoteric, I'll grant. Don't feel bad that you haven't heard of it."

"I want to know about everything," she said.

"Why?"

"The more I know, the better nurse I will be," she said. "And the better nurse I am, the more I can help people. Besides, I hate ignorance and unanswered questions."

"You're not comfortable with the phrases 'nobody knows' or 'I don't know?'" he asked.

"I like answers," she replied.

"Good for you," said Stuart.

"Can anything be done for Joey?"

"Yes. We'll order an MRI of the spine to confirm the diagnosis. Once we have that, you can consult neurosurgery. They can resect the tumor and Joey should do well."

Mary shuffled her feet a little and worked up the courage to ask "What if the MRI doesn't confirm the diagnosis?"

Stuart laughed. "I'll bet you a milkshake that the MRI will confirm my diagnosis."

He offered her his hand. They both grinned and confirmed the bet. Finishing his consultation note, Stuart left the pediatric unit.

Mary giggled a little as she watched him walk away. Wow, she thought.

◆ ◆ ◆

The board room was on the top floor of the university hospital with a view of the outer Sunset district and the Pacific Ocean. Sumptuously furnished with a solid cherry wood board table and luxurious calf leather chairs, the board room pampered the members. The atmosphere and the architecture were deliberately designed to radiate calm and a sense of stability. Board members were supposed to feel comfortable and secure when they made their decisions.

Helen Crawford, Sutro State's hospital administrator and Chief Executive Officer, sat at the head of the table, to the right of the board chairman. She looked forward to the board meetings each month. There was just enough stress to make them challenging. Helen was very good at her job and she knew it. Board members would ask questions about any topic, as if they were probing for her weaknesses. Helen was a master of preparation and had a superb memory for facts. She took great pleasure in having a response to each question. The monthly board meeting was a chance for Helen to show off.

The main agenda item this month was the quarterly financial report to the board. The hospital finances were a very important part of Helen's job. In general, board members knew very little about hospitals or medicine, but as businessmen they understood finances. So Helen had to anticipate that board members would pay close attention and ask detailed questions. While she was confident in her knowledge and preparation, Helen always had the chief financial officer, Bill Henderson, attend the meetings when the financial report was discussed. Having Bill there demonstrated how seriously she took the subject and her confidence in the administrative staff. Bill sat on Helen's right, looking happy to contribute and knowing that Helen would answer all the questions herself.

Helen walked the board through the pages of the report. She discussed patient volumes and the mix of insurance pay-ors. She explained the charts of how many patients had private insurance, how many were on Medicare or MediCal (California's version of Medicaid), and how many were uninsured. She showed how much each hospital service and department cost and how much, if any, revenue was generated by each. Helen was masterful and Bill Henderson smiled with admiration.

At the end of the presentation, Helen demonstrated that the hospital had brought in far more in revenues than it had spent for the quarter. A university hospital could not use the word "profit," but that is what it was.

"A quarterly total of revenues over expenses of three mil-lion dollars does not seem like great financial success to me," said Mr. Davenport with a scowl.

Helen thought that Davenport might be the smartest member of the hospital board. He was a successful trial lawyer known for his scathing cross-examinations and tough presentations in the courtroom.

"It isn't bad for what is supposed to be a non-profit enterprise," said John Wright, chairman of the board.

"May I respond to the question, Mr. Chairman?" Helen asked. She loved this sort of challenge. For Helen, the game was on.

"Of course."

"Sutro State University Hospital must be seen as part of the university itself," she explained. "Unlike a private hospital or a business, we cannot make a profit and there are no stockholders to pay. As part of the state university, we are a public institution. We are obligated to accept patients who cannot pay at all and also patients whose insurance coverage is poor, resulting in lower compensation to the hospital for medical care. A private hospital can be more selective regarding which patients to treat with respect to insurance coverage. In addition, our hospital is a teaching facility for the students and residents of the university. Some expenses are higher in teaching hospitals than in private ones."

"You mean that we have to pay our interns and residents salaries," said Mr. Wright.

"Yes, Mr. Chairman," Helen replied, "but also it has been shown that interns and residents tend to order more tests than private practitioners. Since many insurance companies pay a flat rate to the hospital depending on the diagnosis, ordering more tests tends to increase our costs."

"Why not restrict the interns' and residents' ability to order tests?" asked Davenport. "Put them on a kind of diagnostic budget."

Helen smiled. She loved this sort of repartee. "This is how they learn, Mr. Davenport. The residents learn by ordering lots of tests and discovering which ones they actually needed to make the diagnosis. And, because they are still learning, interns and residents can't zero in on the correct diagnosis is well as the more experienced faculty."

"Why don't we let the faculty make the diagnosis and order the tests?" asked Davenport. "We sure as hell pay them plenty of money."

"Because our mission is to teach the students and residents," Helen replied, "and young doctors learn best by doing, not just watching."

Davenport was beaten and he knew it. He shifted his gaze to the papers in front of him and harrumphed. "It still seems to me that we could have done better."

The chairman, Mr. Wright, folded his arms across his chest. "Well, are there other questions or comments about the financial report?"

Silence.

"Hearing none, I move that we accept the quarterly financial report with our commendation to Ms. Crawford and her staff."

The board continued its meeting, discussing their upcoming off-site meeting on the Big Island in Hawaii. Serving on the hospital board was considered an honor. Board members received no monetary compensation, but the perquisites in travel and entertainment were lavish.

Helen paid little attention to the discussion. She would, of course, attend the meeting in Hawaii. What, after all, would these distinguished gentlemen do without her to lead them? The fact that all the board members were men did not escape Helen's attention. Perhaps that was one reason that she enjoyed the job so much.

Fundamentally, Helen thought of the hospital as a business. She preferred the title of CEO to hospital administrator. As CEO, Helen had to walk a financial tightrope, maximizing revenue, minimizing costs, and, at the end of the year, somehow not showing a profit. Helen was very skilled at her job. At the end of each fiscal year, the books needed to be balanced and no profit could be shown.

The board moved on to a discussion of the hospital endowment fund. The fund was worth about two billion dollars. As long as the hospital could generate revenues to support its operation, the endowment fund could simply grow. However, the excess revenues needed to be spent each year in order for the books to balance. How those revenues were spent was a frequent topic of dispute at board meetings.

"We should have a financial reserve for rainy days," said Davenport. "Goddammit, we're always being asked to spend our money on new buildings, MRI machines, and other high technology crap that's obsolete before it's paid for."

Davenport was notorious for opposing every new project that Helen and her staff proposed to the board. Helen respected him for his intelligence and enjoyed the intellectual sparring at the meetings. She had put up with his insults and profanity for years. He still managed to annoy her. He was so negative so often that she wondered why he served on the board at all. With all the self-control that she could muster, she remained calm, looking to see if Chairman Wright would respond.

"I've told you a hundred times, Jim," said Wright, "it's essential that the hospital keep current with modern health care technology. We're training the leaders of the future in medical science here. Our students and residents must be familiar with the current state of the art."

"Bullshit," said Davenport. "The equipment our students learn on at the hospital is obsolete before the ink dries on their diplomas. This is just a kind of medical shell game, a con. We buy all this shit that is intended to create a profit. The educational value of it is just a sham. More profits, which we can't call profits, make more income so we can buy more shit. And our administrative staff gets bigger and bigger, drawing down higher and higher salaries and obscene bonuses."

"Do you actually have anything positive to contribute to this discussion, Mr. Davenport?" asked Wright.

Davenport frowned and folded his arms across his chest.

Helen was relieved. John Wright was one of the good guys.

"I'd just like to say that I think Ms. Crawford and her staff are doing a marvelous job," said Mr. Clay Ross. "This hospital provides excellent care to the patients in this community. In spite of providing a lot of free care to uninsured patients, we manage to take in a lot of revenue. And, we can be proud that we have never had to ask the taxpayers for more money."

"Well said, Clay," said Wright. "Helen, I really don't know how you continue to maintain such high standards of care while taking care of so many medically indigent patients. We on the board are very proud of you."

Wright led the board and a hearty round of applause. Davenport snorted and scowled.

"Thank you, Mr. Chairman," said Helen. She did like recognition for her efforts.

"The next item on the agenda is a proposal from our orthopedic department to build an orthopedic and sports medicine institute," said Wright. "Wayne, has your committee had a chance to look at the proposal?"

Wayne Patterson was a veteran member of the board. He was a respected businessman in the San Francisco community, owning a chain of high end supermarkets which catered to both the gourmet and the snob. He was chairman of the powerful Planning Committee of the board. A thin, distinguished man with grey hair, impeccably dressed in his tailored suit and sporting synthetic emerald cufflinks, he tapped the stack of paper in front of him and addressed the board.

"Thank you, Mr. Chairman," he said. "We have not had an opportunity to study the proposal in detail, but on the surface it appears to be a good idea. The orthopedic department is asking for the hospital to purchase some old warehouse space a few blocks from here. They'll build a state-of-the art outpatient clinic with same-day surgery suites. There will be a special sports medicine rehab facility as part of an extensive physical therapy department. So many wealthy people think that they are twenty year old athletes. They love their recreational sports and they'll line up for appointments. With excellent insurance, they'll pay handsomely to sustain their illusions. The orthopedists think that this institute will be a gold mine that will pay for itself in seven years. In addition, the department should be able to provide care to sports teams of many of the local schools. This kind of activity also enhances our reputation in the community and brings in even more patients."

"How much will this cost?" asked Davenport.

Helen was not surprised at Davenport's question. He was like a bloodhound. When it came to money, he believed that his job on the board was to treat each of the hospital's dollars like it was his own. She also knew that Davenport disliked Wayne Patterson personally.

"We're not sure yet, Jim," replied Patterson. "The figures aren't all in. I'm guessing that when it's all complete we'll be looking at about thirty or forty million dollars."

"Jesus," said Davenport, "you *think* it will be thirty or forty million dollars? Christ Almighty, Wayne, shouldn't you *know*?"

"Helen, what do you think about the orthopedic proposal?" Wright asked.

Helen could sense that Davenport annoyed the Chairman. Mr. Wright was struggling to remain civil. She knew that Wright was asking her to restore some calm to the meeting, perhaps by deflecting Davenport.

She wrinkled her brow and tapped her pen gently on the papers in front of her. "Well, Mr. Chairman, as Mr. Patterson points out, we haven't had enough time to completely study the proposal, but I have a few concerns."

"Concerns?" asked Davenport. "No shit."

Helen ignored the comment.

"Well, the purchase of the property could cause some problems. The community is worried about traffic congestion and parking in a part of the city where traffic is already a serious problem. And I fear that the cost estimates may be overly optimistic. While our revenues have been steady, I'm not sure that the board wants to commit such a large amount of money over what may be many years to this project. It may preclude growth in other, more important programs. Lastly, while the orthopedic department may be correct that there are lots of potential patients who would utilize the facility, my staff is conducting an extensive needs assessment study to get more specific facts."

"I thought that Wayne said that the orthopedic department already looked at the population and concluded that the patients were there," said Davenport. "Why does your administrative staff feel compelled to do its own study? Is the orthopedic department wrong?"

"Well," said Helen, "the orthopedic department has done some work investigating the potential patient population and demographics which would utilize the proposed institute. When I and my staff looked at their proposal, it seemed to us that our orthopedic doctors have not taken into consideration the attraction of patients to Stanford. Many patients from the San Francisco area go to Stanford for their orthopedic care, because of the prestigious reputation of that institution. Stanford is particularly popular with residents of the wealthy East Bay suburbs. We want to look at the numbers ourselves so that we can make the most professional, and most accurate, recommendation to you, the board, who must make this serious decision. So, we've decided to do our own needs assessment study."

"So, you're against it?" asked Patterson.

"No," replied Helen, subtly biting her lip. "It's expensive and I have some concerns, but I wouldn't make a judgment until our needs assessment is completed and we've all had a chance to study the proposal further. We need to be patient."

"I appreciate your concerns," said Patterson. "It is a lot of money and we need to get this right. As you say, if we go forward with this plan, it may tie up our excess revenues for many years. To make sure that we can afford this, it would be prudent, I believe, for us to commission a full audit of the hospital's finances before we go spending this sort of money on an orthopedic institute. A full audit of current operations and a projection of anticipated revenues and expenses."

"Damn good idea," agreed Davenport.

This was not what Helen wanted to hear, even though she had expected it. Planning for all contingencies, she was already at work to deal with this. She distrusted Davenport as much as he distrusted her. She knew that he was suspicious of doctors, especially surgeons, and had represented clients suing for medical malpractice. She doubted that he cared much about the orthopedic institute one way or another. She did not welcome the idea of Jim Davenport rooting around in the hospital financial data. She was about to speak when the chairman cut off the discussion.

"Tabled until next month," said Chairman Wright. "Wayne, were there any other proposals put before your Planning Committee?"

"Well," said Patterson, "Dr. Phillips, our chief of the medical staff, mentioned to me that he was working on a proposal for a new and modern medical staff library, but he hasn't finished a final proposal yet."

"A library?" snorted Davenport. "Christ. You can be certain that a library won't bring in a dime of revenue. He probably just wants a room that he can put his name on, to memorialize himself forever. Shit, who would use it? Nowadays young students can get all the information they need out of their cell phones."

"Maybe we should let Dr. Phillips present his proposal before we begin our criticisms, Jim," said Wright.

"Dr. Phillips regrets that he could not attend the board meeting today," said Helen, "but he assures me that he will be here next month. Perhaps he can elaborate on his plans then."

"Good," said Wright, "If there is no further business, I believe we are adjourned."

As the board members filed out, discussing good places for drinks and dinner or reporting on their latest triumphs on the golf links, Helen Crawford caught John Wright's attention.

She knew from the way he looked at her that Wright admired more than just her administrative skills. She always dressed like an executive, with business suits expertly tailored to hide the bumps and bulges that came with age. Her jewelry was large, but simple in design and expensive with lots of gold and large stones. Today's outfit looked particularly good.

Helen could use many skills to achieve her goals in life. Including flattery. "I always enjoy watching the way you run a meeting. Very efficient. Much better than your predecessor. You show authority, command respect. You were in the military."

Wright held the door for her. "Marine Corps, two tours in Vietnam. Company commander. Thank you for noticing. Are you from a military family?"

"Army brat. Moved every two years as a child growing up. My father was a Master Sergeant. I had my first rifle before I had my first pair of high heels."

"Was your father in Vietnam?"

"No. His war was Korea. Silver Star and two Purple Hearts."

"God bless America," said Wright.

THREE

KEITH LEANED OVER the desk at the nurses' station on the orthopedic unit and smiled at the pretty nurse. "Eva, which room is Valerie Kraft in?"

"You mean Dr. Warren's patient?"

"Yeah."

"She's in twenty-five, Keith. She's in strict isolation, you know. MRSA."

"Figures," he said.

"Do you want the chart?"

"No, thanks. I'm really just a visitor."

There was a yellow cart in front of the door to room twenty-five and lots of signs warning that isolation precautions were in place because of the dreaded super-bacterium MRSA. Keith put on paper shoe covers, a yellow paper gown, vinyl gloves, a paper cap and a surgical mask before knocking on the door. A feint female voice invited him in.

Valerie Kraft was a slender young woman with long blonde hair whose face was puffy from much crying. She lay in the bed with her leg elevated. The whole leg was wrapped in a massive dressing of gauze encased in ACE bandages. Heavy tubing ran into and out of the bandages. A mechanical pump forced saline solution laden with antibiotics into the knee while a large plastic bag collected the outflow. Keith noticed that the liquid in the bag was cloudy and tinged with blood.

"Ms. Kraft, I'm Doctor Grant," he said.

Valerie studied the masked face and squinted. "Who?"

"Dr. Grant," he said, "from the emergency room the other night. I did the surgery to drain your knee."

"Oh, now I recognize the grey eyes. My memories are a little blurry from that night."

"That's all right. How are you feeling?"

"The pain is actually better, but I can't say that I feel good."

"The pain should improve since we got all that swelling and pus out of the joint," he said, "but the knee isn't going to really feel good with those drains in there."

"Did you put those tubes in?"

"Yes," he said, "after we washed out the joint."

"When do they come out?"

"When the fluid in the bag looks clear, like the fluid going in"

"Why did this happen to me, Dr. Grant?"

Keith dreaded that question, though he expected her to ask. "Your knee got infected with a nasty bacterium."

"Did the infection happen here at the hospital?"

Keith couldn't lie. Besides, most of the public knew that MRSA usually was found in hospitals. "Probably."

"Will my knee get back to normal?"

No chance, he thought. Keith thought that the best answer was to be tactful, not to take away the woman's hope.

"It's hard to tell at this point. We'll see as you get past the infection and start with physical therapy."

"Dr. Warren said that the risks of this surgery were minimal. He might have said 'negligible.' He said I'd be back running in just a few weeks."

"Dr. Warren has a very high success rate with surgery like this," Keith said. "Complications like this are extremely rare. Obviously, though, they do happen. He didn't lie to you."

"I never imagined," she said, starting to cry.

"I'm very sorry, Ms. Kraft," he said. "We'll do everything we can to get you better."

Keith left the room and discarded the isolation clothes in a biohazard bag. This infection shouldn't have happened.

♦ ♦ ♦

Mary had to concentrate on cutting the chicken without taking off one of her own fingers. Her hands were shaking and her mind was preoccupied with anxiety about the evening.

Keith was coming to dinner at her family home in Daly City. She had invited him to meet her family and she was terrified at what might happen. The little brothers and sisters weren't the problem. It was her parents that she was concerned about. They were immigrants from the Philippines, unsophisticated, poorly educated. Old fashioned simple people who worked hard at menial jobs. Mary loved her parents with all her heart, but she hoped they would not embarrass her tonight.

She whispered a prayer that God would make her parents like Keith and that Keith would like her family. She didn't want to even think about what she would do if this evening was a failure.

Mary looked at her mother, Felicia DeGuzman, who was preparing the meal with her in the kitchen. They spoke in Tagalog.

"Are you all right with this, Mama, I mean having Keith over for dinner?" she asked. "Does it bother you that he's not Filipino?"

Felicia put down her measuring spoons and looked at her daughter. "It's alright that he's not a Filipino. We're in America and your father and I have to accept that you'll meet Americans. They seem to come in all shapes and colors."

Mary smiled. "Yes, Mama, they do."

"Do a lot of the nurses date the doctors at the hospital?" Felicia asked. "Like on TV? Are your friends dating doctors?"

"Not too many of my friends are dating the doctors," Mary said. "It happens. Not as much as on TV."

"Your father and I worry a little that the doctors might take advantage of the nurses," Felicia said. "That they might use their position to, well, you know. And a pretty girl like you is so vulnerable."

Mary had to laugh. So that's it. My parents are watching too much TV.

"Mama, you can be certain that Keith is not taking advantage of me," Mary said. "I can take care of myself. You raised me with pretty strong values and I know how to defend them."

"Tell me again how you met this man," said Felicia.

Mary rolled her eyes a little. She and Keith had been dating for months and she had told this story a dozen times. It wouldn't hurt to tell it again. It might make her feel better, less anxious. Maybe that was why her mother asked to hear it again. Her mother was very wise and very insightful.

"Well, there was a little girl with a terribly broken elbow," Mary explained. "Keith operated on the little girl, fixed the bones and put her in a cast. He was worried that the swelling from the injury and the surgery would get so bad that the circulation to the girl's hand would be cut off. He and I stayed with the child all night watching her. Keith was prepared to take her right back to surgery if things got bad."

"So you spent most of a shift with him," Felicia said. "And how did the little girl do?"

"She's fine," smiled Mary. "The swelling went down and she went home in a day or so. But I got to know Keith and I was impressed with not just his knowledge, but his compassion for the little girl. He really seemed to care. So, when he asked me out, I was happy. And he's really good looking, too."

"Are you serious about him?"

Am I ever, Mary thought. But she couldn't say that, not to her mother. Not tonight.

"I don't know. Maybe."

"But you've invited him here for dinner tonight."

"Yes. I wanted you and Dad to meet him. And I wanted him to get some idea about my Filipino family. And, please, speak only English when he's here. We don't want to insult him."

"He's a white man, you said," her mother continued. "Is he from California?"

"No, he's from Connecticut," Mary said. "He was an athlete in college, a football player. He got a scholarship to go to the Collage of the Holy Cross."

"So, he's at least Catholic?"

"You know he is, Mama. We've been going to Mass together. With all the suffering he has to deal with at work, Keith finds some comfort in his faith. He has a very hard schedule, so he can't attend every Sunday. He's a really nice man. And he's a doctor. You and Dad should be happy about him."

"I thought he wasn't a real doctor, just a student."

"He's the chief resident. And yes, he's a real doctor. He's in his last year of training to become an orthopedic surgeon, although he'll probably add another year of sub-specialty training in either pediatrics of trauma. But he has a real license to practice medicine. If he had chosen a less rigorous specialty, he'd already be in practice."

The rumble of the Harley-Davidson outside the modest tract home in Daly City where the DeGuzman family lived announced Keith's arrival. Mary and her father met him at the front door. Mary invited Keith to remove his shoes and to don a pair of slippers from a basket in the hallway. Mary introduced Keith to her parents and her four younger siblings, two brothers and two sisters.

Supper was family style around a large, but inexpensive, dining table which was the center of the DeGuzman family life. Keith, as the guest of honor, was seated at one end of the table, with Mr. DeGuzman at the head. Felicia sat at her husband's right hand, Mary next to Keith. The other chairs were randomly occupied by children.

"Let us begin with grace," said Mr. DeGuzman. Everyone bowed their heads. "Bless us, O Lord, and these Thy gifts which we are about to receive from Thy bounty."

Everyone made the sign of the cross. Felicia and Mary hustled to the kitchen to bring in the food.

"Mary and I made this dinner together," said Felicia, placing a heaping bowl of food in front of her husband. "It's a traditional Filipino dish, called adobo."

Mary produced a huge bowl of rice in front of her father. "Adobo, Keith, is a marinated chicken spiced with garlic, soy sauce, and vinegar."

"Looks and smells great," said Keith.

Everyone was served before anyone took a bite. Keith found the food delicious. He gave Mary a subtle thumbs-up sign.

"What kind of doctor are you?" asked Marcus, Mary's ten year old brother.

Mary shot her brother a nasty look, but the youngster ignored her.

"I'm a doctor for bones," said Keith.

"Like if somebody breaks their arm, you fix it?" asked Marcus.

"That's right."

"Do you put on casts?" asked twelve year old Lydia.

"Yes," said Keith.

"Do kids get to pick the color cast they want?" Lydia asked.

"Usually," said Keith, "if we have the color they want."

"I would want a purple cast," said Lydia.

"I want a black one," said Marcus, "Do you have black ones?"

"Yes," said Keith.

Mary noticed that Keith's plate was empty. A kind of giddy delight made her grin.

"You seem to take to Filipino cuisine, Doctor," she said.

"This is great," Keith replied. "My compliments to both of the chefs."

"Seconds?" asked Mary.

Keith blushed. "Yes, please, if there's enough."

Felicia beamed. "There is plenty."

Mary shared big grins with both her parents.

"Why do you drive a motorcycle?" asked Marcus.

"Oh, I love that motorcycle," said Keith with a smile. "I love the feeling of the wind on my face when I ride. Besides, it's easy to park in San Francisco."

"Was it expensive?" asked Felicia.

"Not really," said Keith. "I got a great deal on it. The man who originally bought it decided that he didn't want to ride it after all and sold it quickly, with little mileage on it."

"Why didn't the man want it?" asked Marcus, "Was he scared to ride it?"

"I would be scared to ride on it," interjected Lydia. "I think Mary is scared of it, too."

Mary blushed with embarrassment.

"As far as I can tell," said Keith, "your sister Mary isn't scared of anything."

"Are you scared of it, Mary?" asked Marcus.

"Well, I don't like it," Mary replied. "It's loud and uncomfortable and it smells bad."

"Mary doesn't like the stinky motorcycle," said Marcus in sing-song.

They all had a laugh. Mary was happy to see that Keith laughed, too.

Dessert was leche flan, a kind of custard dish. Mary was relaxed by now. Her family was obviously comfortable with Keith. And Keith seemed to be enjoying them. She was feeling that the evening was a success.

"Do you have brothers and sisters?" asked Lydia.

"No," said Keith, "My parents just had me."

"Do you have a pet?" asked Amelia, who was only six.

"Yes, I have a pet bird."

"Is it a boy bird or a girl bird?" asked Amelia.

"She's a girl."

"What's her name?"

"Her name is Baby."

Amelia giggled.

"What sort of work does your father do?" asked Mary's father.

"He sells insurance," Keith replied, "My mother works as a bank teller."

"Did they both go to college?" asked Mr. DeGuzman.

"Yes."

"Mary is the first person in our family to graduate from college," said Mr. DeGuzman. "We are very, very proud of her."

"You should be very proud indeed," said Keith. "Mary is a terrific nurse."

Mary smiled and gave Keith's hand a little squeeze.

"Our brother Alex is in prison," blurted Marcus. "He's a burglar."

Mary blushed. The family was not supposed to talk about Alex in front of guests. Theirs was a traditional Filipino family. Alex was her favorite brother. He wanted a quicker and easier path to material wealth and became a thief. He taught her how to pick a lock and even gave her a set of picks for Christmas one year. Unfortunately, Alex was not very good at burglary. He was in prison for the second time.

There were a few moments of awkward silence.

"We love all our children," said Felicia. "Besides the five you see tonight, we have two older sons. Marcus has already told about Alex. Our other son works in construction here in the Bay area. We hope that Mary's example will inspire the younger ones to go to college as well."

"Were you both born in the Philippines?" Keith asked.

"Yes, we came here to have a better life for our family," said Mr. DeGuzman. "All of our children were born here in California."

"Have any of you been to the Philippines?" Keith asked the children.

They all shook their heads.

"Do you speak Tagalog?"

Mary laughed as the children exchanged grins.

"In our house, we always speak Tagalog," Mary said. "Once we're out the door, we're as American as bubble gum."

"Mary tells me that you are almost finished with your medical training," said Felicia. "Will you go into practice next year?"

"I don't think so," Keith replied. "I think that I would like to do another year of very specialized training. It's hard to decide, though. I am interested in trauma and also in pediatrics."

"Trauma?" asked Amelia. "What's that?"

"That's accidents and shootings and explosions and stuff," said Lydia.

"Like on TV?" asked Marcus.

"Yeah, like on TV," Lydia replied. "Are you going to be a doctor like on TV?"

Mary caught her breath. She knew about her parents' fears about doctors and nurses on TV. "No. Keith is never going to be like a TV doctor. In any way."

Keith gave her a puzzled look. "Well, trauma is a lot about accidents and injuries. From the surgeon's point of view, it's pretty exciting. You never know what is going to happen next. You have to think fast and operate faster. I like the challenge."

"The other option is pediatrics," Mary said.

"You seem to have a very good way with children, if tonight is a fair example," said Mary's father.

"Thank you," Keith replied. "I like kids a lot. They're innocent and honest and just want to get better."

"If you take care of kids, you and Mary can work together," said Amelia.

Out of the mouths of babes, Mary thought.

"That could be an important consideration," Keith said.

Keith and Mary shared a warm glance. Mary's parents shared one too.

The younger children dutifully volunteered to clean up after the supper. Keith and Mary chatted with her parents for a while, then Keith excused himself, pointing out that he had to be in surgery very early the next morning. Mary followed him onto the front porch.

"Well?" she asked.

"You cook even better than you kiss," he said.

"Wanna bet?" she replied, kissing him tenderly.

Somehow Mary knew that one of her little brothers was peering between the living room curtains, so she let Keith depart after just one kiss. When she got back inside, her parents were sitting in the living room. So were the other kids.

"What's the verdict?" Mary asked.

"Marry him quickly, before he gets away," said Felicia.

◆ ◆ ◆

Scott Osborne could not wait to see his mother arrive on her flight from Atlanta. Scott had been asking her to come visit him in San Francisco for years. In a way, he was looking for her blessing, her approval of him. Scott wanted so much to know that his mother still loved him. To know that, even though he was gay and was living in San Francisco, he still was grounded in his mother's love.

Scott strained his eyes, watching the passengers come through the gate. At first he was not certain that he was looking at his mother. Mabel Osborne had gained nearly a hundred pounds since he had last seen her. Still, he thought she was beautiful. He ran to her as she waddled across the airport past security and gave her a huge hug. Then he hugged his brother Mike, who had accompanied their mother on her visit to The City by the Bay.

"Scott, you look thin," said Mabel. "Don't you eat right out here in California?"

"Mom, you look great to me," said Scott. "I sure would give anything for a taste of your fried chicken."

"And maybe a slice of homemade peach pie?" she teased.

"Maybe two slices," Scott smiled.

"You may be thin, but you look prosperous," said Mike. "Nice clothes. Nice watch."

Scott straightened his jacket and held his head high. "I've had a certain success here in the last four years."

"What business are you in now, Scott?" asked Mabel.

"I own a sort of nightclub with entertainment," Scott answered.

"Oh, can I visit?" she asked.

"I'm pretty sure you wouldn't like it, Mama," Scott replied. "Loud rock 'n' roll music and all that."

Mike rolled his eyes, turning his face so that Mabel could not see. Mike and Scott had been sibling rivals as children. The rivalry had diminished some with the years, but was not gone.

Pulling his brother aside, Mike whispered "Oh, shit, Scott, do you own a fucking gay bar?"

"Shhhh," Mike said. "Mama doesn't need to know."

Scott and Mike retrieved the suitcases from baggage claim. Scott guided them to a limousine that he had hired for the trip to the hotel.

"Oooh, Scott, look at this car. I feel like a movie star," Mabel said.

"You're more important than any movie star, Mom."

The limo pulled out of the airport and onto the freeway.

"Is that the Pacific ocean over there?" asked Mabel.

"No, Mama, that's San Francisco Bay," said Scott, "I can ask the driver to take us past the ocean on the way to the hotel, if you'd like."

"Is it on the way?"

"Well, not exactly," Scott confessed.

"You know, Scott, I'm so very tired from the long day of travel, I believe that I'd just like to go to the hotel. Maybe we can see the ocean tomorrow."

"Of course, Mama. We can go to the ocean tomorrow morning if you'd like. I have a tour with the Grey Line bus scheduled for tomorrow afternoon. We could see the ocean in the morning before the tour."

"Where are we staying, Scott?" asked Mike.

"I've reserved a suite for the two of you at the St. Francis. It's right on Union Square."

"Sounds expensive," said Mike.

"You know, I've waited more than four years to see my mother visit me here in my new home," said Scott. "I can't really tell you how happy I am right now. There is no better way that I can think of to spend my money than making sure she has a pleasant trip."

◆ ◆ ◆

"This is a wonderful party, Wayne," said Helen Crawford, "It's so kind of you to host these events for the hospital board. Is that a new painting?"

Helen was referring to a small oil depicting sawgrass and a bush with white flowers bent over in the wind. The sky behind the plants was reddish grey, like the sunrise over San Francisco Bay before the daily fog had lifted.

"Yes," said Wayne Patterson. "It's good of you to notice. The artist is a local Bay area woman. Eleanor discovered the piece at a gallery in Sausalito."

The entire board was present in the lavish home of Wayne Patterson, a mansion in the exclusive Sea Cliff neighborhood of San Francisco. Helen loved the old mansion and always enjoyed her visits there. Near the Golden Gate Bridge, the house had an impressive view of the rocks and the shores of San Francisco Bay. Helen liked to stand out on the patio and watch gentle waves break over large boulders. This evening, the water was mostly grey-green with little flashes of turquoise as the last rays of sunlight caught them. Wispy fingers of fog floated by on their daily journeys, adding a sense of mystery to the peaceful setting.

Feeling the chill of the incoming fog, Helen wandered back inside. The large room featured hardwood floors covered generously with expensive Middle Eastern rugs. The furnishings were classical in style, clearly expensive. A long bar of American walnut accented with a brass railing took up most of one interior wall. Parties at the Patterson home were regular events for the board, a chance to socialize and politic about hospital issues. As CEO, Helen Crawford was frequently invited. The wives of the board members were all there, decked out in formal dresses and dripping with fine jewelry. Everyone was dressed to impress. Helen herself wore a designer dress, tasteful and professional, but displaying a hint of cleavage. Her best necklace and earrings enhanced her appearance. She thought that she was more than just competitive.

It seemed as though everyone was talking and nobody was listening. Tongues loosened with alcohol told exaggerated stories and outright lies, but no-one seemed to mind.

"You seem to be out of Chivas Regal, Wayne," said Clay Ross, "but I see an unopened gift box with a fifth of Johnny Walker Black. Would you mind if I opened it?'"

"I would be delighted if you did," said Patterson, watching Ross make his way unsteadily toward the bar.

Helen watched the interaction with interest. Clay Ross was drunk again, as usual. Helen thought that Wayne Patterson was both annoyed and disgusted. He could not be upset that Clay had drunk all of his Scotch. Wayne was incredibly rich. He owned a chain of supermarkets and he got the Chivas wholesale.

Clearly, Clay's alcoholism was getting worse. Helen thought it was sad, but potentially useful. Clay Ross was a successful businessman in San Francisco, well liked and well respected. Witty and funny and the life of any party. As his drinking accelerated, Clay couldn't hold his thoughts together and no longer made a lot of sense when he talked. His business was beginning to suffer as well, not to mention his contributions to the hospital. His attention to details on the board was decreasing, which made him an uncritical supporter of Helen's proposals.

Wayne Patterson's own wife Eleanor was sliding down that same slippery slope. Eleanor, the love of Wayne's life, now started her drinking when she got up in the morning. She was fairly well loaded by noon and incoherent when he got home from work. Helen knew that Wayne's heart was breaking. Helen had some experience with an alcoholic spouse, but she didn't know if she should say something to Wayne. Even now, she saw Eleanor stumbling across the room toward Wayne, a foolish smile on her face and an empty glass in her hand.

"Darling," said Eleanor Patterson, "be a doll and get me another drink?"

"I think you may have had enough," said Patterson as his wife nearly fell off her high heels. She was a slender woman who had seen better years. Weekly trips to the hair stylist and manicurist were not enough to slow the deterioration of body and mind that came with too many years and too much alcohol.

"Allow me," said John Wright, interrupting with a smile for Eleanor. "Cream sherry, isn't it?"

"Thank you, John," she said. "At least there's still one gentleman here."

Eleanor staggered after Wright toward the bar. Wayne Patterson was left standing with Helen, who nursed a glass of white wine.

"Cream sherry, cream sherry. She's the only person I know who drinks that stuff," said Wayne. "I think she may drink a gallon a day. Buys it by the case, you know. I order it for her from the same distributor that I use to stock my supermarket. Christ, she goes though it faster than my store in Diamond Heights."

"But she's such a sweet person," said Helen, "and just the perfect hostess."

"You're very kind, Helen," he said, "and I apologize for my use of language. And I apologize again for complaining to you about personal matters. My personal issues are not your worries."

"It's alright," she replied. "I really do understand. My second husband was an alcoholic. I know how much you hurt inside."

Patterson looked at her intently. "You do?"

"You love them so much and you just want to help them," she said. "You feel guilty because you think maybe something you did or failed to do is the reason for the drinking. When my husband was sober, he didn't want to talk to me. It was as though he was so ashamed that he couldn't face me."

"Exactly."

"And, after he had a few drinks he would talk, but he usually denied that he had a problem. He insisted that he knew what he was doing, that he was in control, that he could quit any time he wanted to."

"That's just what Eleanor does. What did you do? Did your husband get help?"

"I didn't know what to do," she said. "I just cried myself to sleep at night, with him passed out in his recliner in the living room. And no, he never got help. One morning I woke up and found him dead in the recliner. I thought he had drunk himself to death. The doctor said it was probably a heart attack."

"Oh, Helen, I am so very sorry."

"Thank you, Wayne, you're a kind man. It took a while to get over. You know, I never stopped loving him. And I wondered for a long time if there was anything I could have done. To help him, I mean, so that maybe he'd still be alive."

"The prospect of losing Eleanor scares me terribly," said Wayne. "I feel just the way you're describing. I'd do anything to help her."

"After Philip died, I learned that there are support groups for people like us, people whose lives are being torn apart because of the disease our loved ones have. The best known is Alanon."

"Alanon? Never heard of it."

"I didn't know about it when I really needed it," Helen said, "but I went to a couple of meetings after Philip passed. I'm not sure that it will help Eleanor, but it might do you some good."

"I'll try anything at this point," he said.

"I can get a contact list for you. Please stop by my office when you're at the hospital and I'll give it to you."

"Thank you," he replied, "I'll do that. Now, if you don't mind talking a little business, do you have time to discuss the proposal for the orthopedic institute? Since the board meeting I've read more of the details and it looks very, very good to me. If we go ahead with the full audit of the hospital's financial status, and, if it looks like we can afford it, why not build it? Are there other problems that I am not aware of?"

"There are a few, Wayne, and we can certainly talk about it here, or in my office next week," said Helen. "Let me just get another glass of wine and we'll find a quiet place to sit and talk."

Helen made her way to the bar, smiling and shaking hands with every board member and wife she encountered. It did not bother her at all that she was the only woman at the party who was not married. She enjoyed the fact that she was one of the most powerful and important people in the room. When she got to the bar, she noticed the large collection of gift bottles at one end. Her own gift, enclosed in a fancy box, was lost in the crowd of elegant and colorful bottles. It was ironic, she thought, that so many people, including herself, made gifts of strong drink to a home being torn apart by alcoholism. Surely it would be hard for poor Eleanor Patterson to get sober in the midst of so much expensive booze. Perhaps she should come up with a different, non-alcoholic gift in the future. Pouring herself a glass of chardonnay, she returned to Patterson. They found a quiet corner and sat down.

"It is not just the orthopedic institute," Helen began, "but the commitment of so much of the hospital's revenues over such a long time. There are many more, less expensive, projects that have been proposed. If all the money is tied up in one project, many other things may be neglected."

"And that's why Jim Davenport and I think that a full audit would be necessary before we proceed," he replied.

"We don't need an extra audit," said Helen. "The regularly scheduled full audit comes in a year and a half. Audits take a lot of time to complete and place an enormous burden on my staff, particularly in the financial offices. Scheduling an additional audit is, in my view, wasteful and unnecessary. I know more about the hospital finances than anybody. I can answer the questions that the board has without the time delay or expense of an audit."

"Hmmm," said Patterson. "There are some members of our board who would agree that an audit is not needed. But Jim Davenport and I have been talking. We both think that the hospital is at a crossroads right now. As you say, it's not just the orthopedic thing, although that is an important part. Jim and I think that a complete review of the financial picture would be invaluable to the board going forward."

A slight commotion from across the room caught their attention as Eleanor Patterson tripped over a ten thousand dollar Persian rug and went sprawling. Wayne Patterson rushed to her side. Eleanor was giggling and struggling to get up.

Dr. Richard Phillips was already at her side. As chief of the medical staff at the hospital, he was the only physician invited to board parties. Phillips helped Eleanor into a comfortable chair. Looking concerned, he checked her pulse.

"Thank you, Doctor, but I'm fine," she said. "Really. I'm just fine. The only thing injured is my pride."

Phillips scowled.

"We really have to get that rug replaced," slurred Eleanor. Turning to her husband, she smiled.

"Ooh, I seem to have spilled my drink. Be a dear and get me another, please, my love."

◆ ◆ ◆

A certain amount of engineering was required to get Mabel Osborne into the Grey Line tour bus. Once she was hoisted up the stairs, she needed two seats to accommodate her enormous girth. Scott and Mike sat in the seats behind her. Scott supplemented the tour guide's narrative with little anecdotes. He pointed out his favorite Italian restaurant, the best jewelry store in San Francisco, the location of his own travel agent.

"The tour will begin with Chinatown, which is right around the corner from Union Square," said the guide.

"Chinatown?" asked Mabel. "Is it a whole section of San Francisco?"

"There's a large Chinese community here in San Francisco," said Scott. "The Chinese came over in the nineteenth century. Between the commercial port and the Gold Rush, there was a great demand for labor."

"Well, would you look at that," mused Mabel, staring out the window. Scott was pleased to see the smiles and interest his mother showed for the crowds of people on the streets, the trinkets and souvenirs set out on tables right on the sidewalks, the Chinese characters that were displayed on large colorful signs. San Francisco was every bit the exotic delight he hoped to see in her eyes.

The tour went on for two hours, the bus struggling on narrow streets in traffic that was perpetually jammed. They saw Coit Tower, the monument to the firefighters who struggled to save San Francisco after the 1906 earthquake; the beautiful Palace of the Legion of Honor, constructed for the World's Fair to show the world that the city had recovered from that earthquake. Elegant houses with spectacular views that sold for tens of millions of dollars. As the sun was setting, the bus pulled into a slot near the famous Cliff House restaurant right on the ocean.

"This is a lovely spot," said Mabel.

"It should be the perfect place to take a photo for the family back home in Alabama," said Scott.

"Yes," agreed Mike, "I'm sure we could get the tour guide to take our picture together with the setting sun over the ocean. That would be a picture the whole family would love."

For most of the tour, Mabel had mercifully stayed in her two seats, although other tourists got off the bus from time to time to see the sights up close and shop for cheap souvenirs. This photo opportunity, however, was just too good to pass up.

After all the other tourists had disembarked, Scott and Mike went to work to extricate Mabel from the bus.

"I'll get off first and stand outside the door," said Scott, taking charge. "Mike, stand behind Mama and help her."

Mike put an arm under Mabel's armpit to steady her as she rose. It was quickly apparent that she could never clear the narrow steps and door heading straight down.

"Turn sideways, Mama," said Scott, "that'll make it easier to get down the steps. Careful now. Just another step and take my hand."

Mabel's knee gave out and all four hundred pounds of her tumbled toward Scott. Instinctively, he side-stepped and Mabel landed on the concrete.

"Ahhhh!" she cried. "Oh, my God! I think I broke my leg. Why didn't you catch me, Scott?"

Why indeed? he wondered.

FOUR

EACH NOTE OF Jefferson Airplane's "Embryonic Journey" was perfect and Dr. Raymond Stuart made the old Gibson acoustic six-string sing. Fingers flew over the strings, directed by muscle memories and the song in Ray's heart. The only accompaniment to the guitar was the sound of the waves. Funny, he thought, he no longer played most of the old songs. Casualties of the accident? Maybe, in a way. The lively rock songs died well before the crash. After his body healed, he sold all the electric guitars, part of his recovery, or part of his penance. All he had left were this old Gibson and his Guild twelve-string. Those two instruments were sufficient for now. Most of the songs were quiet, many sad.

As the last notes faded away, Ray looked down at his fingers. Both hands worked very well. They had been spared injury. Both legs shattered, now full of hardware installed by his friend Felix Romano and working almost normally. The right eye gone, of course. That seemed like justice to Ray. But the hands worked well. For a few minutes, he thought about returning to surgery. He could do the operations, his hands still highly skilled. He knew that. But he would not operate again and he knew that, too. No more surgery. It was part of his penance.

Raymond Stuart had flashbacks to the night two years earlier when he was driving his sports car along the curvaceous Highway 1, a narrow two-lane road a hundred feet above the Pacific Ocean. Now he could clearly see the tree directly in front of him, illuminated by his headlights. After that, there was no memory.

So here he sat, all alone on his wooden deck overlooking the Pacific Ocean, picking his guitar and watching the waves. It was quiet and peaceful at his home on the coastside south of the city. His legs worked well. He walked with no limp. He was used to seeing things with one eye. Other senses seemed keener than ever, like his hearing, perhaps in compensation for the eye. But he still had a lot of healing to do.

◆ ◆ ◆

"Well, did you like it?" Keith was very proud of his first effort to cook a meal for Mary. Now that they had eaten, he was looking for a compliment.

The kitchen table in Keith's apartment was adorned with a tablecloth which began its career as a curtain. Both dinner plates were of matching patterns. Keith had, with some difficulty, assembled matching settings of utensils. All of this represented the best table setting that he could produce. Mary was the most special dinner guest he could host. Most of this was lost on Mary because the only lighting in the apartment was from the two candles in the center of the table.

"It was, well, different," said Mary as she got up from the table to start the kitchen clean-up. She flicked on the overhead light in the kitchen area.

"It's called hamburger stroganoff," said Keith. "Kind of a beef stroganoff for poor people. I got the recipe from a book on a hundred ways to cook hamburger."

"It was kind of spicy," she said.

"You know, they don't teach us in medical school what 'tsp' stands for. It could be 'teaspoon' or it could be 'tablespoon.' It's just ambiguous."

"You don't know that 'tsp' means 'teaspoon' and 'tbsp' means tablespoon?" she asked.

"No, I didn't know that."

"Somehow that explains things," said Mary. "How much salt and pepper did you put in?"

"Well, I couldn't figure out if it was teaspoons or tablespoons, so I sort of split the difference and eyeballed it," Keith said.

Mary laughed, then gave him a big kiss.

"I do love you," she said. "It's a good thing you decided to be a doctor rather than a chef. I'll help you clean up. And I need another glass of water."

"Thanks," Keith said. "Maybe I should stick to simpler things than cooking. Like surgery."

"Good idea. Next time we'll have dinner again at my family's house."

"Oooh. I'd like that. Could we have some of those lumpy things? I love the Filipino food your mother makes."

"Hey," she said, "I did most of the cooking last time. And they're called lumpia. They are meat, usually pork, cooked in pastry. They're hard to make and we usually serve lumpia only for special guests or on special occasions."

"If I come over for dinner again, that would be a special occasion."

"I'm not sure that it would be special enough to justify all that effort in the kitchen. Especially if you're going to give my mother all the credit."

"Whatever, I like them," he said. "Speaking of your family, is it all right for you to tell me a little more about your brother Alex? It seemed like an awkward topic when I was there for dinner."

"Yeah, my parents don't like to talk about him. They're embarrassed. But Alex is my brother and I love him very much. We're pretty close'"

"And he's in prison, right? Is it all right for me to ask about what he did?"

"It's alright with me," said Mary. "But I wouldn't suggest you bring it up around my parents. Alex is impatient. He wants it all and he wants it quick. So, going to school, getting a job, saving up his money, well, they don't appeal to him. He started playing the lottery as soon as he could figure out how to con someone into buying a ticket. He routinely lost his allowance on lottery tickets. He got this idea that he could steal things. He broke into a few houses. Not far from our house, but never within a block or so. He took some money mostly. He learned how to pick locks."

"How do you learn to pick locks?"

"A friend taught him," she said. "He bought his own lock picks and practiced on the locks at home. Then he practiced on the locks at our school and eventually on other people's locks. He even taught me how to do it."

"Seriously?"

"You have to understand that Alex and I are very close. We totally trust each other. I'm the only one that he ever told about his lock picking and his burglaries. Honestly, I was really afraid for him. I begged him to stop. I worried that he would get caught. He just laughed at me. He wanted to teach me to pick locks and he bought me a set of tools. Just to show him that I loved him and appreciated his attention, I learned. Though I would never, ever do anything like that."

"Alex got caught, though."

"Yeah, twice," she said. "The cash he was stealing from houses wasn't enough and he was getting pretty confident. So he broke into a convenience store one night. The alarm went off and he couldn't outrun SFPD. He did two years for that."

"And he got out?"

"Yeah, but he didn't learn his lesson," Mary sighed. "Alex went right back to burglarizing houses. Just like before, he usually took only cash. Eventually he broke into a really nice house in Pacific Heights. The owners had a burglar alarm and he knew it. He was long gone before the police arrived. What he didn't know was that the owners also had security cameras. So he's doing five more years."

"Do you visit him?"

"As often as I can," she said, her eyes getting moist. "I pray for him every day. I can't tell you how many candles I've lit at St. Anne's for him."

Mary gave a little sad laugh. "You know, I still keep those lock picking tools Alex gave me. In my purse. Kind of a reminder of him."

"I hope he's learned his lesson," said Keith. "And I hope that maybe the two of you can go to the beach and throw your burglary tools in the ocean."

"Me, too," she said. "Alex has two strikes, two felonies. If he does this again, he may never get out of prison."

"I'll pray for him, too," he said. "Sorry to bring this up. The memory is painful for you."

"It's okay. We need to trust each other."

Keith gave her a supportive hug. For a minute they just held onto each other. Then Keith spoke. "To change the subject, your director of nursing has started to work out at my gym."

"You mean Ms. Roberts?" asked Mary.

"Yeah," he said. "Kind of petite, attractive in a way, getting up in years. The guys are calling her 'The Cougar.'"

Mary giggled.

"Some of my co-workers on the unit say that she's trying to snag a resident for herself," she said. "Nasty rumors. She's old enough to be their mother. But I've been raised to treat both my superiors and my elders with respect. My parents are old fashioned."

"She sure dresses well," said Keith, "like a woman half her age. Fancy shoes and lots of bling. Not on the gym floor, of course, but coming and going from the street. She's been coming regularly for a couple of weeks now."

"I wonder why she chose your gym. I think she lives over in the Marina district. There are closer places."

"Maybe it was suggested by that financial guy in administration. He's been coming to the gym for a couple of years."

"You mean Mr. Henderson," said Mary.

"I just call him Bill," said Keith. "He seems nice enough. Kind of nerdy, like you would expect for an accountant. He tries pretty hard in the gym. Not an athlete, but you have to admire his tenacity."

"Maybe he suggested the gym," said Mary, "but maybe Ms. Roberts is having some sort of career make-over. She's totally changed her management style in the last six months. It used to be that we staff nurses never saw her. Maybe you would see her in the parking garage coming and going, dressed to the nines. Never on the units or the operating room or any place where there were actual patients. We weren't sure that she knew that we had a pediatric unit. Now we see her at the most unexpected times and the oddest places. Dressed in scrubs and sneakers as well. The other day she showed up in Central Sterile, where they sterilize all the surgical instruments and things, at the beginning of the day shift. Just hanging around, watching everyone work. It's kind of creepy."

"Well, good for her," said Keith. "It's good for the top administrative people to get out of their fancy offices and see what happens on the front lines of the hospital."

Keith's phone rang.

"Dr. Grant, it's Kyle Swanson at the hospital." Swanson was a junior orthopedic resident on call that night, a smart young doctor but a bit unsure of himself. "Dr. Romano is asking if you could come in and help us with a case."

Felix Romano was the professor in charge of the orthopedic trauma service. Romano was totally fearless. He was a superb surgeon who seemed to be able to fix almost anything the patients and society conspired to break. Keith recalled a case of a homeless man who had stumbled in front on one of San Francisco's famous trolley cars and almost literally broke every bone in his body. As a young resident, Keith had assisted Romano in a ten hour marathon that resulted in full restoration of anatomy and function. Keith loved the action of trauma surgery and the creativity required to come up with complex solutions to difficult problems right in the heat of the moment.

"I'm not on call," said Keith. "What's the big deal?"

"Well, 'big deal' is more true than you think," said the junior resident. "We have this woman who's visiting the city from Alabama or Mississippi or one of those states. It's her first day in San Francisco and she tripped and fell out of the tour bus over near Land's End and broke her hip."

"A hip fracture? That's pretty routine. Why does Romano want me?"

"Well, she's pretty big, Dr. Grant," said Swanson, "probably more than four hundred pounds. She's seventy years old. Dr. Romano thinks that this case may be pretty tough and he would like some help from somebody with more experience than I have."

"Okay," said Keith, "but you owe me one. I'm going to have to leave the prettiest girl in the world to come in there, operate on the fat lady, and look at you instead of her."

Keith met Drs. Romano and Swanson in the surgeon's locker room. They looked at the x-rays on the computer terminal in the lounge.

"It's a pretty straightforward femoral neck fracture," said Romano. "The real problem is that she weighs almost a quarter of a ton."

"What would you do with this, Kyle?" Keith asked the junior resident. As a chief resident, Keith always felt an obligation to teach the juniors. Every new case was a teaching opportunity.

"I would suggest a bipolar prosthesis," answered Swanson.

"Why?"

"Well, the blood supply to the femoral head goes up along the neck," responded the junior resident. "With complete displacement, it's all torn. So, the femoral head is almost certain to die. The patient is in her seventies, so a bipolar will last her the rest of her life. And, with her size and other medical issues, like her obesity, it would be best to get in and out quickly and only have to do one operation, not a revision somewhere farther down the line. A bipolar would be quick and accurate. This lady would be tough to x-ray for a pinning. We wouldn't need x-ray with a bipolar."

"Very good," said Professor Romano, praising the junior resident's knowledge and problem solving skill. Swanson smiled at the compliment from the chief of the trauma service.

"Kyle, in this particular case, you're going to have to assist Keith and me. You're going to have to retract six to eight inches of fat so we can get down to the bones. Sorry, but you may not see much."

"No problem, Dr. Romano," said Swanson.

"Which room are we in?"

"OR 10, sir."

"Who's doing anesthesia?" asked Romano.

"Dr. O'Brien is the attending, sir, with Kevin Williams as the resident," said Swanson.

"That means that Williams is doing the anesthetic," said Romano, shaking his head. "I haven't seen O'Brien get his hands dirty in the OR for years. Oh, he shows up to look at things, so he can say he was here when he submits his bill. But the work will be done by the resident. As usual."

Mabel Osborne, sedated and stripped of all dignity, lay on a hospital gurney, only partially covered by a hospital issue gown. The unfortunate woman was immense. Her hair and her skin were as white as the linens on the operating table, which was way too narrow to accommodate her girth. It took all three orthopedic surgeons and the anesthesia resident to position the patient on the operating table, lying on her side to expose the left hip area.

Keith felt sorry for the patient even though he had never actually met her. He imagined how embarrassed the poor woman would have been if she could have witnessed herself being positioned for surgery. Great sheets of fat spilled over the edges of the narrow table. Enormous pendulous breasts flopped over the edge. In order to expose the skin where the incision would be made, Keith had to use tape to hold back a big roll of fat. While Keith and Swanson were securing the safety straps, the door to the operating room burst open and O'Brien, the attending anesthesiologist rushed in.

"Jesus Christ," shouted O'Brien, "she's falling off the left side of the table!"

Charging in closer to the operating table, O'Brien continued to shout.

"Jesus Christ, she's falling off the right side of the table!"

O'Brien stopped in his tracks.

"Jesus Christ, she's falling off both sides of the table," he paused. "Je-e-e-sus Christ!"

Everyone but the anesthesia resident, Williams, burst into laughter. Keith thought that maybe Dr. O'Brien should spend a little more time in the operating room. The surgeons were really laughing at the anesthesia professor.

Williams was frowning, looking from the patient to the monitor on the anesthesia machine. He was grumbling quietly, cursing something and adjusting the dials on the oxygen flow meter.

"Dr. O'Brien, we have a problem," said Williams. "Her O_2 sats are falling dramatically."

"Did you increase the oxygen, Kevin?" asked the anesthesia attending.

"She's at 100% oxygen and her saturations are still falling, sir."

"Is your tube in the trachea?"

"Yes, sir, I'm sure of it. Good breath sounds on both sides."

"Are you having trouble ventilating? Is she in bronchospasm?"

"Air is passing easily, sir," said Williams, clearly worried. "Now the pulse is slowing."

"Turn her on her back," O'Brien shouted to the surgeons. "Get those straps off. We may need to resuscitate."

Keith, Swanson and Romano quickly removed the straps and braces and turned the large woman flat on her back. Both anesthesiologists were frantically at work at the patient's head by now, injecting medications into the IV, listening to the air rush into her chest, glancing at the numbers on the monitor. Alarms were ringing as the monitors recorded the downward spiral.

"Shit," said O'Brien, "I can't detect a pulse."

"Start chest compressions!"

Keith climbed up on the operating table and began to pump on Mabel's chest. His own pulse was racing. He had done resuscitations before, but this one was different. This was a total surprise.

Keith pumped and compressed Mabel's chest. O'Brien and Williams worked feverishly, looking from the monitors to Mabel's face. The two anesthesiologists spoke furtively to each other, then injected one medication after another into the IV.

Swanson stood beside the operating table helplessly. Romano asked Keith if he needed a break from the effort of the chest compressions.

"I'm OK," said Keith between thrusts. He was not tired and didn't need a relief, but he was far from OK. The patient was dying right under his hands.

It was no use. The surgeons and anesthesiologists worked on the patient for half an hour. She was blue and cold and dusky when they finally gave up.

Keith reluctantly got back on the floor. He was devastated.

"Holy shit," Romano asked O'Brien. "What the hell happened? We never even made an incision."

"I really don't know, Felix. Maybe a pulmonary embolus. Maybe some reaction to one of the drugs we gave her," said a perplexed O'Brien.

Sadly and in silence, the doctors helped the nursing staff move Mabel from the operating table to a gurney so that the body could be taken to the hospital morgue. The anesthesiologists, Swanson, and Romano shuffled out of the operating room.

Keith remained behind with the nurses, needing a little time to compose himself. He leaned against a wall, trying to understand what had just happened. The nurses silently packed up the surgical instruments that had never been used. A slender woman with heavy makeup, dressed in scrubs entered the room.

"I heard what happened," said Patricia Roberts, Director of Nursing. "Are you two all right?"

"We'll be okay, Ms. Roberts," said the instrument nurse. "But I'm going to have a stiff drink when I get home."

"It was so sudden," said the circulating nurse. "Everything was going so well and then, well, it seemed like she just died."

"I'm sure you did your best, as did the doctors," said Patricia, nodding to Keith. "Sometimes our best just isn't good enough."

"Pardon me," asked the instrument nurse, "but isn't it rather late for you to be in the hospital?"

"I was working late on some paperwork in the office when I heard about the problem," said Patricia. "I came to see if I could help. Maybe just to provide support to my nurses."

"Well, thank you. It's very considerate of you. But we're okay," said the instrument nurse.

"We need to have this OR shut down until I can get hospital engineering to check out all the equipment and the monitors," said Patricia. "Just a precaution, of course. But use the other ORs tonight."

◆ ◆ ◆

The door to the CEO's office was closed. Only Helen and Patricia attended this daily meeting. The two of them really controlled how the hospital operated.

"Our numbers look great. Our admissions are up and MediCal is paying us promptly, without questioning our billing," said Helen. "I think we've built up some trust there. Or, on the other hand, the MediCal staffers may simply be mindlessly sending us the taxpayers' money."

"As long as they send us money and don't trouble us, I'm happy." Patricia laughed.

Helen enjoyed Patricia's laugh. They were not just professional colleagues, but close friends. They were both highly intelligent professional women. However, they differed in their approach to men.

Patricia had one failed marriage. Her husband left her for a younger woman. This broke her heart and severely damaged her self-esteem. She made every effort to remain attractive, keeping her body in excellent shape with attention to her diet and vigorous daily exercise. Frequent visits to the plastic surgeon for Botox injections, tucks and trims combatted the wrinkles of advancing age. She dressed fashionably, selecting styles that were popular with women much younger than she. And she was successful to a certain extent. Patricia did not like to sleep alone and she was often able to attract partners for one night stands.

Helen was divorced once and widowed by the death of her second husband. She had given up on her physical appearance. To be certain, she made an effort to be attractive to men that she wanted to impress. That, however, was business, not romance. She was somewhat overweight. She was losing the battle with aging. She concentrated on her work, taking satisfaction in her success as an executive. Helen found her professional career to be more than an adequate substitute for personal relationships.

"You know," Helen said, "it's really all about the money. We like to talk about providing quality care to the patients and good education to the students, but we all get measured in dollars. I don't know anybody in health care who gets promoted for giving good care, or fired for being a bad teacher. But, in our business, if the dollars aren't there, you and I are looking for jobs."

"Yes, in the final analysis, that's how we keep score in our society," said Patricia. "Dollars are like points in a game. Whoever has the most dollars, the most points, wins."

"You get it," said Helen, "That's one of the things I liked best about you when we met for the first time."

"You mean my interview?"

"Of course," said Helen. "You were not just some idealistic nurse trying to save the world. You're a realist. You appreciate the importance of the financial aspect of health care. As a result, you know the value of smart management. In health care, it's really management that makes the system work."

"Yes, and I've learned an awful lot from you," said Patricia. "Management makes it possible for good patient care and good education. We're so often vilified and unappreciated, particularly by the doctors. The doctors get all the glory. They have no understanding of how important our work is and no idea of the challenges we face."

"It's not entirely the fault of the doctors," said Helen. "They get no training or education on the topics of management or health economics. They know how to take care of patients, but nothing else about the health care industry. I think that's why we see so few doctors in positions of leadership in health care."

"Nurses, on the other hand, do get some education in health care organization," Patricia said. "And the nature of our profession, being hierarchical, promotes professional advancement through management."

"You're right," Helen agreed. "And you yourself are a perfect example of a nursing professional who has learned so much about management and who has used her knowledge to advance herself professionally and personally."

"So much for our mutual admiration hour," Helen said. "Back to the business of running this hospital. How is the nursing staffing going?"

Helen knew that her own mind worked faster than those of other people. She was often onto a different topic in the middle of a conversation. Thankfully, Patricia seemed to like Helen's little quirks. Helen knew that Patricia trusted her completely in both professional and personal matters. Helen knew herself well enough to realize that she had a kind of charisma, a kind of aura, a sensation of power that Patricia found inspiring and perhaps a bit exciting.

"Tolerable number of vacancies. We're using some registry nurses, but not enough to stimulate us to raise our salary rates for nurses. We're keeping up with other Bay area hospitals, neither sustaining net gains nor losses in staffing because of salary and benefits."

"Good. Then we'll hold salaries for now. We'll only consider raises if the market inequity gets so bad that our nurses are leaving in large numbers for better paying jobs."

"I think we need to add some staff to Five South, though," said Patricia.

"Really?" Helen raised an eyebrow.

"Yes," Patricia replied. "I've been looking at the census reports from each nursing unit. They show an increase in the average daily census on Five South. Now, we are obligated by contract to have a certain ratio of nurses to patients on each unit. Our staffing on Five South is currently too low. We need to add three full time RNs to cover all shifts with an adequate ratio."

"Very well," said Helen, a slight smile crossing her face. "See to it. I heard that a patient died on the operating table during orthopedic surgery. Can you give me an update? Are we going to get hurt because of this?"

"Well, she just died, it seems," said Patricia. "Nobody can figure out why. The autopsy was inconclusive. Did you know that she weighed over four hundred pounds? The family is upset, of course, but I don't think that they'll sue. The hospital is paying to have her body shipped back to Alabama."

"I hope they don't charge by the pound. It could break the budget."

Both women shared a laugh.

"My new approach to my job is going well," said Patricia. "The staff nurses are getting used to me appearing at any unit, any time. They like that I wear scrubs and sneakers, just like them. Oh how I detest those clothes, Helen. They have no style at all. You have no idea what a sacrifice I'm making, wearing those hideous shoes and shapeless rags."

"Soldier on, Patricia. It's for a good cause."

"The best. How is the proposal for the orthopedic institute going with the board?"

"Well, Mr. Patterson is a strong advocate for the project. But he's called for a full audit of the hospital finances to make sure we can afford it. He's supported in his call for the audit by

Mr. Davenport, who is a hateful old bastard. Davenport doesn't trust me. He doesn't like anything I propose. I shouldn't feel persecuted, however. I don't think Davenport likes anyone or any proposal. He wants to see the audit just to stir the shit pot and make trouble."

"That could be a lot of trouble, Helen."

"We'll make sure that it isn't, Patricia. Davenport is scheduled to have a knee replacement in a few weeks. That's a pretty painful operation and should distract him from board business for several months."

"And the other man?"

"Patterson, well, he can be distracted for a while as well. I'm not worried about him."

Helen planned and prepared for everything. Planning was one of the essential elements of her success. Nothing was ever left to chance. Every possible contingency was considered. Helen never had loose ends or questions she could not answer. And Helen selected her top staff with care. She surrounded herself with a close circle of devoted senior managers. People like Patricia.

"How long do we want to delay the orthopedic project?"

"Six months should do it," said Helen, "After that everything should be just fine."

FIVE

IF YOU HAD to come to the doctor, you might as well select one with some style, Ted Wells thought.

"So, my real question is did you make the backhand shot?" asked Dr. Alexander Warren with a grin. Warren was a professor of orthopedics at Sutro State and the head of the sports medicine division.

Warren had the MRI images of Ted's knee up on a computer screen.

"No, it didn't even clear the net," laughed Ted. He was just on the other side of forty, strikingly handsome and remarkably fit. He looked like a Hollywood star, with a perfect tan, perfect teeth, perfect haircut, just the slightest touch of grey above his ears. Nobody would be surprised to learn that he was a very successful talent agent, opening doors to stage and screen for his clients. Ted exuded confidence seasoned with a dash of narcissism.

When Ted hurt his knee playing tennis, he sought out Dr. Warren from Sutro State because he was the best. When it came to his own health, Ted wanted only the best.

"Well, my friend," continued Dr. Warren, pointing at a spot on the MRI, "you've managed to tear your medial meniscus. That's a torn cartilage in layman's terms."

"I knew something snapped when I went for the backhand shot," said Ted. "Do I need surgery?"

"Yes," replied Warren, "but the surgery is pretty minor. It looks like you have a very small tear in the inside cartilage. We should be able to just trim this a bit, clean up any loose cartilage. The tear is small enough that we shouldn't have to repair the meniscus. It will be same day surgery. In and out the same day."

"Do you do this in your office?" asked Ted. There was more privacy in the office than in a hospital. If possible, he would prefer to hide his own vulnerability as much as possible.

"No, we do this in the regular operating rooms at Sutro State University Hospital, but you won't have to stay overnight. You'll come in a few hours before surgery, fill out some insurance forms, be examined by the resident and the anesthesiologist. We'll have you asleep for the procedure, which should take about an hour. When you wake up you can go home."

Ted didn't want to look like a cripple after the surgery. That didn't fit his image of himself. "Will I need crutches?"

"We'll give you a set. I want you to make an appointment with my sports medicine physical therapist before the operation. She'll fit you with crutches and teach you how to use them. Using the crutches after the operation is optional. If you feel comfortable, you don't need to use them. When you see the PT, she'll set you up for a few post-op therapy sessions."

"I don't want to seem like a wimp, Alex, but how much does this hurt?" asked Ted. He really, really didn't like pain.

"Not much. It's a little uncomfortable," said Warren. "I'll give you a prescription for some Vicodin, but I doubt that you'll need it. Everything is done with the arthroscope, you see. We don't make much of an incision, just a couple of small stabs to get our instruments inside. No big cuts in muscles or ligaments or things that cause pain. And, very little scarring."

"That's nice to know," said Ted.

"You'll not be allowed to drive on the day of surgery," said Warren. "You'll probably be a little woozy from the anesthetic. Is there someone who can drive you to and from the hospital?"

"Sure, my girlfriend can do the driving," said Ted.

"Any other questions?"

"A couple," said Ted. "When will I be able to play tennis again?" Ted had been blessed with good health all his life. He had never had any sort of surgery. This whole episode with his knee was unnerving.

"We'll have you back on the court in about four weeks," said Warren. "About six weeks after the procedure, you should be back to your usual quality game."

"That sounds reasonable," said Ted. "I should be back in action for the club tournament in three months. One more question?"

"Sure."

"Well, when can I have sex? Wendy is some kind of hot."

Warren laughed.

"Whenever you want, Ted. Right after surgery if you wish. Any other questions?"

"No, that's about it."

"Do you want me to schedule the surgery?"

"By all means. Let's get it over with," said Ted. "Can we do the surgery early in the morning?"

"I can make you the first case, if you like," said Warren.

"Thanks," said Ted. "Let's get this over with so I can get back to my life."

♦ ♦ ♦

The basement of the hospital was somewhat unfamiliar to Keith. It seemed a little cold. The halls were stark and grey, lit by fluorescent bulbs that were just a bit on the blue side of white, it looked, well, industrial. Keith thought that the hospital was probably saving money on décor, since no patients ever came down here. At least no living patients.

Keith was there to see his best friend, Dr. Matt Harrison. Despite many differences, Keith and Matt had become close in medical school at Tufts. Keith was straight and Matt was gay; Keith was liberal Democrat and Matt was Republican; Keith was Catholic and Matt was an atheist. Still, they had an odd chemistry together and became roommates during the last two years.

Matt was a tall, slender man who was now the senior resident in pathology. Matt wanted to do his residency in San Francisco so that he did not have to hide his sexuality. Keith supported his friend, but they agreed that they would not share living quarters in San Francisco. Matt wanted some freedom in his social life and Keith would have been an awkward companion.

Normally they would meet upstairs in the sunlight or in the hospital cafeteria. Each was a frequent guest in the other's apartment for dinner. This time, Keith needed to talk to Matt about a clinical case.

"What can I tell ya, Keith? She had morbid obesity, some coronary artery disease, Type II diabetes, a hip fracture, and a few broken ribs, which I suspect you gave her when you tried to resuscitate her," said Matt.

Matt had recently finished the autopsy on Mabel Osborne. They were in Matt's cubbyhole office, down the hall from the autopsy rooms. Matt looked over his rimless glasses at Keith.

"What was the cause of death?" Keith asked. "Did she pop a pulmonary embolus? Was there a big old clot in her pulmonary artery? Was there some drug reaction?"

"No. Nada. Nothing that we could find," said Matt. "I signed her out as 'hypoxia' for cause of death."

"Hypoxia? She didn't have enough oxygen? Shit, Matt, anesthesia had her on 100% oxygen," said Keith. "That's bullshit and you know it."

"I've got to put something on the death certificate and that's the best guess I have based on the lab tests and the autopsy findings. Did you have some other idea?"

"No. I have no idea. And that's what bothers me the most. Well, losing the patient bothers me the most. Did you look at the anesthesia record? Is there something in that to indicate what went wrong?"

"Yeah, I checked it out, and I queried the memory of the monitor as well" said Matt. "It looks like her pulse, blood pressure and O$_2$ saturations started to go down slowly right after her intubation. My guess is that you guys were positioning her on the table for a while, which caused some interference with the measurements and monitor recordings. Then, when Dr. Williams became worried, things just continued to spiral downhill."

"Is there nothing we can learn from this?" asked Keith. "This poor lady came all the way from Alabama to see our City by the Bay, falls out of a goddam tour bus and breaks her hip and winds up dead. What a tragedy. She was halfway across the country, away from family and friends. And nobody can even learn from this? God, that's pathetic."

"My friend, sometimes fat old people just die," said Matt.

♦ ♦ ♦

Dr. Richard Phillips was totally comfortable in Helen Crawford's office. As chief of the medical staff, he felt superior to the administrator and her middle managers. In Phillips' view, the entire hospital staff existed to serve the doctors. After all, patients did not come to the hospital because of the reputation of the management group. People came because the hospital had excellent doctors. And, as chief of staff, he represented the doctors.

"What did the board decide about the proposal for an orthopedic institute?" Phillips asked.

"They haven't made a decision yet," Helen replied.

"Clay Ross told me the other evening at the Patterson's party that it was going to be approved," said Phillips.

"Was that before or after Clay got drunk?"

"What do you mean?"

"Clay Ross is a hopeless alcoholic." said Helen. "I thought he was probably drunk before the party even got started. So, Richard, it would be smart to take anything that Clay says with a grain of salt."

"So it's not decided?"

"Wayne Patterson seems in favor, and he heads the Planning Committee," she said, "but nobody has looked carefully at the needs assessment study that the orthopedic department prepared. The issue is tabled until I and my staff complete our own needs assessment study."

"If the board approves the orthopedic institute, that will tie up the hospital's money for years to come," said Phillips.

"Yes, it will," she said, "which is one reason why the board must be careful in deciding to approve the project."

"You know that I would rather see the money go to building a new medical staff library. One that is totally modern, with lots of internet connections and printers. A library that will benefit all the medical staff, the residents, and the medical students.".

"Yes, Richard, I know that's a priority for you," Helen said. "You'll just have to wait until the board makes its decision."

"I'm not happy, Helen. Not happy at all."

Dr. Anthony Green was always comfortable in the combined departmental library and conference room. It made him feel proud of the orthopedic department that he chaired, proud of the excellent patient care, research, and teaching that his program was known for. In addition to modern computers and DVDs illustrating surgical techniques, the library portion of the room proudly housed handsomely bound volumes of orthopedic journals going back almost a century. The stacks of bookshelves were made of the same walnut as the paneling and the large conference table.

Green usually enjoyed the monthly meeting of is faculty. It was a time to contemplate the success of the program. Green enjoyed being the man in charge of all this. Normally the faculty sat comfortably in black wooden armchairs with the seal of Sutro State University in gold at the top.

Today's meeting of the faculty was not going to be comfortable. Green felt his stomach acid gnawing at his insides.

"Not a great week for the orthopedic department all around," said Green, calling the meeting to order. "Felix's hip fracture patient's death has been selected for review at surgical M & M's. The three MRSA infections in routine arthroscopy cases are under investigation by the hospital Infection Control Committee. And our proposal for an orthopedic institute is meeting considerable opposition at the board level."

Morbidity and Mortality Conference, or M & M, was a monthly meeting of all surgical faculty and residents to study preventable complications. It was held in a large amphitheater-style classroom in the medical school across the street from the hospital. While in general the meeting was constructive and looked for ways to improve the quality of patient care, it could be an Inquisition. No surgeon looked forward to having her or his cases brought up for discussion and criticism. Everyone agreed that the M & M conference was the most effective way for the surgeons to spot problems with the quality of care and for good colleagues to make suggestions with the good of both patients and surgeons in mind. Every surgeon thought the discussions were fair, unbiased, and constructive. Except the surgeon whose complication was up for discussion.

"I never even laid a knife on that lady," said Romano. "How can it be an M & M case?"

"You brought her to the OR, Felix," said Green, "so it's classified as a surgical death. What is the story on the infections, Alex?"

Alexander Warren was the sports medicine surgeon. The three infected joints were all his patients.

"I'm totally baffled," said Warren. "I've looked at all three cases and I can't make any sense at all of it. Two knees and one shoulder. I did all three. Nothing went wrong. They were fast, uncomplicated operations. My only guess, and it's just a guess, is that there is some source of MRSA that has contaminated the residents. Maybe something in the call room."

"The residents?" asked Green.

"I have no data, but that's the only thing I can think of," Warren replied.

"May I suggest that we ask Keith Grant to have a look at these cases?" said Dr. Stuart. "He's a very smart young fellow with good problem solving skills. He's a chief resident, somewhere between a junior resident and a faculty member and he's on the adult reconstructive service now. He didn't scrub on any of the sports cases, except to clean up the last infection. Maybe a fresh set of eyes with minimal personal involvement will be able to see something that you've missed. Keith is a sharp guy, the best resident we've had here in ten years."

"Sounds like a good idea, Ray. It would be better if we could explain this and take some corrective action," said Green. "Otherwise some asshole from administration will claim that we don't cover our noses or wash our hands when we operate."

"I'm afraid that is already beginning," said the senior faculty hand surgeon. "We've been notified by Infection Control that every attending surgeon and resident in the department must go to employee health for a nasal swab culture."

"So they think we are spreading MRSA all over the hospital in boogers? Christ," said Amelia Howard, the current head of pediatric orthopedics. Howard was a petite woman with short hair, a winning smile, and a sense of humor in all situations. She was Stuart's protégé and hand-picked successor.

"It's embarrassing," said the hand surgeon. "The news is all over the hospital. Staff and visitors are talking that maybe it's not safe to have an orthopedic operation here."

"Damn," Green said. The stomach acid was getting worse. "Let's see if Keith Grant can help with this. We'll discuss it again when he's finished his investigation."

"And you say that our proposal for an orthopedic institute is in trouble with the board?" asked Warren. He was the principle architect of the plan and, as head of sports medicine, had the most to gain from its implementation, both in personal fame and monetary fortune. "We put a lot of work in on that."

"Well, I talked with Wayne Patterson of the board," said Green. "His committee is the one that has our proposal. He's pretty excited about our idea. He presented it to the board at their last meeting. It sounds like Helen Crawford wants to do her own needs assessment study to see if there really is enough demand in the community to make such an institute profitable. Patterson and Jim Davenport have demanded a complete financial audit to make sure the hospital can afford the institute."

"Hell, we did the needs assessment part," said Warren. "There's plenty of demand in our community. We'll have patients lined up the day we open the doors. This is a gold mine."

"Well, Ms. Crawford has other concerns as well," said Green. "She thinks our cost estimates are too low and that the institute will cost so much that the hospital won't be able to afford both it and the other projects that she wants to do."

"Yeah, like fat bonuses for herself," said Warren. "Do we have enough political clout to get that bitch fired? She seems to obstruct everything we try to do."

"She's no friend to the orthopedic department," agreed Green. "I don't know why. We bring in plenty of money to the hospital, lots of patients. She should love us. But I'm not sure we could get her fired if we wanted to."

"Especially not now, with the infections and stuff hurting our reputation in the hospital," added the hand surgeon.

Green's stomach was in revolt. He needed to end the meeting and find an antacid. "We need to do good work, solve this infection problem, and hope for the best."

SIX

KEITH SAT ALONE, contemplating a cup of coffee.

"You look perplexed," said Mary as she set her tray down on the table across from Keith in a corner of the hospital cafeteria. "You didn't even see me coming."

"Sorry," said Keith. "Dr. Warren and Dr. Green asked me to review all these MRSA infections that we've had. I've been immersed in the hospital charts all morning. I've got a spreadsheet of data and all kinds of notes, but I just can't figure it out."

"What have you got?" she asked. "Can I help?"

"Well, I'd appreciate a fresh set of eyes," said Keith.

"How about a fresh set of ears? I've only got half an hour for lunch. Tell me what you have so far."

"OK, but I'll be surprised if you can figure this out in half an hour while eating lunch when I can't solve it with four hours of concentrated work."

"You would be surprised about a lot of things that I can do," said Mary.

He laughed. There was no doubt in his mind that Mary was full of surprises. He was really falling in love with her.

"Here goes," Keith began. "There are three MRSA cases. Two women and one man. Two knees and one shoulder. All young with minor injuries. All athletes, but different sports. One knee is a young woman who's a runner. That's the one I had to clean out in the middle of the night when I was on call. The other woman, a tennis player, had a shoulder scope for some minor labral tears. The man is a college student, a football player with a partial meniscus tear. No intraoperative complications in any case and no recorded breech of sterility on any of the notes. Anesthesia records show uneventful, fast procedures. The only person who was present for each operation was Dr. Warren himself. The nurses, techs, anesthesia staff, residents, students appear in different combinations, but nobody other than Warren was at all three operations. All were same-day surgeries and the patients were discharged from recovery doing fine. The only thing they have in common is that they were all first cases of the day."

"How about recovery room staff?" she asked.

"Good question. I looked at that and each had a different nurse. And it would be very unusual for a recovery room nurse to remove a surgical dressing. I can't find any hospital personnel who might have transmitted the MRSA to all the patients except Dr. Warren."

"Well, has he been checked out?" asked Mary.

"Yeah, and he's not a carrier of MRSA," said Keith. "Warren has implied that there is some MRSA infection in the residents' call room. He's trying to pin the blame on the residents. That figures. I don't really think that Dr. Green believes that the residents are to blame. And I'm certain that Dr. Stuart doesn't buy that. Anyway, it seems like there is a kind of witch hunt on. That's part of the stimulus that made the department ask me to do the review. Hospital Infection Control is investigating this as a threat to patient care. In addition to a massive raid on the call rooms and resident lockers, they've already done nasal swabs on every faculty surgeon and resident in orthopedics, looking for MRSA carriers."

"You, too?"

"Oh, yeah," said Keith. "It was a little embarrassing. Like I was some sort of suspect for the San Francisco Typhoid Mary."

"I wish I could have watched that," said Mary. "Or better yet done the swab myself. I'd have stuck the swab deep, making sure I had a good sample."

"You're a sadist," said Keith. "You probably would have enjoyed sticking a Q-tip up my nose."

"Yep. Would've been fun. But let's get back to your mystery. You looked at the health care providers. How about the patients themselves? Do they have anything in common?"

"Nothing at all," said Keith. "The runner lives here in the city and works in a retail clothing store. The tennis player lives down in San Mateo and works for an insurance company. The football player lives on campus in the East Bay and is a college student. The runner and tennis player are white, the football player is black. The insurance coverage is different for all three. No prior history of MRSA infection in any of them. No MRSA reported in the football locker room at the college. There's no evidence that any of the patients knew each other before their operations or that they have met since. You know, if word gets out that Infection Control is suspicious of substandard care in the orthopedic department, there could be some lawsuits."

"Bummer," she said, "but lawsuits aren't your problem. Your issue is trying to find out how this happened. You've looked at the hospital personnel and the patients. How about other things, like maybe the suture used in each case."

"You're thinking like an operating room nurse," said Keith. "Dr. Warren uses the same suture on all his arthroscopy cases. Two different operating rooms were used in these cases. The two knee cases were done in OR 6 and the shoulder in OR 10. Even though the suture was the same, the boxes in each room probably came from different manufacturers lots. He used a 2-O suture on the football player and a 3-O stitch on the runner. So the sutures in all three cases came from different lots. And there are no other MRSA surgical infections from anywhere else in the hospital during this time. Nice thought, though. Are you beginning to see why I'm stuck?"

"Hmmm," said Mary. "So, personnel, patients, equipment. Have you looked at the bugs?"

"The what?"

"How about looking at the germs themselves?" asked Mary. "There are different strains of MRSA. Are they different in each case too?"

"I don't know," admitted Keith. "That's one thing I didn't compare. I wonder if the lab keeps a record of those things."

"Matt would know," she said. "The clinical lab is under the pathology department. Matt could get access to any data about the bacteria that aren't on the chart."

"I'm going to check that out," said Keith, "right after lunch. I have a few minutes before I'm expected in clinic."

"You know," said Mary, "you might consider running all this past Dr. Stuart as well. He was up on pediatrics the other day for a consultation. I got to accompany him. Honestly, Keith, he is amazing. He did this examination on a little boy and it looked like the two of them were playing games. Then he made this exotic diagnosis that nobody had even thought of, right there on the ward. An MRI was done yesterday which confirmed his diagnosis, just exactly the way he predicted. I owe him a milkshake."

"A milkshake?" laughed Keith, "You made a bet with Stuart?"

"He's really nice," said Mary. "I've worked with him before. He teaches me so much. And he said that I was really sharp."

"Well, Stuart was certainly right about that," said Keith. "He's pretty approachable and he sure is good at solving problems that nobody else can solve. Maybe I'll stop by his office this afternoon as well."

Keith found the hospital charts right where he left them in his resident cubicle. Quickly he turned to the laboratory reports on the cultures from each infected case. There was a list of possible antibiotic resistance and sensitivity for each culture. They were identical. Keith called his friend Matt Harrison in pathology.

"Hey, Matt," he asked, "does the microbiology lab keep cultures going of MRSA cases or are those destroyed?"

"They keep them going while the patient is still in the hospital," Matt answered. "Then maybe for a week after discharge. After that I think they destroy them."

"Damn. Do they do specific typing on MRSA that they don't put in the chart? I mean, it's such a problem and risk in the hospital."

"Actually, the lab does typing on the MRSA and even phage typing, for just the reason you mention," said Matt. "We're doing our best to learn about MRSA infections, particularly in the hospital, so we can try to prevent these things."

"Phage typing, too?" asked Keith. "That's pretty serious."

Phage typing was a sophisticated test that examined the viruses that infect the bacteria. It was an excellent way to determine the exact strain of bacteria.

"We take MRSA pretty seriously, my friend," said Matt. "Why do you ask?"

"My faculty has asked me to look at three MRSA cases in routine arthroscopic surgeries that we have had recently. Could you look up the lab data on the bugs from these three cases for me?"

"Sure," said Matt, "give me the records numbers and I'll have the information to you by the end of the day."

"Thanks, man," said Keith, "I gotta spend all afternoon in clinic."

When Keith returned to his cubicle after clinic, he found a disturbing e-mail from Matt. Keith felt a little sick in his stomach as he read:

"All three infections were caused by identical strains of MRSA. It was ST-239-MRSA-III. The phage typing was identical in all three cases. These bacteria certainly come from a single source. Please call me as soon as possible."

♦ ♦ ♦

The sight of Wendy Petridis actually took Dr. Warren's breath away for a moment. She looked like a swimsuit model, which she actually was. Warren was not sure he had ever seen a woman so beautiful. Ted Wells had all the luck. Wendy was probably an aspiring movie star, looking to Ted for her ticket into the big time. Warren thought that he would go to see any movie starring Wendy.

"Ms. Petridis?" asked Warren, regaining his focus but still staring at her. "Ted is fine. Everything went exactly as planned. We took out a small loose piece of his knee cartilage. He's in the recovery room now, sleeping off the anesthetic. You can take him home in a couple of hours."

"Thank you, Doctor," said Wendy.

The long eyelashes over soft brown eyes seized Warren's attention again. He knew it was unprofessional, but he was overwhelmed. He never heard what she said next.

"Doctor?" she asked.

"Oh, yes," said Warren, "you were asking?"

"What can I expect from Ted?"

"Well," Warren began, "he may be sleepy this evening, as his body washes out the anesthetic drugs. He's allowed to eat.

I don't want him drinking any alcohol if he is taking the opiate pain pills."

"Does Ted have a follow-up appointment?"

"Yes. The nurses will give you a paper with his appointment. I want to see him in about a week. We'll start his physical therapy after the office visit. There are written instructions. He can walk without the crutches if he's comfortable. There's a prescription for some Vicodin, but I doubt that he'll need any. Probably a couple of Tylenols will control his pain."

"Thank you, Doctor," said Wendy, flashing a smile that drove Warren crazy.

Warren didn't want her to leave. He knew that he had four more operations to do. He just wanted Wendy to stay, to talk to him. So he could continue to look at her. But he couldn't think of anything else to say to her.

"If there are no more questions," said Warren, "I need to get back into surgery. If anything comes up, please don't hesitate to call me."

Warren was not thinking of Ted at all when he gave Wendy his phone number. He had no idea how he was going to concentrate on his next procedure. He wondered if there was time for a cold shower before the case began.

◆ ◆ ◆

SFPD Detective Duane Wilson saw the flashing lights of the patrol car parked ahead. In the ritzy Sea Cliff neighborhood, patrol cars with flashers were about as common as black detectives, like himself. Wilson took a perverse pleasure in the situation.

"What's up?" asked Wilson, approaching a young patrol officer standing near the front door of the Patterson house. "Why did you call me?"

"Duane, something just doesn't seem right with this," said the officer. "There's a dead body. Maybe you don't need to be here, but, well, I really want you to look at this for yourself."

"Fill me in."

"Apparently the cleaning lady found the body," said the officer. "Today was just a routine day. No sign of break-in. Nothing missing according to the husband. By the way, Mr. Patterson owns Elegant Markets, all of them."

"The high-end supermarket chain?"

"The very same."

"That explains the Sea Cliff address," said Duane. "Keep talking."

"Well, according to the cleaning lady, the neighbors, and the husband, Mrs. Patterson, er, the deceased, was quite a drinker," said the officer. "Even this early in the day it wasn't unusual for her to be getting started on the day's drunk. When the cleaning lady showed up, she found Mrs. Patterson, still in her nightgown and housecoat, lying on the floor in the parlor. A spilled glass was on the floor with her. At first, the housekeeper thought that Mrs. Patterson had just passed out drunk. That has happened before. So she tried to wake the woman and found that she was dead. The housekeeper called 911 and we responded in about 5 minutes."

Duane took out a paper notebook and a pen. The young officer was being very attentive to details. Duane sensed that the patrol officer was suspicious about this case. Duane wanted to take a few notes.

"Where was the husband?"

"At work. He came over immediately when we called."

"So, was anyone in the house when the housekeeper arrived besides the deceased?"

"No. The doors were locked. The housekeeper has a key and the code for the alarm system, which was on. Just what she expected. The cleaning woman said that it was not unusual for her to let herself in. Mr. Patterson was often at work and Mrs. Patterson might still be sleeping off the previous night's drunk. Or, it could be that the lady of the house was out of bed and already into the bottle."

"So you have an old lady alcoholic who is found dead in the family room with an empty glass nearby," said Duane. "Nothing disturbed, nothing stolen, no signs of break-in. Why isn't this a case of the woman drinking herself to death? So far, this doesn't sound like much of a mystery. Why call homicide?"

"Like I said, Duane, this may be just what you say," said the patrolman. "But please have a look for yourself."

"Okay. Something about this bothers you, doesn't it? Care to tell me what?"

"Just take a look."

The late Eleanor Patterson was sprawled on the carpet in a most undignified pose. There was dried saliva on her face, along with quite a bit of blood on her face and the carpet. The blood seemed to have come from her mouth. Duane thought he could see deep cuts in her tongue. A few feet from the body lay an empty cocktail glass. Without disturbing the glass, Duane got down on the floor and sniffed inside. The sweet odor of cream sherry was still strong. Duane got into a crouched position and studied the corpse. No blood on the hands. No marks on the face and neck. But, for a woman who had been dead for at least several hours, Mrs. Patterson's skin looked awfully pink, almost red.

"Does her skin look odd to you, officer?" Duane asked.

"That's what I noticed, too," he replied. "It almost looks like a carbon monoxide poisoning. But here in the family room? How could that be?"

Duane was on his feet and looking around the room.

"Did anybody disturb the bottles on the bar?" Duane asked.

"No, sir."

"Hmmm. There's a bottle of cream sherry with the cork pulled. It's almost full. I don't see any other open bottles."

Duane crouched down again and looked at Eleanor Patterson's face.

"The blood, I think, came because she bit her tongue. Combine that with the dried saliva all over her face and I would think that maybe she had a seizure."

"Did she get so drunk that she had a seizure?" asked the uniformed officer.

"I don't think she was drunk," said Duane. "The glass contained cream sherry. And the bottle has just been opened. I think she was on her first drink. And I think you are a very smart cop."

"Really?" asked the officer.

"Yeah," said Duane, "one of the signs of cyanide poisoning is a red, ruddy skin. I think that old Mrs. Patterson may have been poisoned."

Duane declared the Patterson mansion in Sea Cliff to be a crime scene. Forensic teams were summoned as was the coroner. Soon TV camera crews began to arrive, like flies attracted to a fresh pile of poop.

Duane was no stranger to the art of managing a crime scene. Usually homicide scenes were in the ghetto. There were lots of curious neighbors who would scatter if a police officer approached. The killings of poor people were so common that the media generally left them alone. Things were a little different in Sea Cliff. The streets were narrow and the houses were huge mansions. The neighbors remained indoors. The limited parking was taken by the coroners van, the crime scene investigators, and dozens of TV, radio, and print media vehicles. Duane handled them all firmly and with authority. He kept the media confined to the sidewalk across the street. He allowed no interviews at all.

Uniformed officers kept Wayne Patterson confined in the living room. The thin elderly gentleman in the three piece suit was pacing the floor, obviously upset. When Duane approached, he detected a mixture of grief and anger. Duane was fairly certain that there was also a hint of a special kind of contempt, racial contempt, in the face of Patterson.

"Mr. Patterson, I'm Detective Wilson," Duane said, offering his hand.

Patterson looked at the proffered hand with distaste. He made no effort to shake it. "Are *you* in charge of this?"

"Yes. This is my crime scene."

Patterson's face reddened. "Crime scene? What the hell are you talking about? And who the hell are all these people? This is my home and I want these people out of here."

"Mr. Patterson, I'm sorry for the loss of your wife, believe me," Duane said, "but it is possible that this was not an accident or a natural death. We need to figure out what happened here."

"What happened here is that my wife finally had one drink too many and it killed her," Patterson said. He paused for a moment and then turned away. Duane saw him shake with a sob.

"I am sorry," Duane said. "I'm sure you loved her very much."

Patterson composed himself. "You have no idea, Detective. And I want you to leave now. Leave me alone to mourn my wife. Get all these reporters out of here. They're vultures. They'll ruin my reputation and my business in their quest for sordid gossip."

Two attendants from the coroner's office pushed a gurney with a shrouded corpse toward the front door.

"Where the hell are you taking Eleanor?" demanded Patterson.

"To the morgue, sir."

"Like hell you are," ranted Patterson. "Take her to Sutro State University Hospital. I'm on the board of the hospital. I will not have my wife in the morgue with all those junkies and winos and homeless bums. She deserves better than that."

"It's okay," said Duane. "I'll call the coroner's office. Take her to the university hospital. Let the coroner and the pathologists at the hospital work it out. Let's give Mr. Patterson a little break."

Duane did not mention that his partner of two years was a pathology resident at the university hospital. In addition to calling the coroner's office, he would call Matt. He should have the preliminary data on the autopsy delivered in person when they got home that night.

"Thank you," said Patterson, genuinely relieved to have been afforded even this slight courtesy. "Why are you taking all the bottles from my bar? Eleanor only drank cream sherry."

"Just a precaution," said Duane. "We'll return your property after we've tested it. Now, I'm sorry about this, but I have a few questions for you. Would you prefer to talk here or back at the station?"

◆ ◆ ◆

Stuart was busy in his office. When he was alone or with close friends he wore a black patch over his right eye. It was more comfortable than the glass eye which he inserted for more formal occasions. Stuart did not like to be confined and had the office door wide open. The professor was behind his desk, poring over several yards of paper with wiggly lines. Still he sensed someone in the doorway. He turned and saw Keith Grant.

Stuart smiled and beckoned. "Come on in, Keith. I've got something to show you. Each of these lines represents the contraction of a specific muscle in a child with cerebral palsy. We have fine wire electrodes, about the same diameter as a human hair, inserted into the muscle. We take the electrical signal of the muscle contraction, amplify it, and transmit it via FM telemetry to our recording devices. This can be done while the child is walking normally. The kids don't like the electrode insertion, because we do it with a needle, but once they're in, they don't hurt at all and the kids walk normally. Well, normally for them. By studying the abnormal muscle contraction and looking at the motion of the child's legs as she walks, I can discover which muscles contract at the wrong time or failed to contract at the right time. With this information, we can explain why the child has so much trouble with walking and might give a clue as to how we can intervene to improve function."

"Your research has made a big difference to the kids," Keith said.

Stuart looked up from his papers. "But you didn't come here to talk about my research."

"Do you have a minute, sir?" asked Keith. "Well, to be honest, it may take more than a minute."

"Sure, Keith, have a seat," said Stuart. Keith was one of the best residents that Stuart had ever seen. The young man had an inquiring mind, excellent memory, attention to detail, and a real love of people. Ray Stuart was trying to gently nudge Keith into a career in pediatric orthopedics. And Stuart suspected that he was having an effect on the young resident.

"I wanted to discuss some recent complications with you," said Keith. "They're not on the pediatric service, but I'm puzzled and, well, you really impressed my girlfriend, a nurse on pediatrics, the other day. She suggested that I talk to you about these cases."

"Is Mary DeGuzman your girlfriend?" Stuart asked.

"Yes."

"Good choice, Keith. She's one smart young woman."

'Thank you, sir," said Keith. "She thinks very highly of you as well. Can I tell you about these cases?"

"You can fill me in," said Stuart. "I know something about them from our faculty meeting. In fact, it was I who suggested that you be assigned the investigation. Sorry about the extra work, but I thought that yours was the best mind to put on the project."

"I guess that I should thank you for your confidence," said Keith, "but I'm afraid that I'm going to disappoint you. We have three infected routine arthroscopic operations done on the sports service. All Dr. Warren's cases. All routine, uncomplicated. All infected with MRSA."

"Any other MRSA infections on the sports service?"

"No, sir."

"How about on other orthopedic cases?"

"I don't think so. Have you ever heard of anything like this?"

"Are the cases related in any other way besides being Alex Warren's scope cases?"

"Not that I can find. Nothing in common except that Dr. Warren is the attending surgeon and each operation was the first case of the day. Mary suggested that I look at the infecting organism. Dr. Matt Harrison is a good friend of mine and a pathology resident here. He looked at the microbiology lab data in pathology, the stuff that doesn't make it to the chart. It turns out that the infecting organism is the exact same strain of MRSA in each case. Even the phage typing is identical. But how the infections occurred is baffling. And it's driving me nuts."

"Well, Keith, I've never heard of anything similar, and I certainly didn't know that the organisms were identical," said Stuart. "In a way, I'm actually glad that you're bothered. It shows me two good things. First, it shows me that you actually care about the patients, even though they're not your own. That means that you have not become so hardened by your training to forget the compassion for others that attracted you to medicine in the first place. Don't let that part of you change. Second, it shows me that you have intellectual curiosity. Cases that do not make sense, or seem way out of the routine, pique your interest. You're not comfortable not knowing. That's good. In surgery, we often forget that we're still doctors. We get all caught up in the techniques of surgery, selecting the right metal implant or doing the operation faster than our colleagues. We often forget that it's more important to understand the disease, to make the right diagnosis, than it is to do the latest fad operation. Do you want me to look into these cases?"

"I would really appreciate that," said Keith, "and, well, there is another case that has me puzzled. And this one I was involved with, but we never really did an operation."

Keith described in detail the case of the Mabel Osborne, the heavy old woman from Alabama, including every detail from the operating room and the results of the autopsy as Matt had related them to him.

"It just doesn't make sense," said Keith. "This poor woman came here as a tourist, broke her hip, and died. And she had a name. She was Mabel Osborne, not just some fat lady from Alabama. The whole thing makes me, well, a little angry. She died for no apparent reason. And we haven't learned a thing. It's just a waste, it happened for nothing."

"Hmmm," said Dr. Stuart. "I heard a little about that one at the faculty meeting, too. This one is intriguing. And you've told me all the data that we have. I can't explain this death. You're right. She was a person and she had a name. Most likely somebody loved her. That should bother more people than you and me, Keith. I'll look into this also, if you don't mind. I agree with you that people should not die for no reason. We won't advance the science of medicine by simply shrugging our shoulders and saying that sometimes old people die."

"Thank you, sir."

"Hey," said Stuart, "say 'hi' to Mary for me."

SEVEN

WENDY WISHED THERE was something she could do. She hated seeing the man she loved suffer.

"God damn, this knee hurts," said Ted, "Dr. Warren said it wouldn't be bad. Am I some kind of wimp?"

Ted was sitting on the couch with his leg propped on the coffee table.

Wendy snuggled up to him and purred. She was not a nurse, but she had an idea that had been successful before.

"You're not a wimp, Ted. I can vouch for that. Can I make you feel better?" she whispered.

"Later, baby, right now I need one of those Vicodins."

An hour later, Ted's knee was still killing him. Wendy made him a Manhattan, his favorite drink. Wendy knew he was not supposed to mix Vicodin and alcohol, but, if it put him to sleep, maybe he would feel better when he woke up.

Using his crutches clumsily, Ted hobbled into the bedroom and slipped under the sheets. Wendy handed him his drink. Ted loved her Manhattans. He seemed to relax, but didn't stop breathing or anything, so Wendy felt justified in combining the alcohol and the opiate. Soon Ted dozed off.

Ted slept fitfully for a few hours. When he woke up, he cried out in pain. He grabbed his knee with both hands and rubbed gently. Ted was obviously suffering.

Hearing the shout and the motion in the bedroom, Wendy glided over to him, dressed only in a silk robe.

"All better?" she asked, bending over to kiss him and brushing her naked breasts against his chest.

"Better with you here," Ted said, trying to rally.

Wendy ministered to his body expertly. She knew just where to touch, just where to kiss, the best places for her tongue.

Ted just could not respond.

Wendy knew that her lover was sick.

♦ ♦ ♦

Helen stood by the window of her corner office, admiring the view. She had a few minutes to relax and think. Helen's office was furnished in a futuristic modern décor. Abstract art adorned the walls. One whole wall was windows with a view of the Pacific Ocean.

Bill Henderson, the hospital CFO, tapped on the doorframe.

"Excuse me," he said, "can you and I talk privately for a while?"

"The board chairman will be here in ten minutes," said Helen. "Can we deal with the issue before then?"

"I think I'll need more time than that. This may be pretty important and we need time to talk."

"My schedule runs until five today. The office staff goes home then. Can you stay late?"

"That would be perfect," said Bill. "It will just be the two of us. I'll come back at five."

Soon, Mr. Wright arrived. Helen greeted him, friendly, but professional.

"Good to see you, John," Helen said. "Terrible news about Eleanor Patterson. Was it from her drinking? She looked fine at the party the other night. Was she sick?"

"Wayne tells me that the police think she may have taken poison," said Wright. "Wayne is very upset."

"Poison?" said Helen. "Do they think she took her own life?"

"Possibly," said Wright, "Or homicide. The police haven't decided. In addition to losing his wife, Wayne is afraid he may be a murder suspect. He's not doing well. In fact, that's what I wanted to talk to you about. Wayne has asked for a leave of absence from the hospital board and I gave it to him. Under the circumstances, I think that's the least I can do to ease his suffering."

"It's the right thing for you to do."

"I'm thinking of asking Clay Ross to take over the Planning Committee," said Wright. "What do you think?"

Perfect. Helen's thoughts raced. Ross was an alcoholic whose mental abilities and business enterprises were both circling the drain. Helen could get him to do anything she wanted and have him convinced that it was his own brilliant idea.

"Clay would be an excellent choice. He's smart and pays attention to details. He keeps an open mind and asks good probing questions. I and my staff would look forward to working with him."

"The only real issue before the Planning Committee is the proposal for the orthopedic institute," said Wright. "Are you and your staff up to speed with that?"

"As a matter of fact, John, I was just looking at the needs assessment study that we did on the orthopedic institute," Helen pointed to a folder of papers. It was a masterpiece and she just wanted to hug it.

In fact, no real study was ever done. Helen and Patricia Roberts had created the report out of thin air, whole cloth, and wishful thinking. The result was a polished presentation, complete with colored pie charts, lots of graphs and tables, and fifty pages of narrative. It was a masterwork of fiction. Always attentive to detail, Helen had every possible item covered. Unless someone actually did the basic research, there was no way to tell from reading the report that it was a fabrication. Helen was confident that no board member would check any of the so-called facts. They would be content to read the conclusions and recommendations. If they read it at all. It was more likely that they would ask her for a verbal summary.

"Oh, it's done," said Wright. "You worked quickly, Helen. Good for you. How much did it cost? Did you have to hire outside consultants?"

"No, John," said Helen. "You know how I dislike paying consultants their exorbitant rates. I and my staff did this. It was hard work, digging out all the data, but I'm confident that the report is complete and thorough. And we didn't have to use any extra budget money at all."

John Wright beamed with joy. She was sure he would remember this effort when it came time for salary bonuses.

"You are a treasure, Helen. And, if you don't mind, what does it show? I don't need the details, just the big picture."

"Well," said Helen, "the big money in orthopedics is in spine surgery, sports medicine, and total joint replacements. And, of course, the private insurance companies pay better than Medicare and MediCal. Pediatric orthopedics is generally a money loser as is tumor surgery. Trauma will probably break even, but that is going to come in through emergency services rather than an orthopedic institute. In the Bay Area, we are looking at the private sector, UCSF, and Stanford as our main competitors. Kaiser Permanente takes care of its own and doesn't enter into the equation. Looking at the national demographic statistics, the volumes by diagnosis, and waiting times at the competition, I just don't know where the patients are going to come from to make the orthopedic institute proposal a financially viable enterprise. Perhaps with time and the good reputation of our orthopedic staff it could become competitive, but I think it'll take at least ten years before it hits a financial break-even point."

Helen knew her facts. She was an expert at the business of health care in northern California. She knew what was the best course of action, for the hospital and for herself. No real needs assessment study was required.

"Really?" asked Wright. "Wayne Patterson was so enthusiastic about this proposal. He said that the orthopedic department had done research and they believed that the institute would turn a profit within the first several years."

"I'm not sure where the orthopedic department got its data," said Helen. "They may be good doctors and excellent surgeons, but that doesn't qualify them to make a good business plan. Perhaps their sampling methods were not that thorough. Or perhaps they didn't look at the volumes at Stanford, since it's so far south. But lots of Bay area patients go to Stanford because of its reputation for excellence. I don't know what to say, John. I wish that the facts were different, that they supported the orthopedic institute. But I can't change the facts."

"Would you mind sending a copy of your needs assessment study on to Clay Ross?" asked Wright. "He'll need to look at it in detail."

"Of course," said Helen. She knew that Clay Ross would look at the cover and the conclusions at the end and nothing in the middle. Not that the fool would understand it anyway.

Later, when all was quiet in the administrative suite and the staff had gone home, Bill Henderson knocked on Helen's door.

"Can we talk now?"

"Yes, Bill. This is a good time. Come in and have a seat."

Bill carried a handful of papers and sat down in a chair at the conference table that took up most of the space.

"I was looking at some of our MediCal billing information," Bill said, "and I found some things that don't make sense."

"In what way?"

"Well, I was looking to see what the time delay was between when we submitted our bills and when we actually received payment," said Bill. "And a curious thing appeared. It looks like the hospital sends out a large number of MediCal bills on the last Monday of every month. Most of the time, the bills are sent out pretty evenly through the month. I mean, there are about the same number of bills sent out each working day of each week. A little variation, but nothing striking. However, I noticed that on the last Monday of each month there's this surge in billing."

"That's odd," said Helen. "Is it just a coincidence?"

"At first that's what I thought," said Bill. "I looked back and the same thing has been happening on the last Monday of the month for almost two years. Every month without fail. I talked to my people in the billing office and they said that they didn't know of any reason why so much billing should take place on one specific day of the month. They say that billing is pretty steady all the time."

"Does this make any difference?" asked Helen. "Is there any significance to it?"

"I don't know," said Bill. "If I noticed it, then MediCal auditors may find it as well. It seems to me like we should have some sort of explanation in case they ask. So, I'd like to investigate this in more detail. I want to look at the specific bills that go out on the last Monday of the month and see if I can get to the root of this."

"Of course, Bill," said Helen. "I suspect that there is a good explanation. But you're right. If MediCal auditors see something unusual, we need to have a ready explanation. Those pencil pushers are always looking for some excuse to not pay us for taking care of the indigent patients. Get on this right away. And let me know what you find."

"Thanks, Helen," said Bill, "I knew you would agree with me."

"Oh, Bill," she added, "can you keep this confidential between you and me? Until you find the explanation, that is. I hate hospital rumors and there's no reason that anyone else needs to know about this."

"Sure," said Bill as he left the office.

Helen hated questions she could not answer. She liked things to be in order. She wanted to control everything in the hospital. Damn, she thought.

◆ ◆ ◆

Phillips popped two Tums and tried to think of something positive. He just could not get the idea that Anthony Green and his orthopedic department were about to get the best of him once again. All he wanted was a new medical staff library. The old one was a dinosaur. Modern medical libraries had lots of computers, internet access, devices to play DVDs and other electronic media. The old one was just a dark room full of old texts and journals. But, no, Tony Green needed a big, shiny new building so he and his cronies could bilk money out of a bunch of rich crybabies who really suffered from minor inconveniences in life, not real diseases. He and his internists treated real diseases, the kind that required education and intelligence to diagnose and knowledge of physiology and pharmacology to treat.

Phillips hated Anthony Green. Not just because Green was chairman of orthopedics, although that probably would have been enough. But there was a personal grudge as well. Green had opposed Phillips in the election for chief of the medical staff. Green had said some very nasty things about Phillips in the run-up to the election. And Warren Phillips was slow to forget an insult, even slower to forgive.

♦ ♦ ♦

Keith had just finished his morning rounds when the saw Dr. Green, the department chairman, heading his way.

"I want you to help me on the total knee this morning, Keith," said Green. "I apologize in advance that you're not going to be the surgeon. You'll be first assistant and we'll have a junior resident as a second assistant. The patient is a VIP and I really don't want anything to go wrong."

"Of course, Dr. Green," replied Keith. "I still have more than a few tricks to learn. I don't need to actually be the surgeon every case."

"You're a good resident, Keith," said the chairman. "The patient is James Davenport. He's a member of the hospital board. And he's a trial lawyer, for God's sake. I think he'd sue his own mother if he didn't like her peach cobbler. He's ornery and mean and a son of a bitch. He distrusts doctors and nurses and hospital people in general."

Keith could barely contain a laugh.

"So, if he hates health care people that much, why is he on the hospital board?"

"Beats me," said Green. "Maybe he thinks that as a board member he will get better treatment."

"Sounds like he's right."

Keith went to visit Davenport in the pre-op holding area. A review of the hospital chart told Keith that Davenport was 62 years old and in remarkably good health. No diabetes or heart disease. Kept his weight down and exercised regularly. No smoking. Social drinking. Divorced and living alone. The right knee had been injured playing high school basketball. He had undergone arthroscopic debridement six years earlier for the arthritis. Dr. Warren had gone in using the arthroscope and trimmed some loose tissue, removed a few loose fragments of cartilage, and tried to clean things up. It was an operation designed to delay the inevitable disintegration of the joint. The arthroscopic procedure gave him considerable relief for about five years, but the deterioration of the joint was relentless. It was time for a new knee.

"Mr. Davenport," said Keith, "I'm Dr. Keith Grant. I'm the chief resident in orthopaedics. I'll be assisting Dr. Green on your operation this morning."

Davenport scowled at Keith and declined his out-stretched hand.

"I don't want some goddam student doing my surgery."

"I can assure you, sir, that your surgery will be done by Dr. Green. I'm just there to assist him. To make things go faster and smoother."

"Green better do it," said Davenport, "or I'll sue his ass and yours. I know how you bastards lie to patients. The only people who are bigger liars than you goddam doctors are the goddam hospital administrators. Bunch of liars and crooks they are."

"Mr. Davenport," said Keith, "I'm sure that Dr. Green told you this, but the total knee replacement surgery is quite painful. I would like to ask the anesthesiologists to start you on a drug called ketorolac while you are still in surgery. It's a non-steroidal anti-inflammatory drug, which is the same class of drug that includes aspirin and ibuprofen. I see from your record that you have taken ibuprofen for a long time without any side effects. You have no history of heart disease or peptic ulcer disease."

"I don't have ulcers," said Davenport. "I give other people ulcers."

Keith totally believed this.

"So, sir, as I was saying, using ketorolac for the first couple of days after your surgery should give you better pain relief with a very low chance of side effects. And, you avoid the side effects of the opiate analgesics like morphine, which include nausea, drowsiness, and constipation."

"I hate constipation," said Davenport. "And I want to be fully alert to make sure none of you people tries to kill me. So let's try your new drug, Dr. Grant."

Oh boy, thought Keith. This one is going to be fun to take care of. Maybe he shouldn't have suggested the ketorolac. The nurses and residents might be happier if this asshole was a little sedated.

EIGHT

THE EMERGENCY DEPARTMENT at Sutro State was complete bedlam, as usual at seven in the evening. There were screaming babies, drunks vomiting on the floor, people coughing and crying, junkies shaking with the early signs of withdrawal. One little boy sat sobbing with his mother, holding his arm. Despite the splint, the gross deformity of the forearm made the diagnosis of a fracture obvious. A fat, dirty woman lay sprawled lengthwise over three chairs and snored loudly. Not a single seat in the waiting room was empty.

Wendy was horrified at the collection of human misery in the ER. Even with his crutches, Ted had to lean on her from time to time, trying to bear the pain in his knee. They had to wait in a slow-moving line just to register. Wendy was certain that she was going to contract some horrid disease from the people in that room. This, indeed, was a test of her love for Ted.

Eventually, the clerk took Ted's insurance information and told him and Wendy to take a seat and wait. Fat chance. They stood in a corner of the overflowing ER and tried not to make eye contact with any of their fellow sufferers. Each time the nurse opened the door, all eyes and ears were riveted on her, hoping desperately that she would call their name.

Some cried out, "Nurse, nurse, what about me?"

This has to be one of the deeper circles of hell, Wendy thought.

After what seemed to Wendy to have been an eternity, Ted's name was called and he was taken into a cubicle separated only by a curtain from a wino who had not had a bath since high school. The curtain was nominally closed, but there was a gap through which it was easy to see the patient in the next cubicle. Wendy and Ted tried not to look, but it was impossible to ignore their new neighbor. The wino coughed up some awful green stuff into a basin and eyed them with hostility.

"Hop up onto the gurney, Mr. Wells. Take your clothes off, all of them. Put the clothes in this bag." said the nurse. "Put this gown on, open in the back."

The nurse glanced at Wendy.

"Do you want to wait with him, Mrs. Wells?" she asked.

There was no chance that Wendy was going to correct the nurse with regard to her relationship with Ted. The idea of returning to the waiting room was terrifying.

"Yes, ma'am," said Wendy.

"Dr. Adams will be in soon," said the nurse as she left.

Ted and Wendy waited an hour and nobody came. Ted's knee was swollen to twice its normal size. It felt hot and red and like it was about to explode. Ted lay flat on his back and groaned in pain. Wendy tried to comfort him and fought to control her own impulse to panic and just run away. The wino coughed and coughed on the other side of the curtain.

Eventually, Dr. Kevin Adams came to see Ted. Adams had Ted's chart and did not look up.

"Your surgery was yesterday morning, right?" asked Adams, still studying the chart.

"Yes, Doctor," said Ted, "Can I please…"

Adams ignored him, pulling down the sheet and looking at the knee. Adams put on a pair of vinyl gloves. He gently removed the bandages. The knee was red and greatly swollen. There were four small incisions where Dr. Warren had inserted his arthroscopic instruments. All four of them were held with small sutures which looked like they were about to snap under the pressure. Adams pushed softly on the knee.

Ted screamed in pain. Adams withdrew his hand.

"What is it, doctor?" asked Wendy through her tears.

"I'm afraid that the knee may be infected," said Adams. "We'll get a few lab tests and have the orthopedic resident on call come down and see you."

Adams tossed the gloves into a hazardous waste container along with the surgical dressings. He went straight to the nurses' desk.

"Get me a complete blood count, a chemistry panel, and a urinalysis on Mr. Wells," Adams told the nurse, "and call the orthopedic resident. Another one of Warren's arthroscopies has gotten infected."

◆ ◆ ◆

Duane loved the Castro district. People always seemed happy. One might say that they were "gay" in more ways than one. There was so much color everywhere, in the houses, in the shops, and in the people. In the Castro, a person could be themselves. Nobody had to wear a mask. Everyone was accepted and there was really no prejudice, no judgement. He and Matt had a spacious apartment right on Castro Street. Duane was always happy to come home.

"Hey, what's for supper?" asked Duane as he entered the apartment. Matt's hands were wet and messy from chopping vegetables, so Duane just hugged him gently as they kissed.

"It's pasta primavera," said Matt. "Something healthy. A change of pace for a cop."

Duane got a beer out of the refrigerator and removed his jacket and tie.

"And I have a nice Pinot Grigio to go with it," said Matt. "Something with more style and grace than beer."

"Somebody in this relationship has to have some class," said Duane.

"And it certainly isn't going to be you," said Matt. "God knows that I've tried to teach you. I guess that you can take Duane out of the ghetto, but you can't take the ghetto out of Duane."

"I'll bet that I learned more on the streets of Hunter's Point than you learned in your fancy house in Providence, following your daddy to work in the bank."

"At least I had a father to follow around," countered Matt.

Duane chuckled. This sort of insult was a part of their relationship. He tried unsuccessfully to steal a piece of carrot from the chopping board.

"Yep, and he hates your skinny white faggot ass," he said. "I think I was better off without a daddy."

"Well, you sure did well with your mom," conceded Matt. "She's some kind of lady."

"Oh, yeah," said Duane, "she is tough. Did I ever tell you about the time she chased a gang banger down the street, swinging an axe at him? Jesus, I'll take the image of her running with that axe with me to my grave. Nobody messed with Mama Wilson. Not me either. She insisted on me going to school. If I ever came home with a B on the report card there would be hell to pay. Shit, she might have taken that axe to me."

"But you owe her. If it hadn't been for her you'd have wound up in a gang or in prison."

"I don't think I would do well in prison."

"Maybe some graveyard," said Matt. "I don't think that the gang bangers like gay members."

"I think I'd be smart enough to stay in the closet if I joined the Crips, man."

"Seems to me you still are in the closet."

Duane was a respected young police detective who was rising rapidly in rank and reputation through SFPD. Duane was very, very private about his personal life when he was at work.

"Look, man, you don't understand," said Duane. "It's one thing to be a white doctor in San Francisco who happens to be gay. Shit, half the white doctors in San Francisco are gay.

Nobody cares. But it is something else altogether to be a black cop in San Francisco who is also gay."

"San Francisco is the most tolerant city in the whole country," said Matt.

"Maybe," said Duane. "The cops of SFPD are pretty tolerant of black people and gay people. Just not black, gay cops. Not one of their own. Shit, Matt, it's hard to get our own families to accept who we are. Don't push it with the cops."

"Okay," said Matt. "I understand. Or I try to."

Generally, Matt and Duane did not talk about work when they were at home. Tonight, Duane had to make an exception, since he had engineered Matt to help him with his latest case. The serious conversation began as they finished up their supper and polished off the last of the wine.

"Say, did you catch the Patterson woman we sent over from Sea Cliff?" Duane asked.

"Sure did," said Matt. "Real VIP. Husband is on the hospital board and richer than Croesus. The coroner sent over one of his assistants to do the post. I helped with it. I figured it was your case and I got all the details that are available at this time."

"So, give," said Duane.

Matt didn't hesitate to talk about the case. Duane was the detective in charge of the investigation and he would learn the findings sooner or later. Besides, Matt trusted his partner completely. They had no secrets.

"Well, you were right. Cause of death was cyanide poisoning," said Matt. "She was an alcoholic, with fatty liver and early cirrhosis, but not much else on the autopsy that you wouldn't expect for a woman of her age who drank too much. Alcohol levels were really low in her blood. So it looks like the first glass of cream sherry was the one that killed her."

"Cream sherry," said Duane. "How can anybody drink that shit? Her husband said she went through one or two bottles every day. Nobody else in the family drank it."

"Do you think that her husband poisoned her?"

"He had the means, the opportunity, and probably a motive, but, no, I don't think he killed her. He's just too distraught. I think he actually loved the old broad. Cream sherry as the vehicle for the poison sure indicates that this was deliberate. If the poison was in a different bottle, who knows who might drink it? But cream sherry was Mrs. Patterson's personal pick. Anything on the autopsy to suggest she did this to herself?"

"Like a cancer or dementia or something? No, nothing that I could see that would make her want to take her own life. Did she leave a suicide note?"

"No. Actually most suicides don't leave notes or letters. That's a myth."

"I think the coroner is going to sign it out as a homicide," said Matt.

"Yep. My guess is that it's murder," said Duane.

"If the husband didn't do it, who did?"

"I'm not saying that he's innocent," said Duane. "Just that my instincts tell me he didn't do it. The Pattersons entertained a lot. And a lot of the guests do a lot of drinking. Bringing bottles of booze as gifts to the host seems to have been pretty common. There were lots of different liquors in the bar, some still in gift boxes. Anybody who was a guest in the home who knew about Mrs. Patterson's fondness for cream sherry could have brought a bottle as a gift with a pretty good idea of who would drink it. Hell, your whole hospital board was over for a big party a few days ago."

"So, why would somebody on the hospital board want to kill Mrs. Patterson?" asked Matt.

"I don't know," said Duane. "Senior citizen's lover's quarrel? We have a lot of work to do. This killer is pretty sophisticated, I think. Not my usual street junkie or gang banger."

"You know, I like it better when we don't talk about work at home," said Matt. "Work talk spoils a nice evening. We've had a fine supper, if I do say so myself. I have a full belly and a nice warm feeling from the wine. I'm heading for bed. Care to join me?"

"I'm all in," Duane replied with a smile.

♦ ♦ ♦

Helen and Patricia did not restrict their meetings to the office.

"I'm thinking of firing Bill Henderson," said Helen. "The man just cannot focus on the important issues facing the hospital. He ignores the big issues and farts around with his computer all day, engaging in mathematical mental masturbation."

"Oooh, that's harsh," said Patricia Roberts. "I thought he was doing a good job."

Helen's apartment was on Nob Hill, with a spectacular view of The City and the Bay. From her living room, they looked down on the Fairmont Hotel and Grace Cathedral. It was breathtaking. Helen, like many San Franciscans, measured a person's worth largely by the view from the person's dwelling place.

"I used to think he was, well, adequate," said Helen, "but the longer I work with him, the more obvious it becomes that he's just not smart enough."

"Too bad," said Patricia. "When do you plan to let him go?"

Firing staff members was not unusual under Helen's leadership. Many employees thought that she fired people just for sport. Helen knew that was very close to the truth

"I haven't quite decided. I'm not sure yet. I thought I'd run it by you."

"Well, personally I don't care," said Patricia. "You know I admire your management style. A certain amount of uncertainty among the staff is good for productivity. And you haven't fired anybody at the senior management level in a long time. It would demonstrate that no-one is immune from scrutiny and that everyone must be held to your high standards. I really like the way people respect your style. I'm using it myself with the nurses. I already notice an increase in attention to detail. Documents are properly filled out. The nursing units are cleaner and neater. Fear is a great motivator of productivity."

"Hmmm. My thoughts as well," said Helen.

Helen sipped her drink and enjoyed the view. She enjoyed Patricia as a friend as well as a professional colleague. There were many things they could talk about besides work. So she changed the topic.

"Have you seen the new BMWs?"

"No, not yet."

"I just bought a new x6, with the TwinPower Turbo engine," said Helen. "It rides like a dream, is appointed like a Rolls Royce, and flies down the road like a jet fighter. I just love it."

"But you have a beautiful Lexus and it's not very old," said Patricia.

"I was tired of the Lexus," said Helen. "It was nice, but slow. I want something with speed, responsiveness. That's where my life is going now. Life is exciting, maybe a little dangerous. So I traded in the Lexus. This new BMW is just perfect for where I am in my journey right now."

"How much did it cost?"

"Mine was $65,000, but well worth it."

"You deserve it," said Patricia.

Helen took another sip and stared out the window. "You know, I think I do. You only go around once, they say."

"Might as well seize the opportunities that we have," added Patricia.

"You know, people like you and me work very hard. We had to study and compete to get the education we have. The business world is very demanding."

"Not to mention that the business world is still dominated by men," Patricia said. "As women, we have to be so much better. We can't afford to fail. Or even look like we're weak."

"Right," Helen said. "I get so uptight about little details. I get stressed out when there are loose ends. I need to feel like everything is under control, all the time. It's hard for me to sleep when some issue is unresolved."

"So you need a few material things to help you relax," Patricia said. "All of us do. That's why they make BMWs."

"And apartments with views," Helen smiled.

"And twelve year old single malt Scotch whiskey," said Patricia, pouring two fresh drinks.

They clinked the crystal glasses together.

"To the successful women of San Francisco," Helen said.

The two women enjoyed their drinks and the view of the city. Mostly they talked about travel. Each enjoyed seeing the world, visiting exciting new places, especially ones with beaches.

When the bottle of Scotch hit the halfway point, Helen became pensive.

"By the way, Wayne Patterson resigned from the board today. John Wright told me."

"Because of the business with his wife's death?"

"Yes. Apparently the police think she was murdered. And Patterson is a suspect."

Patricia, a little tipsy, chuckled.

"Like on TV. The husband is always a suspect."

"Yeah. Too bad for Wayne. He's a kind man. His wife's drinking was tearing him apart. I actually felt sorry for him. Besides, Wayne was usually supportive of my proposals. Until this damn orthopedic institute thing and the hospital audit. Anyway, John gave Wayne's committee to Clay Ross, who's a complete fool."

"Is that bad?" asked Patricia. "I mean that Clay Ross is in charge of the committee.?"

"No, it's fine. Ross is in the process of pickling his brain. He doesn't think too well. He'll do whatever I tell him."

"Well good, then. Except for Mrs. Patterson," Patricia's words were starting to slur. "Let's drink to Mrs. Patterson."

"I think that would be inappropriate." Helen said, "and I think you've had enough. We both have to work tomorrow, Patricia. Let's call it a night."

NINE

MARY WENT STRAIGHT to the birdcage. Baby was sitting on top.

"Wee-oo-weet," whistled Mary.

Baby cocked her head and looked at Mary.

"Wee-oo-weet," Mary whistled again.

"Wee-oo-weet," chirped the bird.

Mary stuck out her finger and the little yellow parakeet hopped on. Mary brought Baby up close to her lips to give the bird a kiss, but Baby promptly flew off and took her usual spot atop the curtain rod.

"She likes me," said Mary.

"I'm surprised," said Keith. "She's usually pretty skittish with anybody but me. And she is very, very jealous of other females who compete for my affections."

Keith took Mary in his arms. The little kiss was a celebration of how happy they were when they were together.

"I got some Chinese take-out," she said. "You really have to go back to the hospital?"

"Yeah, I need to check on the post-ops. And the junior resident did a reduction on a forearm on a kid in emergency. In an hour or so, they'll have the cast on and the new x-rays. I need to see if she got it right."

"Well, we'll eat fast then," said Mary, opening the boxes and distributing chopsticks. "Do you remember that you told me Ms. Roberts was working out at your gym?"

"The Cougar? Yeah, she started a month ago. She's still coming pretty regularly. Still trying to hit on younger guys."

"Like you?"

"Maybe," he said, "but she seems interested in guys with more money and fewer tattoos."

Mary lightly punched his shoulder.

"You're taken," she said. "And you only have one tattoo."

"That you know about. There are places you haven't looked, you know."

Mary blushed. "Well, I was starting to tell you about Ms. Roberts. I'm sure that she's having a major make-over. She was on our unit this morning at the beginning of shift. Not in her fancy clothes, but scrubs and sneakers. She went around and saw a few of the kids with the nursing staff. She never did that before. And a friend of mine told me over lunch that Ms. Roberts was in Central Sterile even earlier in the morning. It's amazing."

"Was she critical of people?"

"No, she just seemed interested in what we were doing. She asked a few questions about how we might improve the nursing on the unit."

"I don't really pay any attention to the administrative types. They never seem very interested in what we're doing with the patients. I never really see them in the clinics or on the wards. I'm not sure I'd recognize them if I did. Except for The Cougar and Bill, the financial guy who works out at the gym. Hey, I need to thank you for your suggestion about the bacteria in the infected arthroscopy cases. It was brilliant."

"Did you figure it out?" she asked, grinning. "Now that I gave you the most important clue."

"Not yet, but the bacteria seem to be a common denominator," said Keith. "I asked Matt to look at the lab tests more closely, following up on your idea. It turns out that the bacteria in every case are identical."

"Well, they're all MRSA," she said.

"More than that," said Keith. "They're identical in type, subtype, and phage type. That's no coincidence, Mary. These bugs came from a single source."

"Have you found the source?"

"Not yet, but the only other thing that all three cases have in common is that they were all first cases."

"Did you ever run it by Dr. Stuart, like I suggested?" she asked.

"Yes, I talked to him about it," said Keith. "He agreed to look into things as well. I'm glad for this. I kind of think that he'll take over the investigation, like when a junior resident gets in over his head in surgery and the senior surgeon bails him out."

"And you feel over your head?"

"Pretty much," said Keith. "He thinks highly of you. You really impressed him on the ward the other day."

Mary had a mental picture of Stuart consulting on the unit. There was something special about that doctor. At the same time, there was something not quite right, something sad.

"He's a legend on pediatrics," she said. "All the nurses know about him and many of us have seen him in action. He gets consulted on really difficult cases. I remember one kid who came in with leg pain, all in one shin. No history of trauma. The pediatricians thought that the kid might have an infection. They got all sorts of labs and x-rays. The kid had no fever. The x-rays were weird, but nobody could figure them out. Finally, they called Dr. Stuart, asking him to do a biopsy of the kid's bone. He looked at the kid for a long time, then at the labs and the x-rays. He said that there was no need for a biopsy of the tibia. He said the kid had leukemia. The pediatricians scoffed at him, because the white blood count was normal. Dr. Stuart said that this was a case of 'aleukemic leukemia,' which is leukemia with a normal white blood cell count. Have you ever even heard of that?"

"I vaguely remember reading about that in med school, but I've never seen it and I don't know anybody who could make that diagnosis, especially not an orthopedic surgeon," said Keith.

"Well, Dr. Stuart was right," said Mary. "They treated the little kid for leukemia and put him into remission. I remember this case really well. It was shortly after I started working at Sutro State. The little boy was my patient. And Dr. Stuart has the most wonderful way with the little kids."

"He really made an impression on you," said Keith.

"How well do you know him?" Mary asked.

"Why?"

"I don't know," she said, "There seems to be a deep sadness in him, like he's been badly hurt. He hides it, mostly. When I've seen him on pediatrics, he is always kind and very professional. I just get the sense that he's experienced some great sorrow."

"Maybe," said Keith, "I don't know him that well. The car accident was certainly a source of sorrow and sadness. He was banged up pretty bad. Broke both legs and lost his eye."

"You're probably right. Somehow, I sense that it's more than that, though."

"That accident was pretty bad," he said. "It happened before I did my pediatric rotation, so I never got to operate with Dr. Stuart. Everybody tells me that he was a brilliant surgeon, the best hands anyone had ever seen."

"Well, I don't know about his hands," said Mary, "but he sure is a brilliant doctor. And he's so kind and understanding. Make sure you keep him in the loop on this infection problem, if you learn something before he does."

"Good idea. I'll do that."

Keith gulped down the last mouthful of noodles and got up.

"I really need to get back," he said.

"Let's clean up and I'll drive you, so you don't have to move the motorcycle from its parking place," she said. "It'll give us a few extra minutes together as well."

"Thanks. You're the best. I really do love you."

"More than that little yellow parakeet?" she said, pointing to the curtain rod.

"Well, maybe," said Keith. "You are both about the same size and she has soft feathers, but I think you have prettier legs."

Mary laughed and gave him another love tap on the shoulder.

Mary dropped Keith off at the emergency entrance at the hospital. A quick peck on the lips as he left the car. Mary headed for home in Daly City. As she was pulling out of the parking lot, she noticed Patricia Roberts coming out of the hospital and heading to the parking lot. Mary thought that it was odd that Roberts was working so late. Most of the administrative higher-ups were gone by four o'clock and it was after seven. Roberts walked quickly and deliberately to her car. Mary noticed that she had not exited the hospital from the doors near the administrative wing, but on the other side of the building, where a bank of elevators went up to the patient units.

♦ ♦ ♦

Keith went into emergency and checked the x-rays on a child with a broken arm. He congratulated the junior resident on the fine alignment of the bones, but pointed out that she had made the cast way too thick. Only three layers of fiberglass were really necessary to hold the fracture. All the extra layers were supporting was the resident's peace of mind, not the child's injury. Keith explained to her that it was common for junior orthopaedic residents to put on casts that were too thick, as if more cast material would keep the bones in place. Once the young doctor became more confident with her fracture reduction, she would make thinner casts. Convinced she had learned the lesson, Keith took the elevator to the seventh floor, where the orthopedic patients were housed.

"Dr. Grant," shouted a nurse as the elevator doors opened. "come quickly! Thank God you're here."

"What is it?" asked Keith as they ran down the hall.

"It's Mr. Davenport, Dr. Green's total knee patient," she said. "He's having a seizure."

Davenport was indeed exhibiting the repetitive jerks of a grand mal seizure. As they entered the room another nurse arrived pushing the crash cart of emergency medicines.

"Should we call a code?" asked the nurse.

"No, not yet," said Keith, noticing that Davenport still had a working IV. "How did this start?"

"He was complaining of feeling jittery, and sweating a lot," said the nurse. "Then his skin got cold and clammy and his eyes rolled back into his head and then the seizing started."

"Get me some D 50 from that cart," said Keith.

"Do you want some IV Valium?"

"Not now, maybe if this doesn't work," said Keith. He quickly injected a 50% glucose solution into Mr. Davenport's IV. As the sugar ran in, the seizures slowed, then stopped.

"Do a finger stick blood sugar," Keith told the nurse. "Add a half liter of D 50 to his IV."

"Jesus," said the nurse as she read the blood sugar on the meter, "his sugar is 35. And that's after your infusion."

A blood sugar of 35 was dangerously low. It had probably been even lower when the seizures began. Such a low level could be fatal.

"How did you know, Dr. Grant?" asked the nurse with the crash cart.

"It was the jitters and the sweating, classic signs of severe hypoglycemia," said Keith. "And I knew that he had no history of seizures before the surgery. I helped Dr. Green with his case and I knew his history. And there's no harm in a test dose of D 50, while IV Valium might have killed him. The real question is why his blood sugar is so low. Let's keep the D 50 running in his IV. Call the internal medicine resident. We may want to have Mr. Davenport transferred to the medical ICU for observation."

"Yes, sir," said the nurse with the crash cart.

But Keith didn't really understand what had happened at all. There was no medical reason for this patient to develop low blood sugar to this life-threatening degree. None at all. Keith had reacted, made a decision and a decisive action. That was how surgeons acted in a crisis. But he really had not thought it through. That was lucky. If Keith had stopped to think about it, Davenport might have died.

Turning to the nurse who was caring for Davenport, Keith asked, "Did you or somebody else give Mr. Davenport an injection of insulin?"

"No, sir. Mr. Davenport is not diabetic, Doctor."

"Yes, I know. But how else can I explain this?"

Davenport slowly regained consciousness with a full broadside of profanity.

"Goddam, fucking, douche bags are trying to kill me," raged Davenport. "Get these goddam wires off me! You can all kiss my hairy ass! Everybody here is going to be sued! I'll have your asses hanging on my fucking wall!"

The on-call resident from internal medicine came and conferred with Keith. They agreed that the smartest thing would be to transfer Davenport to the medical intensive care unit. Most likely, the immediate danger was passed, but in the ICU it would be much easier to monitor his blood sugar and keep a close eye on him for signs of additional seizures. While Davenport cursed and insulted the staff who transferred him to the gurney for transport, Keith said a quick prayer for the poor ICU nurses. He caught a bus back to the apartment, still trying to understand what he had just witnessed.

Baby had flown down from the curtain rod and was sitting on a perch in her cage by the time Keith got back. Keith turned on a light in the kitchen which provided just enough illumination into the living room for them to see each other. There was a peaceful, trusting relationship between man and bird. Keith automatically relaxed when it was just himself and Baby. He could almost sense his heart rate coming down. This evening was scary. Davenport could have died. He got lucky with the D50. Keith had no idea what it all meant. He would have trouble falling asleep, but he had to try.

Gently he closed the door to the cage. Kneeling, he pressed his nose between the bars. Baby hopped over and rubbed her beak on the tip of his nose.

Keith quietly pulled the blanket so it covered the cage. He could hear the bird hop onto the swing where she liked to sleep.

◆ ◆ ◆

Patricia closed the door to Helen's office. The office personnel knew never to interrupt when the Director of Nursing was meeting with the CEO behind a closed door.

"What a mess," said Helen. "How did this happen? Davenport already hates me and all my senior staff. He thinks we cost too much money and don't do enough for patient care. Now he gets a huge complication."

"The orthopedic chief resident was right there. He must be one smart son of a bitch. He saved Davenport's life," said Patricia. "Nobody on an orthopedic floor would have thought of hypoglycemia as a cause of seizures. They're not that intelligent. In a few minutes the old bastard would have been dead. And at least it would not have been a problem for us."

"Davenport will blow this all over town. He may even sue us. He'd love that, to make a big deal out of suing the hospital of which he himself is a board member. He's nasty enough to do just that. He'll have a field day."

"We should be able to contain this," said Patricia.

"We need to act swiftly, decisively," said Helen. "show everyone that we're in control, that we can respond. I want the nurse taking care of him last night fired."

"Fired?" asked Patricia. "Why?"

How naïve can this woman be, thought Helen. Do I have to think of everything? It was time for action, not dithering. Who gave a damn about some staff nurse?

"We're going to spin this as a medication error by the nurse," said Helen. "Incompetence on the part of one nurse. If we act today, Davenport will think we're on top of things. Maybe he'll be impressed enough to not sue us. Or at least he'll settle with us for a relatively small amount. It'll be harder to ask questions of a nurse we fired. Let's make this look like an open and shut case. The nurse screwed up and we in leadership acted with swift and bold decisiveness to remedy the situation. Chairman Wright will love it."

"OK," said Patricia. "The nurse is one of the Filipino girls. I doubt that anyone will make a fuss over her."

"Good. We have quite a few Filipino nurses, don't we?"

"Yeah," said Helen, "they're pretty easy to find. A lot of hospitals don't want to hire them. A lot of people don't think they are as good as American nurses. Some doctors don't want to work with them. They may have foreign sounding accents, which can make patients nervous. But they're actually very good nurses. Polite and rather docile, I think. They had it hard in the Philippines and they don't seem to feel entitled. It's pretty easy to fire them."

"Sounds like a perfect sort of employee, plentiful and uncomplaining. Get us another boatload of them. And fire this woman."

"Consider it done."

TEN

KEITH THOUGHT THAT it was a good sign when the department chairman approached with a big smile and an outstretched hand. The two men were at the nursing station on the orthopedic unit.

"Hell of a good job last night, Keith," said Dr. Green. "You're not just a good surgeon, you're a good doctor. You saved Davenport's life."

"Thank you, sir," said Keith. "I guess I didn't forget everything other than orthopedics that I learned in medical school."

"I just saw the distinguished Mr. Davenport in ICU," said Green. "In between the f-bombs and cursing out the nursing staff, he asked to see you. I think he wants to thank you personally. Any idea why he became so hypoglycemic that he seized?"

"I was on my way there to check on him," replied Keith. "And no, I can't imagine anything in his health history that would account for that severe a hypoglycemia. Other than the possibility that someone gave him insulin. Maybe in his IV."

"You know, they fired the nurse who was taking care of him last night," said Green. "Girl named Carol Ramirez. They say she made a medication error."

"That's too bad," said Keith. "I know Carol Ramirez. She's a good nurse. Frankly I doubt that she gave him the insulin. She was right there when I arrived last night. She was very upset but not at all guilty. She was very helpful last night. Didn't they do some sort of investigation before firing her?"

"This is the work of the dear Ms. Roberts, our Director of Nursing," said Dr. Green. "Off with her head! She learned it from our CEO, Ms. Hitler. No investigation is needed. Facts only slow down the disciplinary process. It's been a hell of a month for the orthopedic department, Keith. What with Warren's infections and the fat lady who died on the table and now this case, we seem to be snake bitten."

"Yes, sir," agreed Keith, "there do seem to be more complications than normal."

Davenport was sitting bolt upright in his ICU bed, yelling obscenities at the nursing staff.

"Get me back to my private room, goddammit," he bellowed. "I don't need to be here. It's too goddam loud. How can anyone sleep with all this goddam racket?"

"We'll transfer you as soon as we get an order from the doctor, sir," said the charge nurse.

"Maybe I can help with that," said Keith. "Let me call the doctor in charge of the ICU and see if the good Mr. Davenport is ready to go back to the loving arms of the orthopedic nurses upstairs."

"Loving arms, my ass," said Davenport. "The bitches tried to murder me last night. And they damned well would have succeeded if you hadn't come along, Grant. You saved my life, goddammit."

"You're welcome," said Keith. He was fairly certain that the orthopedic nurses and the ones in the ICU might not be as grateful to him as Davenport.

"Did they figure out who was trying to kill me?"

"Well, your nurse last night was fired," said Keith. "They're saying she made a medication error and gave you insulin by mistake."

"That little Filipino girl? Are they sure that it was her?"

"I'm not sure how detailed the investigation was, sir. That's a call made by nursing administration. I've worked with her for a while and I always thought that she was a pretty good nurse."

Davenport was calming down and spoke seriously.

"It seems to me that nursing administration is trying to sweep this under the carpet, Grant. You know, act swiftly and fire somebody, then declare the problem to be resolved and move on. If somebody put insulin in my IV, I think they may have been trying to kill me. God knows there are enough people around this hospital who would like to see me dead. Yes, I know that I'm a pain in the ass to everyone from the CEO on down. I have lots of enemies. It comes with being a trial lawyer."

"You may be right there, sir," agreed Keith, "but do you have enemies who would actually want to kill you?"

"Last night's events make me think that I do," said Davenport. "Were the police called in?"

"I doubt it, sir. This is being considered a medication error, not a crime. Like it or not, medication errors do occur. The hospital deals with them internally. The police don't have anything to do with it."

"Look, Grant, I trust you. Shit, you're the only one who has demonstrated any specific interest in keeping me alive. If the hospital isn't going to investigate this any further, I intend to look into it myself. Will you help me?"

"Sure, if I can," said Keith.

Promise him anything, Keith thought. Anything to calm him down and maybe, just maybe, he won't sue Dr. Green and me.

"First, get me out of this goddam ICU," said Davenport. "I can't think in here with all this racket. I don't know if I'll be able to sleep, though. I need to be vigilant. Someone may try to kill me again."

"You could always hire your own private duty nurse," Keith suggested, "if you're nervous about the hospital staff."

"You're damn right I'm nervous."

◆ ◆ ◆

Bill Henderson had a splitting headache.

All day long there had been problems, problems, problems. Bill remembered a management seminar that he had taken a few months before. The facilitator had divided all problems into a big box with four squares. On one side the squares were labeled "Important" and "Unimportant." On the other side, the labels were "Urgent" and "Not Urgent." Most problems, the facilitator had said, were considered "Urgent and Unimportant." These were the things that wore a person down, preventing a person from becoming happy and truly productive. The goal was to move away from these issues and concentrate on the problems that were "Important" only.

The issues that had beleaguered Bill all day were all "Urgent and Unimportant." There were discrepancies in the financial figures in the physical therapy department. The problem was certainly caused by errors in data entry into the computer, but Bill had to identify the errors and rectify the figures. The prices that had been approved for new office carpeting were not the same as on the invoices from the flooring company. This required no fewer than six phone calls. And so it had gone on. All day.

Bill was a man who needed order in his life. He could not tolerate unanswered questions or unsolved problems. There was no peace in Bill's heart when the figures didn't balance. Maybe that was why he was a good accountant. He couldn't stand to have to answer a financial question with "I don't know."

So the issue he had discussed with Helen Crawford regarding the MediCal billing irregularities was driving him crazy. He had no answer. He did not understand. And all the annoying questions and problems that plagued him all day kept him from working on that problem. The MediCal billing issue was "Important and Non-Urgent."

So Bill had skipped lunch to work in his office. And the nuisance problems proliferated. He stayed late after others had left the administrative suite.

Bill mused that nobody would miss him if he worked late. He had no wife or children waiting at home for him. No girlfriend. No drinking buddies. Nobody really. He had a cat in his apartment, but Bill was smart enough to know that cats were really incapable of love. They let you pet them as long as you fed them and let them do whatever they wanted. So right now, Bill Henderson was feeling a little depressed. The self-pity was getting to him. His thoughts were stealing his energy, his enthusiasm for tackling the MediCal billing thing.

So he had a headache. He needed to clear his head. Bill thought that maybe a vigorous workout in the gym would help. The endorphins from the exercise might help the headache. Some push-ups might release the anger at the many annoying problems. Bill hated the gym and hated the exercise, but he was sure he would feel better after he sweated and strained for an hour or so.

After the gym he would go home, take a shower, heat himself a frozen dinner in the microwave and get down to the kind of financial problem solving that he really loved.

◆ ◆ ◆

Keith checked on Davenport just before he left the hospital that evening. The lawyer was sleeping in his private room. A personal nurse that he had hired sat at his bedside, bored to death and reading a book. Keith smiled at the thought of the old bastard bringing in his own babysitter. Or maybe he thinks of her as more of a bodyguard. Davenport was actually doing very well, with good progress in physical therapy and normal blood sugars. Keith thought he would probably go home in a day or two.

Workout clothes were stashed in the saddle bag of the Heritage Softail. The V twin engine roared to life and Keith was off to the gym. This day he found himself in a locker close to Bill Henderson. Bill was just getting into his shorts and tee shirt when Keith arrived.

"Hi, Bill," said Keith. "Gonna hit the weights today?"

"You know me," said Bill, "I'm mostly a cardio guy. I may do a few push-ups to release some inner tension and anger. But I'll leave the weights to you muscle guys. You played football in college, didn't you?"

"Yeah, free safety for Holy Cross," said Keith. "I actually love to exercise. It relaxes me. My time in the gym is often the best time of the whole day."

"Good for you," said Bill. "I hate it. I'm just trying to stay alive a little longer and not keel over with a heart attack. I sit on my ass all day doing nothing. But, to be honest, I'd rather be sitting on my ass at my desk with a cup of coffee than sitting on my ass on the bicycle to nowhere."

Keith laughed and the two of them headed for separate sections of the gym.

♦ ♦ ♦

Patricia Roberts was nearly finished with her workout when she saw Keith and Bill emerge from the locker room. She had her usual Zumba class and spent an extra fifteen minutes on the elliptical machine, just to put a little extra firmness in the glutes. With a flirtatious smile, she walked up to Keith, who was starting his stretches.

"Dr. Grant, aren't you?" she said. "You're from the hospital. I'm Patricia Roberts, Director of Nursing."

Patricia extended her hand and Keith shook it. He smiled a little as Patricia applied her best power grip.

"Yes, I am," said Keith. "And yes, I know who you are. You've been working out here for a month now."

Patricia smiled, genuinely pleased that she had been noticed by a handsome, muscular young man.

Nice buns, she thought, and nice guns, very athletic.

The big Celtic cross tattoo on his right shoulder turned her on. She was in her early fifties, just beginning the downhill side of a century. Twenty or twenty-five years ago she had been attractive. She still kept her dancer's petite body in good physical shape, but time worked its mischief on her appearance. Too many wrinkles had been taken out by the knives of plastic surgeons, replaced by a shiny tightness which, combined with many Botox injections, meant that her face had a kind of waxy, masklike appearance. She tried to compensate with makeup and mascara, but it was a losing cause.

"I heard about how you saved the life of Mr. Davenport, an important member of the hospital board," she said. "How fortunate that you came along when you did. And how fortunate for Mr. Davenport that such a smart doctor was around. Excellent job, Dr. Grant."

Patricia was sure that young Dr. Grant would do an excellent job in bed as well. She wondered if she should make a play.

"Thank you, ma'am," said Keith. "I heard that you fired the nurse who was taking care of Mr. Davenport. I know her. I've worked with Carol Ramirez for a couple of years. She's a good nurse. It's hard to imagine her making a medication error that was as serious as this."

Patricia was on her guard. He was going to second guess her decision. She did not want to talk about this with some upstart resident. So much for trying to get him into bed.

"Doctor, that's none of your business," she said. "You do your job and you do it well. I do my job and I also do it well."

Patricia wheeled and headed for the women's locker room.

◆ ◆ ◆

Keith continued his stretching, moving to some cardio, then core strengthening, then upper body weight lifting. He was done in a little more than an hour. He found Bill Henderson getting dressed to leave.

"Good workout?" asked Keith.

Henderson was carrying a heavy briefcase as well as his duffel bag of workout clothes.

"Yes, very refreshing," said Bill. "Clears my head. I have a lot of work to do tonight on some files I brought from the hospital. There are some puzzling financial numbers that I'm struggling with. I was getting confused and needed a mental break. The workout was just what the doctor ordered, so to speak. I feel invigorated and ready to go."

Bill and Keith had taken a few steps outside the gym when Bill's chest exploded. A shower of blood soaked Keith.

Bill coughed and cried out at the same time. Keith's first reaction was shock. What was this? He caught Bill in his arms. Blood was gushing out of Bill's chest. Keith held on to Bill, still confused about what was going on. Bill tried to speak, but more blood came out of his mouth. Instinctively, both Bill and Keith put their hands on the gushing wound in Bill's chest. It was as useless as trying to stop an open fire hydrant. Bill squirmed and wiggled a little, struggling to breathe or talk. His eyes were riveted into Keith's. Keith hung on, focusing on the man in his arms. He saw a face full of fear, bewilderment. At the same time, Keith saw in Bill's eyes that Bill knew what all this meant. After a couple of agonal expansions of his chest, Bill died in Keith's arms. The light of life just flickered and went out of Bill's eyes.

For a moment, Keith just crouched on the pavement, holding the dead man. Keith began to take notice of what was going on around him. While he did not actually hear the shot that hit Bill, he was aware of perhaps half a dozen more gunshots which followed. People were falling everywhere, some bleeding, some crying out, some screaming. Others were running without a particular direction.

Keith reacted, as he had with Davenport. He was a trained surgeon and he responded reflexively. Emotions were suspended. There was work to do.

Ignoring the pounding of his own heart, Keith ran to the nearest victim. She was a young woman, down on the pavement and not moving. She was a blonde, but that was hard to tell. Her hair was drenched in crimson and her head lay in a pool of blood. Keith opened her eyes. The pupils looked normal. She was breathing normally. Pulse was fast, steady and strong. Gently, he probed her head with his fingers. The scalp was bleeding so profusely, that he couldn't see. But he could feel. He expected to find a jagged edge of bone where the bullet had shattered the woman's skull. The puddle of gelatinizing red on the pavement could be not just blood, but brain. To Keith's amazement, the skull felt intact. He probed a little harder. Yes, the skull was intact. Quickly, he saw the woman's gym bag on the ground. He opened it and found what looked like a clean towel. He wrapped it firmly around her head, hoping that the pressure would stanch the bleeding. This was a scalp wound, a pretty bad one, but not life-threatening.

Keith took a deep breath and looked around. There were other wounded who needed attention. Almost anyone who could walk had fled the scene, seeking shelter. He was alone on the sidewalk with the wounded and, of course, Bill. Keith yelled to a man cowering inside the gym door.

"Hey, come out here," Keith yelled. "The shooting has stopped. Bring the first aid kit from the gym."

Glancing furtively around, the man did as Keith ordered. Tossing the kit to Keith, he scurried back inside the gym.

Keith found exactly what he needed. A big roll of sterile gauze. Removing the towel from the victim's head, he gently supported her and wrapped the sterile thick white gauze round and round. The bleeding was still brisk, but slowing. The woman was still breathing well. Keith was pleased when she began to moan. He leaned over and whispered into her ear.

"You're going to be all right," Keith said, not knowing if she could understand him. "I need to help the others. I'll be back."

Keith next found a young black man with a sucking chest wound. He was lying on his back, gasping for breath. A horrible gurgling sound came from his chest with each labored breath he took. The man had both hands on his own chest, trying to seal the wound. He looked at Keith, his eyes pleading for help, as if he knew that he was going to die without a miracle.

Not if I can help it, thought Keith. This is a nasty wound, but we can save this guy if we can get a tube into his chest. Until then….

He saw a security guard inside the gym. He motioned to the guard and the man cracked open the door.

"Get me a clean towel," said Keith. "Soak it in water and bring it. Right now."

The guard rushed away and returned in seconds. Opening the door a crack and glancing at the buildings across the street, he tossed the towel to Keith. Keith jammed the towel against the chest wound. The victim's breathing improved a little. Keith knew that the man needed a chest tube to re-expand the lung.

Keith could hear the sounds of approaching sirens. He recognized the distinctive sounds of both police cruisers and ambulances. This man needed help and he needed it quickly. Keith could use a little help himself.

"Come on, boys, bring me a chest tube," he whispered while pressing the wet towel against the wound.

The police jumped out of their cars, pistols and shotguns drawn. Some set up a perimeter, looking at the buildings across the street, while others hustled to the wounded and inside the gym. All wore bullet-proof vests. A single ambulance arrived and two paramedics jumped out, running to Keith's side.

"I'm a doctor," said Keith to the paramedics. "I need to put a chest tube in this man."

One of the paramedics sprinted back to the ambulance for the supplies that Keith needed to insert a tube to re-expand the black man's lungs. The other went to the side of the woman with the head wound and began a field assessment.

"She has a scalp wound, not lethal," Keith shouted. "Get me more ambulances. We've got multiple casualties."

A police officer got on the radio to call in reinforcements for the paramedics.

It had been a while since Keith had inserted a chest tube. He felt a momentary hesitation as he couldn't remember which rib interval he was targeting. The hell with it, just get the tube in. Skilled hands accustomed to sharp objects slipped the tube in. As soon as it was in, the young man began to breathe easier. Keith left the paramedic who had assisted him to secure the tube, grabbed a handful of large gauze pads, and went to the next victim.

She was a pretty girl with long, sandy hair. She lay on her side, rocking back and forth and sobbing silently. She held both hands over her abdomen.

Gently, Keith rolled the girl on her back.

"It's okay, I'm a doctor," he said. His voice sounded like somebody else, some actor on a medical TV show about emergency rooms. Keith's mind was beginning to reel. How many people were down? How many were going to die? Jesus, keep me focused. Just one person at a time.

The girl was very slender. She had a small entry wound in her lower left abdomen and a large exit wound out her flank. Keith applied pressure to the exit wound, which was larger and was bleeding more. As he looked at the girl's tearful blue eyes, he tried to remember what structures in the abdomen would be found on a path between the entry and the exit wound. Let's see, sigmoid colon, for sure. Maybe a ureter, maybe an ovary and Fallopian tube. Abdominal and paraspinal muscles. Nothing life threatening. He forced himself to smile at the girl.

"It looks awful, but you'll be okay," he said. "We're going to get you to the hospital. You'll need surgery, but you'll get through this all right."

The girl nodded her head and lay back on the sidewalk. Keith wondered how he had done that.

As the only physician on the scene, Keith was in charge of the victims. More ambulances arrived. He saw no more victims. He became the triage officer. There were four shooting victims in all. Bill Henderson was dead and there was nothing to be done for him. The man with the sucking chest wound was the first priority, then the woman with the abdominal wound. He supervised loading them into ambulances, briefing the paramedics.

Keith himself got into the ambulance with the last victim, the young woman with the head wound. She was beginning to regain consciousness.

"Hey," said Keith, drawing close to her, "what's your name?"

"J-J-Jennifer."

"What city are you in?"

"Huh? Who are you? What happened to me?"

"You got shot, Jennifer, and I'm Dr. Keith Grant."

"Where am I? Where are you taking me?"

"You're in an ambulance and we're going to Sutro State University Hospital. And you're going to have a hell of a headache, but you're going to be just fine."

It was a short ride to the emergency department. Keith's clothes were drenched in blood, mostly Bill's, but he quickly assured the doctors that he was not a victim. The blonde woman had been very, very lucky. The bullet hit her head at an angle, ploughing a trench in her scalp, but never penetrating the skull. Scalp wounds bled like hell, Keith knew. They were very scary, but not life threatening. The emergency room staff would order a CT scan just to make sure. They might even keep her overnight as a precaution, but Keith knew that she would recover completely. The man with the sucking chest wound went straight to the operating room. He too would survive to tell the story of how he got shot at the gym to his grandchildren. Likewise the slender woman with the abdominal wound would require surgery, but should be fine. Keith was in the emergency department for three hours tending to the patients, but was unaware of the time. Adrenaline has a way of making time pass quickly.

"Keith, you look like shit," said Detective Duane Wilson. "You look like something out of a horror movie."

Keith turned to look at the handsome black detective, nicely dressed in a suit and tie. Since Duane was Matt Harrison's partner, he and Keith were good friends.

"Hi, Duane. Is this your case?"

"Yep. I'm sorry. I shouldn't be making jokes. Are you finished here at the hospital?"

"There's nothing more I can do here," said Keith. "All the patients are stable or up in surgery. Except poor Bill. He's dead."

"Is your bike still at the gym?" asked Duane.

"Yeah, I hadn't really thought about it."

"Let me give you a ride back to the gym," said Duane. "And I'm afraid I'll have to ask you a few questions in the car."

ELEVEN

KEITH'S HANDS BEGAN to shake as he rode the Harley back to the apartment. As a surgeon, he was trained to hold his emotions and feelings in check during crisis situations. When the bleeding was out of control, he had to be in control. Now that the crisis was past, it was beginning to affect him.

Mary was waiting in the apartment when Keith got home. He saw the shock on her face as she beheld the bloody mess that had been his shirt and pants. She looked into his eyes and saw the horror that he felt. She threw her arms around his neck and held him very, very tight.

"Thank God you're okay," she said.

"I'm alive and not bleeding, but I wouldn't say that I'm okay. Right now I really need a shower."

There are a lot of advantages to a hot shower after an horrific life experience, Keith thought. Not only can you wash some of the blood away, but you can go ahead and cry. Nobody will see your tears. Keith could not get the image of Bill Henderson's eyes out of his mind. Watching another man who knew he was dying, looking into his eyes, and not being able to do a damn thing to stop it rocked Keith to his core.

When he emerged from the bedroom in clean clothes, Keith took the bloody ones and stuffed them into the trash. He never wanted to see those clothes again. He thought he was back in control of his emotions.

"Do you feel better?" asked Mary.

"To be honest, I feel like the bloodstains will never come out," said Keith.

She hugged him close. Nuzzling his face into Mary's hair and holding her tenderly, Keith could not hold back. He cried in the presence of another person, perhaps the first time since he was a little boy. He just held on to Mary as though his life and his sanity depended on it. He shook with sobs and said nothing.

They held each other for a very long time. Keith had kept his composure from the instant the first shot hit Bill Henderson until now. He had been able to act professionally and effectively. But Bill Henderson died in his arms. God, he and Bill had been laughing and talking up until the instant the bullet shattered Bill's chest. And all the other innocent people. Why? The massacre at the gym was a glimpse of hell itself. Blood everywhere. People screaming and running, but not knowing where to hide. His day was drenched in blood. And now here he was, safe in his own apartment, clinging to the person he loved the most in all the world.

Keith looked into Mary's eyes. She had shed some tears, too. Her eyes were so dark brown as to appear black, but sparkling, as though they were made of a combination of onyx and diamond. When Keith looked into Mary's eyes, he felt like he could see her heart, her soul. And it was beautiful. Sweet and pure and beautiful.

◆ ◆ ◆

Helen could tell that Patricia was upset.

"God," said Patricia, "that could've been me out there in front of the gym. You know I just left an hour or so before the shootings."

"Lucky you," said Helen. "These things are random. Senseless killings. A scourge of our modern society. Do they know who the shooter was? Was this terrorism? Or a random madman?"

"I haven't heard. Did you know that Bill Henderson was killed?" asked Patricia.

"Yes, I heard about that," said Helen. "Tragic. The poor man was so young. And trying so hard to get himself into physical shape."

"And you were going to fire him," said Patricia.

"I'm glad now that I hadn't done it yet. Somebody saved me the inconvenience. It also saved the hospital the cost of the severance package."

"I hate to say it, Helen, but in a way, you're right."

Of course I'm right, thought Helen. Patricia had much to learn, but really lacked the character for true leadership.

"I told his assistant that I would clean out his office personally. Nobody would know better than I how to dispose of the work-related things. He had no family, right?"

"Right, none that I know of," said Patricia. "Have the police been here?"

"Not yet," said Helen. "A Detective Wilson is supposed to meet me in my office at ten."

Helen closed the door on Bill Henderson's office and sat down at his computer terminal. As Chief Executive Officer of the hospital, she had a master login code that allowed her full access to any computer files. Swiftly she scanned Bill's entries. In less than half an hour she had found and deleted all files related to Bill's inquiries about the MediCal billing. She logged off and began to go through his desk and file cabinets. She found no hard copies or paper documents related to the MediCal issue at all. Really, with Bill gone there was no reason to leave any trace of the little discrepancy he had found. Such things would just create rumors and disrupt hospital operations. Helen was confident that things were under control. And Helen always liked things to be under her control. No surprises.

At ten o'clock Duane Wilson and another detective arrived at Helen's office. She had her assistant bring coffee and Danish pastries for the officers.

"How can I help you?" Helen asked. "This is all so horrible. Bill was our Chief Financial Officer. He was an accountant. You know, billing, budgeting, purchasing. The business part of the hospital. He was well-liked and respected here."

"Did he have any enemies or rivals here at work?"

"None at all"

"How about his personal life?" he asked. "How much do you know about his activities outside the hospital?"

"Bill's life was his work, as far as I know," said Helen. "I don't recall him ever mentioning any family members. And I can't remember him ever talking about a date or a romantic interest. Funny, I worked with Bill for years and now I realize that I know so little about him. To be honest, I don't know if he was straight or gay. I know that he belonged to a gym and was trying to get his body into shape. He hated every minute at the gym, but said that it would benefit his health. Ironic, isn't it? The gym was the thing that killed him. Why all these questions about work and his personal life. Wasn't this a terrorist act?"

"The investigation is ongoing, ma'am, and I can't comment on that specifically," Duane said. "We don't know who did this shooting or why. No group has claimed credit for the shootings as yet. If you don't mind, we'd like to have a look at Mr. Henderson's office."

"Of course, detectives, you may look at anything you like," she said, "except patient medical records, of course. Those are protected and quite confidential."

Helen had her assistant help the detectives find their way into Bill's office.

Poor Bill, she thought. Poor, thorough accountant Bill. Always trying to do his job just a little better.

♦ ♦ ♦

"Thank God you're home," said Suzanne Burris as soon as she heard the door to the house open.

"Hi, Honey," Leroy replied. "I missed you, too. It's been a long day at the office."

"Gregory is sick," she said. "And I'm scared. Look at him, Leroy."

The eight month old baby lying in the playpen was listless, whimpering quietly. Gregory was normally a healthy, happy and robust baby. Normally he squealed with joy when his father came home, babbling noises that only babies and parents can comprehend.

"Hey," said Leroy gently. "What's up with my little man?"

The baby looked into his father's eyes and cried weakly.

"What's wrong with him?" Leroy asked.

"He just doesn't feel good," said Suzanne. "You know how he likes to pull himself up on the sides of the crib? Well, he doesn't want to be up. He won't nurse. He's fussy and irritable."

"Does he have a temperature?"

"I think so. Feel his head."

Leroy touched Gregory's forehead with the back of his hand.

"Feels warm."

"Is that a fever?"

"I don't know. Babies' heads always feel warm," said Leroy. He was a businessman, not a doctor. "Did you call the doctor?"

"Not yet," said Suzanne. "Do you think I should?"

Leroy bent over to pick his son out of the crib. As Leroy slipped his hand under Gregory's legs, the baby screamed in pain. Leroy quickly withdrew his hand.

"God," he said, "what is that? What's wrong?"

"I don't know," said Suzanne, starting to cry. "He screams every time I try to pick him up."

"We need to call the doctor," said Leroy.

Of course, the office of the pediatrician was closed. The answering service referred Leroy to the doctor on call, who was not Gregory's pediatrician and knew nothing of the little boy's medical history. Leroy put the phone on speaker so that Suzanne could participate. She thought that the doctor sounded tired, or irritated, or both.

"Does Gregory have a fever?" asked the doctor.

"I don't know," said Leroy. "He feels warm."

"Did you take his temperature?"

"No."

"Do you have a thermometer?"

"No."

"Why not? You're parents of an infant. You should have a thermometer."

Suzanne could sense her husband's anger and frustration increasing.

"Look, doctor," said Leroy, "my son is sick and listless. I don't have a thermometer. So I'll buy one in the morning. But for the love of God, tell me what to do with my son!"

"Well," said the doctor, "you should probably take him into the emergency department at Sutro State University Hospital."

"He screams when my wife or I try to move him," said Leroy.

"Mr. Burris," said the doctor, "if you and your wife can't bring him to the hospital yourselves, call a damn ambulance."

Leroy abruptly hung up the phone. Suzanne was awash in tears.

"What should we do?" she asked.

"Let's take the whole pad from the crib," said Leroy. "We should be able to get him into the back seat of the car without moving him too much."

◆ ◆ ◆

James Davenport went home, cursing and grumbling. Before he was discharged, he gave Keith his phone number and address. The old lawyer still insisted that he would investigate what he was certain was an attempt on his life and he wanted Keith to help him. Keith had no idea how he might help Mr. Davenport pursue his quest. He hoped that time and a few pain pills would make the old goat forget the whole thing.

There were two more infected arthroscopic procedures that Drs. Green and Warren added to Keith's list for study. One knee, which belonged to the talent agent Ted Wells, and one shoulder. The only common factor was once again that each was the first case in the operating room for the day. The infecting bacterium was Methicillin Resistant Staphylococcus Aureus. The strain and phage types were identical to all of the previous infections. Keith was no closer to tracing the origin of the infections than he had been a week before. The hospital Infection Control Committee was now in full frenzy. The administrators, nurse executives, and laboratory managers who ran this committee were now certain that the epidemic of infections was the fault of Warren himself.

◆ ◆ ◆

Helen Crawford had a confidential meeting with Dr. Richard Phillips to discuss the problems in the orthopedic department. Phillips held the office of chief of the medical staff, the highest position for any doctor at the hospital. Helen knew that Phillips' own specialty was internal medicine, though his true passion was in-hospital politics. Phillips was an average clinical practitioner, but a master at political maneuvers. As an internist, she assumed that he knew nothing at all about orthopedics. He was undoubtedly aware that the orthopedic surgeons took care of bones and joints and that they made a lot of money. Helen suspected that Philips could only name about half the bones in the human body and was not quite sure where they were located. Phillips probably thought that the orthopedic doctors were all old jocks, lots of muscles but not very smart.

And, of course, she knew that Phillips hated the orthopedists. They were surgeons, not real doctors. Historically, all surgeons evolved from barbers in the Middle Ages. Not intellectual scientists, like the internists. In the United Kingdom, surgeons were not even addressed as "doctor." They were called "mister." Helen smiled at this tidbit of medical historical trivia. She thought that Phillips would agree that the Brits had that one right. The ancient resentments between internists and surgeons could be useful.

She had to discuss the problems that were affecting the orthopedic department. The rash of complications was a topic of gossip throughout the hospital. She knew that negative news about orthopedics would be seen as great news by Phillips. Anything he could do to punish them he would do. The personal hatred Phillips had for Dr. Anthony Green would energize the whole process.

Helen easily built her case that things were not right in the orthopedic department at Sutro State University Hospital. First there were the joint infections, which seemed to be linked to Dr. Warren, who was, after all, vice chairman of the department. Then there was the sudden death of the tourist from Alabama who died on the operating table attended by Dr. Romano, head of the orthopedic trauma division, while being treated for a routine hip fracture. Finally, there was poor Mr. Davenport, a member of the hospital board, who seemed to have been injected with insulin by mistake following a total knee replacement. And Mr. Davenport just happened to be a patient of Dr. Anthony Green, the department chairman. Helen was no doctor, she hastened to mention, but it did seem to her that there might be a problem with the quality of care at the hospital in the orthopedic department.

As Helen expected, Phillips was horrified.

"These cases are awful," said Phillips. "This is not the standard of care that we expect here at Sutro State. There seems to be a serious threat to the welfare of the patients in this hospital. This sort of thing can be a black mark against the entire medical staff. I'm embarrassed that I have to learn about these issues from hospital administration rather than our own medical staff quality assurance committees. Good God, what sort of department is Anthony Green running?"

"I'm sorry to have to tell you these things," said Helen.

"Helen," Phillips said, "as chief of staff, I know exactly what needs to be done. I will initiate an investigation by the Medical Executive Committee."

The MEC was the most powerful committee in the hospital. Unlike any other hospital committee, the findings and proceedings of the MEC were privileged. That meant that they were exempt from legal discovery, like the lawyer-client relationship or a priest and his confessing parishioner. An attorney could not get a look at the proceedings of the Medical Executive Committee even with a subpoena. The MEC worked behind closed doors. Only the medical staff leadership participated. There was good reason for the special status of the Medical Executive Committee. It allowed the hospital medical staff to monitor and improve the quality of care in the hospital without either the regulatory authorities or nosy trial lawyers getting any information which might be used to hurt the hospital. Immune from lawsuits or penalties, the Medical Executive Committee could work with honesty and candor for the quality of care and the benefit of the patients. This actually worked very, very well, as it did in most hospitals. But the MEC was a powerful weapon that could also inflict a lot of damage on doctors or departments who were not in favor with the chief of staff.

And Philips was chief of staff. Things were going to get uncomfortable for Anthony Green and his orthopedic department.

TWELVE

"**Bed fifteen, Doctor,**" said the nurse. "Burris, Gregory, eight month old African-American boy, brought in by parents. They report that he's sick and listless, won't eat, cries when you try to move him. They got that part right. He screams bloody murder each time we move him."

"Vital signs?" asked Dr. Kevin Adams, the emergency medicine doctor working that evening.

"Temperature 38.6, pulse 110, blood pressure 90 over 60."

Dr. Adams thought. The normal temperature in centigrade would have been 37, so the baby had some signs of fever, but babies can get fevers for lots of reasons. And, sometimes in babies, severe infections do not cause high fevers. The blood pressure was within normal limits for a baby, as was the pulse. With young crying children, one had always to suspect child abuse. Even the best of parents can be pushed beyond their limits by screaming inconsolable babies.

"Any signs of bruising? Is this abuse?"

"None that we see, doctor."

The overworked young physician drew the curtains and approached Suzanne and Leroy Burris, who were holding the tiny hands of their infant son. Suzanne was still crying.

"Mr. and Mrs. Burris, I'm Doctor Adams. I need to ask you a few questions."

"Certainly, Doctor," said Suzanne.

"Has little, er," he fumbled with the papers on a clipboard, "Little Gregory, shown any sign of sickness? Coughing? Vomiting? Diarrhea?"

"No, Doctor."

"Pulling at his ears?"

"No Doctor."

"When did he start to seem sick to you?"

"Well, he seemed irritable last night when I put him to bed," said Suzanne, "But this morning he really seemed to be, well, just not himself."

"In what way?" asked Adams.

"He just didn't seem to be happy," she answered. "He usually stands up in his crib and babbles and laughs in the morning. He's normally a very happy baby."

"He can stand?" asked the doctor with a raised eyebrow. "He's only eight months old."

"He can pull himself up on the rails of the crib. He holds on and bounces up and down."

"Hmm. I see," said Adams. "Did he fall out of the crib? Or get his legs stuck in the rails?"

"No. I don't think so," said Suzanne. "And another thing. He won't nurse."

"You're breast feeding?"

"Yes."

"Hmm. I see."

Adams put the clipboard down and turned his attention to the baby. Suzanne and Leroy stepped back to allow the doctor space. Their eyes were riveted on the doctor and their little boy. There is no anxiety like that which is experienced by parents of young children in the emergency room.

"Well, big fella," said Adams. "let's have a look at you."

Gregory stared at Adams suspiciously. Adams thought for a moment that this was a smart kid. Only eight months old and he already knew that white coats on white men could mean trouble.

Adams warmed the head of his stethoscope with his hand. First, he listened to the child's breathing, then the heart, finally the bowel sounds of the abdomen. Without a word, he took the stethoscope out of his ears and reached for the otoscope mounted on the wall. Placing a disposable plastic cap over the light, he shined it in Gregory's eyes.

Gregory's pupils contracted synchronously. He opened his mouth to begin a howl. At that moment, Adams got a quick but effective look at the normal pink lining of the baby's throat and tongue. While Gregory protested, Adams tilted his head to the right and to the left to inspect the eardrums. When Adams moved to replace the otoscope in its holder, Suzanne stepped closer and spoke softly to Gregory.

"Good, Mrs. Burris, good," said Dr. Adams. "Keep talking to him."

While Suzanne stroked Gregory's head and softly reassured him, Adams began to move the left leg. He started with the foot and ankle. Getting no response, he began to flex and extend the knee. Slight wiggling of the baby, but Gregory's eyes were locked on his mother's face. Moving the hip made little difference. Turning his attention to the right leg, as soon as Adams flexed the knee, Gregory erupted in a scream.

"What is it, Doctor?" asked Leroy. "What's wrong with my boy?"

"We need to get a few blood tests and some x-rays," said Adams.

◆ ◆ ◆

Keith had a message to call Matt Harrison when he was between cases in surgery.

"Yo, Matt," said Keith, "what's up, man?"

"Hey, Duane asked me to call you. He's working this mass shooting case from the gym. He wondered if he could talk it over with you and me. He has some questions and has some documents he doesn't understand."

"Sure. Anything I can do to help. When does he want to talk?"

"Soon. And it may take a little time. He doesn't want to do it at the police station."

"How about my apartment for supper tonight?" suggested Keith.

"Are you cooking?"

"No, asshole, as a matter of fact Mary is cooking tonight," said Keith.

"Good," said Matt. "I won't need to worry about getting poisoned then. What's she making?"

"Jesus, are you making restaurant reservations or do you want to talk? As a matter of fact, she's planning to make spaghetti with meat balls, so there should be plenty to share with you and Duane."

"A Filipino making spaghetti and meatballs? Is this a good idea? Shouldn't she be preparing some exotic island dish? Especially since she has a distinguished dinner guest."

"She doesn't know that you're coming, Matt. Mary's not Italian. She's as American as you are. Her spaghetti is delicious. Supper is at seven."

"Duane and I will be there," said Matt. "We'll bring a bottle of wine for us and some lemonade for you two party poopers."

Keith called Mary and asked if she minded cooking for four.

Baby started chirping as soon as Keith put his key in the lock. Neither Keith nor Mary could figure out how that little bird knew it was Keith without seeing or hearing him. By the time Keith was inside the apartment, Baby had flown from the curtain rod to the top of the birdcage and was chirping her signature whistle insistently.

"Wee-oo-weet! Wee-oo-weet!"

"Wee-oo-weet! Wee-oo-weet!" Keith whistled in reply.

Before he greeted Mary, he went to the birdcage where Baby waited. Bird and man rubbed beaks together in a familiar greeting. Protocol must be observed and family traditions honored. Baby was happy and stopped chirping. Only then could Keith kiss Mary.

"I do love you," said Keith.

"After you have cleared things with the bird."

"Baby was here first."

As if she knew that they were talking about her, Baby chirped again, then hopped inside the cage and began to attack a dish of birdseed. Keith gently closed the cage door. No more flying this evening, Baby. We have guests for supper.

"Smells good," Keith said, leaning over a pot of spaghetti sauce, "Looks like you made plenty."

"Yep. I love to see Matt and Duane. They're fun. You said they wanted to talk some business about the shootings?"

"Matt was a little vague. I suspect that it's mostly Duane who wants to talk. I really can't imagine how I could help with a police investigation."

Soon there was a knock at the door. Mary opened it and Matt swooped in with his most dramatic gait, swiveling his hips and tilting his chin. With one long arm, he picked Mary off her feet and planted a sloppy kiss right on her lips.

"What are you doing with this dumb jock?" Matt asked. Mary giggled.

"I'd dump him in a minute if I could have you. The greatest heartbreak of my life is that you don't like girls."

"Oh, I like them enough," said Matt. "If I liked them more, I would steal your heart."

"No stealing required," replied Mary. "I would give my heart to you in an instant."

"Hey, what about me?" asked Duane.

"You'll do, given the circumstances," said Matt.

Matt put Mary down and strode over to the birdcage.

"Speaking of cute females," said Matt, "hi, Baby!"

Matt botched a whistle. Baby hopped onto the wall of the cage as far away from Matt as she could get and glared at him with as much hostility as a six inch parakeet could muster.

"Smart bird," said Duane.

"Homophobe," said Matt. "Keith said Mary was cooking. Otherwise we wouldn't have come. I had enough of Keith's cooking when we were roommates."

"Nothing fancy," said Mary, "just spaghetti with meatballs."

"Hmmm, Filipino spaghetti with meatballs," said Matt. "That should be different."

"Oh, yeah," replied Mary, "I make the meatballs Filipino style. I use fish heads."

Supper was delicious. The little table in the apartment only had four chairs and the good friends were close and cozy.

"No offense intended," said Duane, "but why does a single guy, and a former football player have a pet parakeet? It just seems weird."

"Easy answer," said Keith. "The apartment rules say that the only pets allowed are fish and birds. And it just doesn't seem right to be talking to fish."

"You talk to the bird?" asked Duane.

"Oh, yeah, she's my best friend and confidant."

"I thought I was your best friend," said Matt, pouting.

"Not since you and Duane started living together. I know when I'm no longer needed."

"Poor boy," said Matt.

"So Matt was replaced by a parakeet," said Duane.

"It was a good trade, actually," said Keith. "Keep it in mind if you get tired of him."

"How in the world did you two ever survive as roommates in medical school?" asked Mary.

"You do seem to be the ultimate odd couple," said Duane.

"Or queer couple," quipped Matt, "but no, that won't work for Keith. They say that opposites attract. Gay and straight, liberal and conservative, Catholic and atheist, jock and geek. We were perfect for each other. For a while. Until we graduated as young MDs from Tufts."

"I thought he was funny, amusing I mean," said Keith. "And I kind of felt sorry for him. We had this class in our second year at Tufts called Physical Diagnosis. They put the students into small groups and we had to learn how to examine patients and use all the gadgets that doctors are supposed to employ. Matt was the worst. He was so bad that I had to laugh."

"I was better than you might think," said Matt.

"Bullshit," said Keith. "You couldn't see the back of the throat with the light. You tried to use the reflex hammer and bounced it off the knee and onto the floor. You spent half an hour trying to figure out which end of the stethoscope went in your mouth. It was hilarious."

"Keith exaggerates, I assure you," said Matt.

"Why do you think Matt is a pathologist?" asked Keith. "It's the only specialty that doesn't require him to examine live patients or use any of our diagnostic tools."

"Not the only specialty," said Matt. "There's always psychiatry."

"God save us," said Duane.

They all had a good laugh. Everyone pitched in to help clean up the kitchen and they retired to the little living room. Eventually, Duane brought up the topic of the shootings.

"Keith, I don't want to ruin your evening, but can I ask you something more about the shooting? Was Bill the first person shot?"

"You know, I didn't even hear the retort," said Keith. "I was standing right next to Bill and his chest just kind of blew up. He collapsed in my arms. Only then did I hear gunshots and other people screaming and shouting and running. So, yeah, I think Bill was the first person shot."

"Did Bill say anything before he died?" asked Duane. "I mean about who might have shot him?"

"No," said Keith, "he didn't say anything. I mean, his lungs were bleeding so much and he was choking on his own blood and, well, it didn't take long for him to die."

"Why are you asking, Duane?" asked Mary. "Do you think this wasn't a random shooting?"

"I'm suspicious," said Duane. "There are some things that don't quite hang together. On one hand, the rounds were all 5.56 mm, which points to the shooter using an AR-15 assault rifle, the favorite of both domestic terrorists and crazies. But the shooter was positioned on the roof of a commercial building across the street. It's a four-story old building with easy roof access through a stairwell. There's a music store on the first floor and rooms on the second floor that are used for giving music lessons. There's no elevator. Nobody saw a shooter or anyone carrying anything that looked like a rifle or rifle case."

"But," he continued, "there are students of all ages and both sexes going up and down those stairs with musical instrument cases all day long. Nobody notices them because there are so many. It would be easy to hide an AR-15 in an instrument case, enter the stairwell on the first floor and just keep going up to the roof. The shooter policed his brass and left no fingerprints or any trace of himself on the roof. When he was done, he just put the rifle back in the musical instrument case and walked calmly back down the stairs."

"Are you sure?" asked Mary.

"Not completely," said Duane, "but this scenario makes the most sense. We're sure about the bullets and the shooter's location on the roof. Nobody remembers seeing anyone suspicious. No terrorist group has come forward to claim responsibility. The whole point of terrorist attacks is to draw attention to their cause. They have nothing to gain by remaining anonymous. They want people to know that they can strike anywhere and at any time. A lot of crazies kill themselves after they have shot others. And the crazies don't usually stop shooting after six rounds when there are at least ten in the clip, then make a clean escape, picking up the shell casings."

"Then, what was the point of this?" asked Keith.

"I think it was a hit," said Duane. "I think the shooter had one specific target he wanted to kill. The other victims were part of a cover up. I think the shooter wanted us to think that this was a mass shooting."

"And the target was Bill?" asked Keith.

"In cases where a hit man takes additional victims, the first person shot is usually the target," said Duane. "The shooter has to be sure that he gets a clean shot at the target. After the first shot, people start running around. The shooter can no longer be sure that he'll get a good shot at his target. But once the crowd panics, there are lots of random targets. And I think that this guy is a pretty good marksman. Maybe a professional."

"You got that right," said Matt. "The bullet went straight through the center of Bill's chest. Took out the major arteries coming off the heart. Bill had no chance."

"The other victims had more or less random wounds. A belly shot, a chest, a head," said Duane.

"That's scary," said Mary. "And the idea of a terrorist was scary enough."

"If I'm right, it's not so scary. If this was a professional hit, the shooter won't do it again. It means that we don't have a crazy shooter out there or a terrorist group who might repeat the shooting without warning. This may be the only shooting."

"Is an AR-15 a normal kind of weapon for a hit man?" asked Keith. "That's the civilian version of the Army's M-16."

"No," replied Duane, "but it's a common weapon for crazy mass killers and terrorists. If the shooter wanted to disguise his assassination of Bill Henderson as a mass shooting, an AR-15 would be a good choice. They're pretty easy to obtain and getting ammunition is very simple. My guess is that our murder weapon is at the bottom of the bay right now."

"Why would anyone want to kill Bill Henderson?" asked Keith. "He was an accountant, for God's sake."

"Good question," said Duane. "Keith, was anyone else from the hospital at the gym that day?"

"A couple of residents who work out regularly," said Keith, "and The Cougar, er, I'm sorry, Ms. Roberts, the director of nursing."

"Was she hitting on you again?" asked Mary.

"Well, yeah, kinda," said Keith. "She was flirting with me until I asked her why she fired Carol Ramirez over Mr. Davenport's complication. Then she got huffy and left. I think she was gone from the gym by the time of the shooting."

"Who's Carol Ramirez and why was she fired?" asked Duane. "And who is Mr. Davenport?"

"Davenport is a cantankerous old lawyer who's a member of the hospital board," said Keith. "He had a total knee replacement recently. Two days after surgery, we think he was given a dose of insulin which might have killed him. The director of nursing has decided it was a medication error and she fired the nurse who was taking care of Davenport."

"That's Carol Ramirez and she is a cousin of mine," said Mary. "She got a rotten deal. She had nothing to do with Mr. Davenport's complication. Nothing. And there was no due process, no investigation. Roberts just capriciously fired her and that was the end of it."

"Don't you nurses have a union?" asked Duane. "Certainly there has to be some sort of due process in your contract. And this woman is your cousin?"

"Yeah, we have a union," said Mary, "But it's pretty ineffective in appealing the firings of nurses. It works well when the hospital lays off groups of nurses, but in individual cases, well, an appeal through the union generally destroys a nurse's reputation and she can't find another job. And I call Carol a cousin because she's another Filipino. It's a cultural thing. We're all related, even though you can't always trace a blood line. All Filipinos are cousins, aunts, uncles, unless they're brothers and sisters."

"It did seem like a rush to judgment," said Keith. "I was there when Davenport had his hypoglycemic seizure. I'm pretty sure that Carol didn't do anything wrong."

"What happened to Davenport?" asked Duane.

"He's okay," said Keith. "He's gone home now. Other than the insulin thing, he had a pretty straightforward total knee replacement. The insulin problem might have killed him, but it didn't. Anyway, Mr. Davenport didn't die and he raised all hell claiming that someone was trying to kill him."

"Keith didn't mention that he saved Mr. Davenport's life," added Mary.

"If you knew Davenport," said Keith, "you might not think that my actions were all that commendable."

"Was Davenport right?" asked Duane. "Was someone trying to kill him?"

"I don't know," said Keith. "He's a world class asshole and had lots of enemies. I suspect that someone injected his IV with insulin to precipitate the hypoglycemia. It could have been an honest mistake. Most of these things are just errors. But I don't know who could've done it. I can't believe it was Carol though. She just didn't act like she'd given him an injection. She seemed shocked with his seizure, not guilty. I doubt that we'll ever know. Ms. Roberts fired Carol and that was the end of the story. Medication error. Case closed."

"Was there anyone else around who might have injected the insulin?" asked Matt. "It's pretty easy to find insulin in the hospital. And if he's the jerk you say he is, he might have had a lot of enemies in the hospital."

"I don't get it," said Keith. "We're off topic here. Duane asked about the shootings and here we are talking about Davenport. These things aren't related."

"Hey, wait a minute," said Mary. "I just remembered something. I dropped Keith off at the hospital that night. As I was pulling out of the parking area, I saw Ms. Roberts getting into that fancy little sports car she drives. Dressed up like a teenager going to the prom as usual. I remember because it was so late. And that same day she had been on the pediatric unit first thing in the morning when my day shift started. I thought that she was putting in some pretty long hours for a big executive. And another thing, she didn't leave the hospital from the exit below the administrative wing. She came out near the other side of the hospital, behind the patient units."

"So this Ms. Roberts was at the gym shortly before the shootings and she was also at the hospital when Mr. Davenport claims that someone was trying to kill him?" asked Duane.

"This seems pretty nuts to me," said Keith. "Maybe she doesn't like Davenport, but nobody really does. But why would she want to kill Bill Henderson?"

"Maybe the briefcase will tell us," said Duane, "Which is the main reason I wanted to talk to you. Henderson was carrying two bags when he was shot. One was a duffel bag full of towels and dirty gym clothes. The other was a briefcase full of computer printouts and hand-written notes from the hospital. I was going to ask Keith if Henderson talked about the documents. We're not sure what they mean."

"He said he was working on some particularly perplexing problem at the hospital," said Keith. "That was about all. He probably knew that I wouldn't understand if he explained in more detail. And, frankly, I probably wouldn't be interested. I knew he had the briefcase. He said he was going to work on it at home."

"We checked his apartment and there was nothing on his home computer related to the hospital. And no written documents. We also looked in his office at the hospital. We couldn't find the files on his computer or any documents to help explain what the ones in the briefcase mean. Keith, would you mind looking at them?"

Duane produced the briefcase and set out piles of paper on the kitchen table. The four of them sifted through the documents. Most of them seemed to be hospital bills sent to MediCal after patients were discharged from the hospital. While unfamiliar to all of them, nothing looked suspicious.

"Look at this," said Mary, holding up a sheet of paper with a hand-written note. "This is weird."

"It says Five South," said Matt. "Why is that weird?"

"Five South is an old nursing unit that administration closed maybe two years ago. They use it for storage now, mostly old beds and chairs and junk. Nobody ever goes there."

"Why would that be of interest to Bill Henderson?" asked Duane.

"You're supposed to be the detective, lover," said Matt.

Other than Mary's observation about the hand-written note, none of them could make much sense of the papers. Finally, Keith had an inspiration.

"I think I might know someone who could help us with these, if you want," he said.

"I could use a knowledgeable set of eyes," said Duane. "Who are you thinking of?"

"The cantankerous, paranoid Mr. Davenport, of course," said Keith. "He's a lawyer and he's a member of the hospital board. The administration is always sending financial stuff to the board. He might understand these files. He asked me to help him figure out who was trying to kill him. I have his phone number and address. Let me show him these. He doesn't need to know that they have nothing to do with his hospital complication and at the very least it may make him feel like somebody is taking his accusations seriously."

THIRTEEN

SUZANNE BURRIS LISTENED carefully to all the conversations and comments made by the hospital staff. She was desperate for news about Gregory.

"Labs are back on the Burris boy, Dr. Adams," said the emergency room nurse.

"Hmm. White count is pretty high," said Adams as he looked at the paper the nurse had handed him. "X-rays?"

"The radiologist said that there might be some widening of the joint space on the right hip, sir," said the nurse. "Otherwise, everything is normal. Chest x-ray is normal, no fractures seen in the leg."

"Call pediatrics," said Adams. "I think maybe this baby has an infected hip."

The pediatric resident arrived in the emergency room in an hour. She repeated all of the questions and all of the examinations that Adams had performed earlier.

"What's wrong with my baby?" pleaded Suzanne.

"I'm not sure," said the pediatric resident, "but we think his hip may be infected. We're going to need an MRI."

"Doctor," said Suzanne, "Gregory has not had anything to eat or drink all day. Isn't there something you can do?"

The pediatric resident looked back at the baby.

"I'll get an IV started," she said. "They'll need that for the MRI anyway."

Another four hours passed while Suzanne and Leroy waited anxiously in the emergency department with Gregory. The pediatric resident was very skilled at starting the IV. Suzanne thought that her son looked a little better after getting some fluid in his veins. Eventually a transport orderly arrived and took the family through a maze of corridors to the MRI suite.

Suzanne and Leroy had to wait outside the MRI suite for almost two hours while the test was being performed. Leroy called his office to leave a message that he would not be in to work the next morning. Then he sat next to his wife and put his arm around her shoulders. Suzanne felt better being held, but she knew that her husband was just as anxious as she was.

Eventually they were all returned to the emergency department. Gregory was sleeping, still sedated from his MRI. No-one would tell Suzanne and Leroy what the MRI had shown.

"Hi," said a handsome, tall black man in a short white lab coat with a smile that would light a room. "I'm Dr. Charlie Travers. I'm the resident on pediatric orthopedics. Do you mind if I take a look at Gregory?"

Suzanne and Leroy were relieved that anyone at all was paying attention to their son. Sitting in the emergency room awash in worry and uncertainty was becoming unbearable.

Travers was gentle with the baby as he repeated most of the examination already performed by the other doctors. Gregory slept fitfully from the sedation until Travers moved the right leg. Then the piercing scream returned.

"I'm sorry," Travers said to the Burris family. "I just had to make sure. Can we talk for a while? Perhaps someplace quieter than the ER?"

"We're not leaving our son," said Leroy. "We'll talk here."

"OK," said Travers with a kind smile. "I understand. Let me explain what has happened to Gregory and how we know it. Then I'll explain what needs to be done and I'll answer your questions as best I can."

"Finally, some answers," sighed Suzanne.

"Gregory has an infection in his right hip joint," explained Travers. "His joint is full of bacteria and his own white blood cells. There's a lot of inflammation. This is why it hurts to move the leg and why he won't stand up. The bacteria probably got into his joint from an infection at the top of his thigh bone, where the thigh bone makes the ball of the hip joint."

"How did he get the infection in his bone?" asked Leroy.

"Nobody knows for certain," said Travers. "There are bacteria that float around it our blood stream all the time. Most of the time, our immune system kills them, but every so often a few get lodged in the bones and they can grow there."

"So, will you give him antibiotics?" asked Leroy.

"Yes, in time," said Travers, "but first we have to get the bacteria out of the joint. The toxins in the bacteria can damage the joint cartilage in the hip. We have to drain the joint. It is considered a surgical emergency."

"If it's an emergency, why have we been waiting for eight hours?" Leroy asked, betraying his stress and frustration.

"We had to know what the problem was for certain," explained Travers. "I'm sorry it takes so long, but, well, you've seen how many patients we have here in the emergency department. We certainly wouldn't like to subject a baby to an operation until we were pretty certain that it was necessary. It was the MRI that told us for certain that Gregory has a hip infection."

"So what happens now?" asked Suzanne.

"We need to take Gregory to surgery," said Travers. "We need to open up his hip joint and get the pus and bacteria out. We'll get cultures to identify the bacteria specifically and start antibiotics. Gregory should feel better immediately after he wakes up."

"You're going to operate on my baby?" Suzanne gasped.

"I'm going to assist Dr. Amelia Howard," explained Travers. "Dr. Howard is the chief of our pediatric orthopedic service here. She's on her way in right now."

Suzanne began to tremble. Leroy held her close.

"What are the risks?"

"Well, there is always a risk with anesthesia," said Travers, breaking into a well-rehearsed routine. "There is a risk that we won't be able to eradicate the infection. Both of those risks are very low. There is also a risk that there has already been too much damage from the infection and that the joint is already ruined or that the bone of the ball of the joint has been killed by the bacteria. Those risks are really from the disease, not the treatment."

"What if the joint is ruined?" asked Suzanne. "Can you replace it?"

Travers smiled kindly.

"Not in babies, Mrs. Burris, only in adults. At this point, the most effective thing we can do is get Gregory up to surgery as quickly as possible."

"Let's go, then, Doctor," said Leroy.

♦ ♦ ♦

Dr. Amelia Howard radiated energy and confidence. She was a favorite of the operating room nurses because she was fast, highly skilled, and very personable. It was apparent why Dr. Stuart had personally selected her to be his replacement. Like many doctors who cared for children, there was an underlying kindness to her that transcended her professionalism. Even though it was late in the evening and she had been called away from her own family dinner to return to the hospital, Howard was cheerful and positive. She introduced herself to the Burris's and answered their questions before the operation began.

Assisted by Travers, Howard quickly separated the skin, fat and muscles to get down to the baby's hip. She was quite comfortable operating on tiny bodies where structures were small.

"Here's the hip capsule," said Howard, pushing some tissue off to the side. "Give me a syringe with an 18 gauge needle."

The scrub nurse handed over the needle and Howard removed the plastic guard. She inserted the needle and was rewarded with thick yellow fluid which displaced the syringe as the pressure in the joint was released. Howard moved the needle from side to side, gently, and removed a large amount of pus.

"Just cap the needle and send the whole thing to the lab," said Howard. "Get a stat Gram stain so we can get some idea of what kind of bugs are in this kid. I want all of the pus sent. We don't want the lab to fail to culture because the sample was too small."

"Want to take a guess at the organism?" asked Travers.

"Well, most of these are caused by Staph," said Howard. "But some, especially in babies, can be H flu or Strep. I'd put my money on Staph. Let's get the joint open and get things cleaned out."

The scalpel divided the joint capsule and the surgeons were looking at the shiny, glistening ball of the hip joint, swimming in yellow pus.

"Irrigation," ordered Howard.

"Suction," said Travers.

They washed the joint with sterile saline solution, sucking up the fluid as they worked. From time to time, they would pause to inspect the joint, looking for strands of congealed pus that had escaped the suction. These they would pick out with forceps.

"There's a hunk of junk around the back, Dr. Howard," said Travers. "See it? I can't quite get the forceps on it. The space is too narrow."

"Yes, I see, Charlie," she replied. "Let me have a shot."

Howard was also unable to grasp the nasty bit of debris.

"We need something smaller to get behind the ball here," said Howard to the nurse. "I've got an idea. Do you have a basket forceps? The kind that they use in arthroscopy?"

"Not on this tray, Doctor," said the nurse, "but I'll open an arthroscopy tray for you. There's one right outside, ready for the first case tomorrow morning."

"The sports guys will be mad if we use their instruments," said Travers.

"They'll never know, Charlie," said the nurse. "We'll re-sterilize the tray and put it right back where we found it. When the jock docs get here in the morning, everything will be right where it belongs."

The narrow forceps were just what was needed to get the last of the infected material out of Gregory Burris's hip.

◆ ◆ ◆

Keith found Stuart in the x-ray department, looking intently at some films of a child's fractured leg. Stuart had his prosthetic eye in the socket, so no black patch. Keith could not stop himself from staring at the glass eye, which in color was identical to the normal left one. It looked so normal that Keith wondered why Stuart didn't wear it all the time. The only difference that Keith could see was that the glass one didn't move when Stuart changed his gaze.

'Hi, Dr. Stuart," said Keith. "I wondered if I could make an appointment to talk to you about the infected arthroscopy cases. I have more data now. There are, I am afraid, two more now, bringing the total to five."

"Sure. I'm about done here. We can go to my office and talk. By the way, take a look at these x-rays. Do you see anything unusual?"

Keith studied the films.

"It looks like a fairly straightforward distal femur fracture, sir."

"Look closer."

Keith looked again. The fracture line was a spiral, starting a few inches above the knee and moving up toward the center of the thigh bone. It was angulated and shortened, but not bad.

"You don't see it, do you?" asked Stuart. Then he pointed at a dark area at the lower end of the fracture. "What's that?"

Oh, shit, thought Keith, there's a tumor in the cortex of the bone. No wonder that the bone broke right there.

"Oh, nuts, sir. I missed it," he said. "It's a fibrous cortical defect. A benign tumor that weakened the bone."

"Yes it is," said Stuart. "It goes to show that things that look routine are not always what they seem. Or, sometimes when you hear hoofbeats, there are zebras instead of horses. Let's go up to the office."

Keith laid out all the data on the infected arthroscopic cases. They spent two hours poring over the data. Then Stuart sat back in his chair and looked at Keith intently.

"So, you have five routine arthroscopy cases, all infected with the identical strain of MRSA. And there is nothing else in common except that they were all first cases and the attending surgeon is Alex Warren in each case."

"That's it."

"It looks like you have eliminated all the standard possibilities for the spread of infection inside the hospital," said Stuart. "The standard things cannot be responsible for all these infections. It's impossible. So, as Sherlock Holmes used to say, 'once you have eliminated the impossible, whatever remains, however improbable, must be the truth.'"

"Sherlock Holmes?"

"Sure. Sir Arthur Conan Doyle was a physician, you know. And we can solve a lot of diagnostic dilemmas by applying the logical techniques that Doyle incorporated into his great character, Sherlock Holmes."

"So, do you know what's causing the infections?"

"Yes, I know what's causing the infections. I knew about the last two cases. Since we talked before, I've been looking into these cases. We are looking at deliberate infection, overt acts. Someone is infecting the cases on purpose, Keith. I just don't know who is doing it. Or why."

"Deliberate acts?" Keith was incredulous. "Someone is doing this on purpose?"

"It's the only explanation," said Stuart.

"But who? And how?"

"My guess is that someone is contaminating the arthroscopic surgical instruments with MRSA," said Stuart, "probably sometime after they come out of the sterilizer and before the operating room opens for the day. That's why each infection is the first case of the day."

"Who would do that?" asked Keith.

"It's fairly sophisticated," said Stuart, "Whoever is doing this has a knowledge of microbiology and access to a source of MRSA, since all the infections have been caused by the same organism. The perpetrator also knows how instruments are prepared for surgery and which ones will be used in the arthroscopy cases. The person also has access to surgical instruments after they come out of the sterilizer. Most likely, we're talking about someone who works here in the hospital."

"So a doctor is doing this?"

"Very likely," said Stuart, "a doctor or a nurse."

◆ ◆ ◆

Mary DeGuzman sipped her coffee as she listened to morning report at the nurses' station, taking notes on the patients assigned to her for the day shift.

"Gregory Burris, eight-month-old black male, patient of Dr. Howard," said the charge nurse. "Septic arthritis of the hip. IV running with D5 in quarter normal saline at thirty milliliters per hour. On methicillin and gentamycin pending cultures. He's pretty irritable, just got here from recovery room about 0400. Parents at the bedside. Infectious disease consult in for today."

Mary had Gregory's chart when she entered the room, but her eyes were always on the child and the parents. Suzanne and Leroy were exhausted and emotionally drained. Neither had slept at all. Gregory fussed and wiggled in the bed.

"Good morning," she said. "I'm Mary and I'll be Gregory's nurse today."

She smiled and shook hands with the parents, then checked Gregory's temperature, pulse, and blood pressure. She looked at the IV site in the baby's arm and the level of the fluid in the bag. Only then did Mary look at the chart.

"You two look like you could use some rest," said Mary. "Why don't you go down to the cafeteria and get some breakfast? Take some time to be together, just the two of you. I have a few things to do with Gregory. I'll watch him."

Relieved, Suzanne and Leroy walked slowly toward the door.

"Don't worry," said Mary, "I'll know where to find you if we need you."

"Thank you," said Suzanne.

With the parents gone, Mary donned vinyl gloves and removed the dressing over the incision, which was in the right groin area, just below the abdomen. A vinyl drain protruded from the incision, guiding remaining fluid from the depths of the hip joint into the sterile bandages. Mary immediately noticed that there was a lot of watery, yellowish fluid on the bandages, mixed with streaks of blood. To her surprise, the incision itself looked red and inflamed. This was not what she expected. Making a mental note, she removed the soiled bandages and placed them in a sterile bag, then carefully applied a new sterile dressing.

Dr. Travers made rounds later in the morning.

"How's the baby from last night, Mary?" asked Travers.

"Not as good as I'd like," she answered. "He still seems generally sick. Not like most kids who have had a septic hip drained."

"Fever?"

"Low grade. Thirty eight point two," she reported. "His dressing was pretty soaked with watery, pussy fluid. And the area around the incision is pretty red."

"Let me look," said Travers.

Together they entered the room. The parents had returned. Gregory continued to fuss and squirm, despite Suzanne's attempts to comfort him.

"Dr. Travers, thank you for all you did last night," said Leroy. "And thank you for being so kind to us. I'm surprised that you're still here."

"You're welcome and I'll be going home soon," said Travers. "I just want to check on my little friend before I leave. Can you excuse Ms. DeGuzman and me for a minute? We need to look at the incision and I need to remove the drain we left in the incision to make sure all the pus was out of the hip."

Travers and Mary put on fresh gloves.

The Burrises left again, handing Gregory to Mary. When Travers removed the dressings, Mary saw that the new bandages were already soaked with watery pus. The incision still looked red and inflamed. She shot a glance at Travers.

"I've seen better looking incisions," he said. "But Dr. Howard said to pull the drain and that's what I'm gonna do. Besides, sooner or later that drain could become a two-way street and I don't want anything crawling into the hip."

Travers slipped out the rubbery strip and more watery pus followed. Mary thought that this was not the way that things were supposed to be.

"Put a new dressing on," said Travers. "It should dry up and get better in a few hours. The infectious disease consultant will be by. Show her the incision. And also Dr. Howard when she makes rounds this afternoon."

"Yes, sir," said Mary with more confidence than she felt.

Late in the morning, Dr. Laura Chin, the specialist in pediatric infectious disease, came to the unit to see Gregory. Mary showed Chin to the room and introduced her to the parents.

"Hello," said Chin, "I'm a pediatrician specializing in infectious diseases. Dr. Howard has asked me to consult with regard to the selection of appropriate antibiotics and to help determine how long Gregory will need antibiotic coverage for this infection in his hip. Dr. Howard sent some of the infected fluid to the lab, so we can grow the bacteria and determine precisely the best antibiotics to use. Right now, Gregory is on methicillin which should kill the most likely germs, namely *Streptococcus* and *Staphylococcus*. He is also on gentamycin, which should kill less likely germs like *Haemophilus influenza* that we sometimes see in babies. Once we know for certain which bacteria is in Gregory's hip, we can adjust things. Most likely, he will need a couple of days of IV antibiotics and then we can switch him to oral agents. Then you can take him home. Usually, the children need about six weeks of treatment with antibiotics."

Mary thought to herself that she would have to translate what Dr. Chin had just said into English for the parents after the doctor left. A big part of her job was explaining to families what doctors said in their own esoteric jargon. She couldn't understand why all doctors didn't talk in terms that ordinary people could comprehend. Dr. Stuart needed no interpretation when he talked to families and he was the smartest doctor she knew.

"Thank you, Dr. Chin," said Leroy. He didn't really understand her, but he was respectful and his real question was simple. "Is the treatment usually successful?"

"Yes, Mr. Burris," smiled Chin. "I know this is really hard on you, but we see infections like this all the time and almost all the children recover completely."

"Would you like to examine Gregory, Dr. Chin?" asked Mary, hoping to get the doctor to look at the child, not just the chart.

"Of course," said Dr. Chin.

Suzanne laid Gregory in the bed and Chin listened to his heart and lungs with her stethoscope, then pushed gently on his belly. Gregory just looked at the doctor and whimpered.

"Would you like to see the incision?" asked Mary, trying to be respectful and at the same time draw the doctor's attention. It didn't work.

"No, I'll leave that part for the surgeons," said Chin.

Chin took the chart and went to the nursing station to write her consultation note. Mary handed Gregory back to Suzanne and smiled at her.

"I'll be here with all of you all day," she said.

Mary was disappointed. As the morning went on, she was less and less happy with Gregory's progress.

Shortly after lunch, Dr. Howard made her rounds. Mary caught her as soon as she entered the pediatric unit.

"Dr. Howard, are you here to see Gregory Burris?" Mary asked.

"Yes, and one or two other kids," said Howard.

"Can we start with Gregory?" Mary asked. "I'm a little concerned about him."

Mary got the chart, handed it to Howard, and went to grab some fresh bandages and gloves while the doctor went into the room and greeted the parents. By the time Mary arrived, Suzanne had laid Gregory on the bed. He was sweaty and listless.

"What was his temperature when you last checked?" Howard asked.

"Thirty-eight point nine an hour ago. Pulse was one-forty and blood pressure eighty over sixty," said Mary.

Howard pulled on gloves and swiftly removed the bandages. They were soaked. The skin around the incision was redder and nastier than before.

"What antibiotics is he on?" asked Howard.

"Methicillin and gentamycin, Doctor," said Mary.

"Culture reports back yet?"

"Just a preliminary, Doctor. Lab says most likely *Staph. aureus*, no antibiotic sensitivities yet."

"Well, then we're doing everything right," said Howard. "Put a new dressing on, will you, Mary?"

"Of course, Doctor," said Mary. She thought that Dr. Howard was not happy with this case either.

FOURTEEN

"Knock, knock."

Stuart looked up from the report he was reading to see Amelia Howard standing in the door of his office, tapping on the doorframe. He was always happy to see Amelia, his successor as chief of pediatric orthopedics after Stuart was injured in the auto accident. Stuart had trained her himself and she was one of the sharpest clinicians and best surgeons he had ever seen. Stuart was wearing his eyepatch over his missing right eye. He noticed that Howard looked worried, not her usual cheerful self.

"Come in, Amelia. What's on your mind?" he said.

"A kid I operated on last night," she said. "Eight-month-old boy with a septic right hip. Pretty routine case, I thought. Today, he really looks lousy."

"Those kids usually look like a million bucks once we get the pus out of their joints," said Stuart.

"Yeah, that's the point. This kid still looks sick. One of the first things you taught me, Ray, was to look at the kid from the doorway, before you get fully into the room. You said that you can tell from the doorway if this is a sick kid or a healthy one. And this kid looks sick."

"Are you telling me that the morning after you drained his hip, the kid still flunks the doorway test?"

"Yes," she said. "He's still a sick little boy."

"Anything unusual at surgery?"

"Nothing at all," she replied. "Joint full of pus. We cleaned it out and left a drain. Started methicillin and gentamycin. I expected to see him bouncing all over the room when I made rounds this afternoon. Instead, he's listless. Wound is still draining sero-purulent stuff and looks red and inflamed and, well..."

"Like it's still infected," Stuart finished her sentence.

"Yeah," said Howard. "Mary DeGuzman's his nurse. I can tell that Mary is worried, too."

"Mary's a good nurse, very sharp."

"I know," said Howard. "Ray, would you mind taking a look at him? I'd feel a lot better if I had your advice. This child just doesn't seem right to me."

"Sure. What's his name?"

"Gregory Burris."

◆ ◆ ◆

Keith's Harley Davidson clearly did not fit into the neighborhood. The loud rumble of the V-twin engine echoed in the quiet, elegant street in the St. Francis Wood district. As he dismounted he could see a few frowning faces peering at him from behind curtains. Davenport's house was really more of a mansion. Removing the copies of Bill Henderson's files from the saddlebag, he ascended the walkway between rows of perfectly manicured flowers and rang the bell.

The expression on the face of the woman who answered the door was far from friendly.

"Mr. Davenport, please," said Keith.

"Who are you?"

Keith remembered that he still had his helmet on. He apologized as he removed it, revealing his tousled hair and friendly smile.

"Sorry, ma'am, please tell him that Dr. Keith Grant is calling."

With a look of distrust, she shut the door while she checked with Mr. Davenport. Keith grinned when he heard the deadbolt fall. He waved to an elderly neighbor peering behind a lace curtain.

The deadbolt turned again and the woman opened the door.

"Mr. Davenport will see you in the library," said the unsmiling woman.

As he expected, the house was elegantly furnished, like a museum or something from the movies. Keith had never been in such an opulent house in his life. Until this moment, he was not sure that such places actually existed in reality, just in the imagination of movie producers. Everything looked like antiques, furniture that once belonged to French royalty. Keith really knew nothing about antiques, but this was impressive. His neck craned from side to side as the woman led him to a large wood-paneled library. Davenport was seated in a large wing chair, his operated leg propped up on an ottoman. He was dressed in a silk robe, pajamas, and slippers.

"Good to see you, Grant," said Davenport. "Please excuse me for not getting up. It takes about twenty minutes to get out of this goddam chair and hurts like hell. Have you figured out who was trying to assassinate me in the hospital?"

"Not yet, sir, but the police and I would like your help with something."

"So, you have involved the police in the matter? I was afraid that you were going to blow this whole thing off, like the rest of the hospital. Write it off as some routine medication error. Bullshit. It was attempted murder, I tell you. And if they think that I'm not going to sue their asses off, they are sadly mistaken. They're going to pay for this, oh yes. In good old US dollars and lots of them. Glad you involved the police, Grant. That shows initiative. I like initiative in a young man. Curious that they haven't sent a detective around here to ask me questions."

"Well, Mr. Davenport," said Keith, "this is not exactly about the incident you had at the hospital. And, to be honest, it's not part of an official police inquiry. You see, I have a good friend who is a police detective. One of his cases is the mass shooting outside the gym a little more than a week ago."

"Is that related to the attempt on my life?" asked Davenport. "God, I thought the shooting at the gym was some madman run amok or some religious fanatic terrorist act."

"It's very confusing, sir," said Keith. "The first person shot, and the only one killed at the gym, was Bill Henderson, the CFO at Sutro State University Hospital. He actually died in my arms."

"I knew Bill Henderson, you know, from my work on the hospital board. Seemed like a good enough fellow. Your experience must have been awful," said Davenport. He had lowered his voice and spoke slowly, certainly thinking about Bill. Keith thought that this was the first time Davenport had appeared anywhere near human.

"More than you might imagine," said Keith. "Bill had a briefcase full of hospital papers with him at the gym. Just before he was killed, he told me that he was going home to work on some financial problem from the hospital. The police seized the briefcase as evidence. It seems to contain a lot of computer printouts and handwritten notes about hospital bills and MediCal. The whole thing makes no sense to the police. I suggested that maybe you would have a look at them. You know more about the finances of the hospital than I do. Maybe something will jump out at you."

"You're telling me that the police don't believe that the shooting was an act of terrorism or random insanity," said Davenport. "They think that Bill Henderson was targeted."

"It's possible, sir. That's a theory that my friend the detective is working on."

There was a small table next to the wing chair on which Davenport had a cup of coffee and some books.

"Get this shit off the table and let's see your papers, Grant," said Davenport, "and bring me my glasses from the desk."

Davenport studied the papers for nearly two hours. The grumpy woman brought both of them coffee. Keith silently helped, moving papers from the table to the desk as Davenport directed.

"What's this little note?" asked Davenport.

"It just says Five South," said Keith. "It may not fit at all. The police don't know what to make of it. My girlfriend is a nurse at the hospital. She says that Five South is the name of a nursing unit at the hospital that was closed two years ago. She says that nobody goes there. It's used for storage. No one knows how it might relate."

Davenport looked at Keith and scratched his chin.

"Really? Grant, bring me that stack of papers over there, on the desk," he said. "No, goddamn it. The stack next to it."

He attacked the stack of computer printouts, mumbling to himself.

"Shit," said Davenport. "That's it. Goddamn it."

"Sir?"

"There are some unusual coincidences in these billing patterns. At least it looks unusual. Do you know anything about accounting?"

"No, sir."

"Do you understand how to use a relational database on the computer?"

"A little."

"Well you can sort things out on the computer selecting for different factors. It allows you to look at a big pile of data, group the data different ways and look at separate factors which might otherwise get lost in the multitude of numbers.

To use a metaphor, it allows you to look at little clumps of trees when you can't quite get your eyes off the forest."

Davenport paused, took a breath, and continued. "It appears that the late Mr. Henderson was looking at MediCal billings over the last year. For some reason, he noticed a huge spike in bills which occurs on the last Monday of every month. The number of bills sent out each day to MediCal is more or less random and even, but it appears that on the last Monday of every month a large number of bills are submitted for payment. It doesn't fail. It happens each month in the year for which he pulled records. And the difference in the volume is not small. There's a big spike compared to other days of the month."

"So?"

"The spike in billing suggests a pattern," explained Davenport. "And I think that your friend Bill was going to look at which hospital beds were occupied by the patients who were discharged on the last Mondays of the month. My guess is that he was going to run a query on the bills by nursing unit that night that he was shot. And that's where your girlfriend's observation fits in."

"Five South?"

"Yes," said Davenport. "From the printouts, it seems to the naked eye that a lot of the discharges from the hospital, which coincide with billing, came from unit Five South. It's just an eyeball observation. You would need a database query to look at it in detail and to know for certain."

"But Mary, my girlfriend, said that there are no patients at all on Five South," said Keith. He could not remember ever hearing of Five South. Like all residents, Keith was concerned only with nursing units that did have patients.

"And I certainly didn't know that," said Davenport. "As a member of the board, I never go down into the hospital itself. I take the elevator from the lobby to the executive level where the board room is. And my guess is that your friend Bill Henderson had never been to Five South either. All those administrative bigshots pride themselves on how little they know about what actually goes on in the hospital. That's part of why I hate them all."

"I don't get it," said Keith. "Bill Henderson discovers that there are more bills sent out on the last Monday of the month than other days. You discover that these bills come from patients who were hospitalized on a nursing unit that is used for storage. And for this Bill gets shot?"

Davenport sat and thought for a few minutes in silence.

"Grant, can you get me access to the hospital computer?" he asked.

"Residents have access to the parts of the computer system we need to take care of patients," Keith answered. "We can get medical records, lab and x-ray results, enter orders, write notes, that sort of thing. But if you want to get into hospital billing records, no. I don't have access to those data. Do you think that Bill got killed because he was investigating a bunch of hospital bills? Seriously?"

"Maybe, Grant, maybe," said the lawyer. "I've got to look into those hospital computers."

♦ ♦ ♦

"Sorry to interrupt, Ms. Roberts. I'm Detective Duane Wilson, San Francisco Police. May I ask you a few questions?"

Patricia was sitting at her desk with the office door open. She startled at the sight of the black police detective. Duane noticed the quick look of anxiety. Patricia recovered quickly and shot Duane a flirtatious smile. Duane was a good looking man, well-muscled from the way he filled out his suit. She liked men with big muscles. Subtly, she looked and was encouraged that Duane did not wear a wedding ring.

"Of course, detective," she said. "How can I help?"

"I understand that you have a membership at the gym where the mass shooting occurred," said Duane, "And that you were there working out on the day of the shooting."

"Yes, I left about an hour before the shooting," said Patricia. "I was shocked when I heard the news. Bill Henderson was a good friend of mine."

"Where did you go from the gym?" asked Duane.

"Well, I stopped for dinner at a Chinese place that I like, then I went home."

"Did anyone see you at the restaurant? I have to ask. It's routine."

"Yes," she said. "The servers and owner. I eat there often and they know me."

"Hmmm. Thank you. Did you see anyone or anything unusual when you left the gym? Perhaps in the building across the street?"

"No," said Patricia, "nobody that I recognized. There were people on the street, but no one and nothing unusual."

"One more thing," asked Duane, "do you know James Davenport?"

"You mean the man who's on the hospital board? Yes, I know who he is. We've been introduced, but I don't know him well. What does this have to do with the shooting at the gym?"

"Probably nothing," said Duane, "but please, be kind enough to answer a few questions."

"Well, all right, but I don't see any connection."

"You do know that he had a knee replacement operation a week or so ago," said Duane, "and that there was a complication?"

"It was what we call a medication error," said Patricia. "We don't like those, but they happen. Mr. Davenport was given another patient's dose of insulin by mistake. The nurse who gave the insulin has been fired."

"Which patient was supposed to get the insulin?" asked Duane. "Did that patient have any adverse outcome because he didn't get his insulin?"

"I don't recall exactly which patient was supposed to get the insulin," said Patricia. Her pulse was rising and she could feel a bit of moisture in her armpit. "I could look that up for you if you like. We must, however, maintain strict confidentiality with regard to our patients' medical records. In any event, we investigated the incident and we're confident that Nurse Ramirez made a serious error. That's why she was terminated."

"Did you conduct the investigation personally?" asked Duane.

"Well, yes, under my authority and supervision," said Patricia. "Detective, I'm in charge of a very large nursing staff. I can't recall each specific medication error. If you'd like to make an appointment and come back, I can have the full report for you."

"So there is a written report?" said Duane. "Did you visit Mr. Davenport in the hospital that evening?"

"Of course there's a report," said Patricia, "And no, I didn't visit Mr. Davenport that evening."

"You were seen in the parking lot of the hospital that evening," said Duane.

"I was working late in my office," said Patricia. "We are preparing next year's budget."

"Of course," said Duane, "Thank you for your help."

FIFTEEN

WHEN DUANE GOT home that evening he made a point of asking Matt about insulin injections. How much of an insulin dose would have to be injected into an IV to induce a seizure like Davenport had? Matt told him that it would take a very large dose.

"Frankly, Duane," said Matt, "that seems like an unusual kind of medication error. I was curious about it the other night when Keith and Mary were talking about it, but we got back to the gym shooting and I kind of forgot. It would take a very large dose of insulin to put a man who was not diabetic into such severe hypoglycemia that he would seize. And it would have to be one of the fast-acting insulins. We have all sorts of different insulin preparations, you know. Most stable diabetics who require insulin are on the longer acting preparations. They might supplement with a fast-acting insulin just before a meal, in anticipation of a rise in blood sugar. In hospitals, we might use a fast-acting insulin in the emergency department, to treat a patient who presented in diabetic ketoacidosis. If the patient was injected with one of the long-acting insulins by mistake, he'd get jittery and uncomfortable, but there would be a long time before he had a seizure, if that would happen at all. No, it had to be a large dose of a fast-acting insulin to make the patient crash and seize so quickly. You know, if Keith hadn't made the diagnosis and treated the hypoglycemia, it's likely that Davenport would have wound up on my autopsy table."

"If that was a medication error," asked Duane, "what about the patient who was supposed to get the insulin? Would that patient have symptoms?"

"If there was a patient who needed that much insulin," said Matt, "I would imagine that his or her glucose would have gone through the roof without it. Do you think that Davenport's complication and the mass shootings are connected?"

"No, not really," said Duane, "although Keith says that Davenport believes that someone was trying to kill him. And Mary says that Ms. Roberts was at the scene of both incidents. But Roberts has a perfectly good reason to be at the gym and in the hospital. The only other person that I know who was at the scene of both incidents was Keith. And he seemed to be up to his ass trying to save lives, not take them. I guess that I'm trying to respect Mary by looking into the possibility of the two things being connected. And I'm very curious about how you medical types conduct investigations when things go wrong. From a professional standpoint, of course."

"What do you mean," asked Matt, "how we medical types do investigations?"

"Well, you do everything in house, you investigate yourselves," said Duane, "you don't call the police. All the investigators have a bias. Doctors investigate other doctors. Don't you think that the doctors doing the investigation have an interest in clearing their colleagues? After all Doctor A may investigate Doctor B this month. Next month Doctor B investigates Doctor A. It gives a whole new definition to the term 'professional courtesy.' And when a nurse makes a mistake and nearly kills a patient by dosing with the wrong medication, who does the investigation? Another nurse.

"Shit, man," he continued, "you don't consider all the possibilities. Take the Davenport case. Here is this nasty old man who goes into the hospital to get his knee replaced. As best anyone can tell, somebody puts enough insulin in his IV to kill him. If it wasn't for the serendipitous arrival of Keith, the old guy would be dead. Nobody calls the cops. You all assume that the nurse gave him the wrong medicine. Whoops. Happens all the time. Well, the old guy survived. No harm, no foul. You fire the nurse. The hospital will settle the lawsuit and everything just goes on. Talk about sloppy detective work. God, if the police worked like that we'd be crucified. If I worked like that I'd be fired."

"Why don't you make it a police case, if you're so suspicious?" asked Matt. "You don't need an invitation."

"You know, if I wasn't so overwhelmed with the two cases I've got, I might just do that," said Duane. "As it is, I've got this Patterson cyanide poisoning thing which is going nowhere and a mass shooting which may not be what it seems. And I haven't gotten past square one on either case."

"I'm intrigued with Mary's idea that Ms. Roberts is involved with both," said Matt. "Was she ever a guest at Patterson's house? Could she have left the poisoned sherry? It sure would be convenient if you could wrap everything up with one serial killer."

Duane laughed.

"That would be convenient, and good for my career," he said, "but no, Ms. Roberts was never a guest at the Patterson house. I asked Mr. Patterson. He never invited anyone of less stature than the CEO to be a guest. From the administrative staff, that is. The chief of the medical staff, a Dr. Phillips, was usually invited. Occasionally other important doctors came to the parties, but only Phillips was at the most recent one. There's really nothing to tie Ms. Roberts to the Patterson case and damn little to tie her to either Davenport or the shootings. Frankly, while I like Mary, I think she doesn't like Ms. Roberts. Mostly because she isn't crazy about Roberts' hitting on Keith."

♦ ♦ ♦

Mary felt a strong sense of relief when she saw Dr. Stuart enter the pediatric unit. She was certain that everyone would see her reaction. Stuart had placed his glass eye in the socket and wore a freshly pressed white lab coat.

"Dr. Stuart, are you here to see..?" she asked.

"Gregory Burris, as if you didn't know," he smiled.

"I'll get the chart and some fresh dressings," she said.

Stuart was talking with Suzanne and Leroy when Mary arrived in the room with the supplies. Mary noticed that while Stuart was getting caught up on the whole story from the parents, his gaze never left the little boy who was nestled in his mother's arms, but not at all attentive or alert.

"Do you mind if I take a look at Gregory?" Stuart asked.

Suzanne laid him again on the bed. Stuart and Mary put on gloves and removed the bandages.

"Is this how it looked when Dr. Howard was here?" Stuart whispered to Mary so the parents could not hear.

"It's a little worse," she whispered.

They applied a new dressing. Stuart looked at the rest of Gregory's leg, then the left side, moving every joint. He took out his stethoscope and listened to the chest for a long time.

"Has he been coughing?" Stuart asked Suzanne.

"A little," she said.

"Dr. Howard asked me to look in on Gregory," said Stuart. "She wanted a head with a few grey hairs to render an opinion. Like Dr. Howard, I'm a pediatric orthopedist. I was her teacher back in the day. Dr. Howard is the best I know. So far, it looks like Dr. Howard has done everything right. The treatment is right according to the textbook."

"But?" said Leroy.

"But it seems like Gregory didn't read the textbook," said Stuart. "We would have expected him to be better than this by now."

"So?" asked Leroy.

"We're going to keep a close eye on him, maybe get a few more tests," said Stuart.

Mary followed him to the nurses' station. Stuart took the chart.

"Mary, increase the IV rate to sixty milliliters per hour. I think he's dehydrated. And let's get x-ray up here. I heard some junk in his lungs. I want a portable chest film and an x-ray of the pelvis that shows both hips and the proximal femurs. And let's get the lab up for some blood."

"Yes, sir," said Mary. She was feeling much, much better about the case now that Stuart was here. "Thank you for coming, Dr. Stuart."

"Call me when the tests are done," he said. "Otherwise, I'll be back in an hour."

◆ ◆ ◆

Stuart took the elevator down to the microbiology laboratory. The laboratory technologists were surprised to see the renowned clinician in the lab, but quickly found for him the culture specimens from Gregory Burris, sent the night before.

Stuart looked in the microscope at the bacteria that Howard had pulled out of Gregory's hip. Little blue balls clustered together like bunches of grapes. Classic Staphylococci.

"Where are the cultures?" Stuart asked.

"Over here, Doctor," said the lab tech.

She showed Stuart small round trays filled with a blood red gel. Little yellow dots covered the red surface. Stuart knew that the dots were clusters of bacteria and that the yellow color was also classic for Staphylococcus aureus. "Aureus" meant "gold" in Latin, and was derived from the yellow color of the colonies on the agar plates.

"I wouldn't bet the ranch on it," said the lab tech, "but from what I can tell of the sensitivities so far, it looks like your garden variety Staph, sensitive to methicillin."

"That's the most common bug infecting babies' hips, so I'm not surprised," said Stuart.

"We should have some definitive antibiotic sensitivities by this time tomorrow," said the tech.

"This is one sick little boy," said Stuart. "We can't wait until tomorrow."

Stuart's pager went off. It was Mary, telling him that the x-rays had been taken. Stuart left the lab and headed for x-ray. The images were just coming available on the computer. Stuart took a seat next to one of the radiologists, who was dictating reports and sipping coffee. She looked bored.

"Can we look at Gregory Burris, pediatrics?" asked Stuart.

"Sure," said the radiologist, clicking the mouse to bring up the chest x-ray.

"Looks like some infiltrates in the lungs," said the radiologist. "What's the story?"

"Eight-month-old little boy with septic arthritis. Everybody said his lungs were clear until I examined him a few minutes ago. I heard some junk in there, everywhere, not localized."

"That fits," said the radiologist. "It looks like the beginning of generalized pneumonia."

Stuart looked at the white lines marring the blackness of the lungs on the x-ray. He knew that abnormalities on the x-ray lagged behind what was actually going on inside the patient, so the pneumonia in Gregory was already worse than it looked on the picture.

"Let's see the pelvis film," said Stuart.

There was nothing special to see on the hip x-ray, just some air in the soft tissues which was consistent with the hip being opened at surgery.

Stuart caught the next elevator back to pediatrics. He and Mary returned to Gregory's room. The baby was still sweating, but felt cold to the touch.

"Mary, let's increase the IV to eighty milliliters per hour," said Stuart. "Ask the chief resident in pediatrics to come over and have a look at this boy right now. I'm going to give Dr. Chin a call."

Chin was already home when Stuart called. She did not seem happy to be interrupted.

"Laura, this is Ray Stuart. I'm with little Gregory Burris. Yes, the boy with the septic hip. He's clearly getting worse. I think he's septic."

"He's on methicillin and gentamycin, right?" said Chin.

"Yes, and I've been down to the lab. The cultures look like Staph which is going to be sensitive to methicillin."

"So, stay the course," said Chin.

"What do you think of adding clindamycin or vancomycin?" asked Stuart.

"Those are usually for MRSA," said Chin. "We have no reason to suspect that this kid has MRSA."

Stuart was starting to feel a cold, creepy sensation in his skin. Perhaps there was a reason to suspect MRSA. The other cases had all been adults who had arthroscopic surgery and were first cases in the morning. This was a baby operated on at night. Still….

"I know," said Stuart. "I've never seen MRSA cause septic arthritis in a kid. Or even read of a single case. But this little boy is not responding to our normal treatment."

"There's no scientific reason to change antibiotics," said Chin firmly. "Stay the course, Dr. Stuart. Give the drugs time to do their work."

No, thought Stuart. There is no scientific reason to suspect MRSA. But there is a sinister possibility.

The pediatrics chief resident was at the bedside, listening to Gregory's chest when Stuart returned. He looked worried. Mary had brought the crash cart with emergency medications. Stuart could see the fear in her eyes, but she remained focused on her professional responsibility.

"Gregory's temperature has fallen to thirty-six point eight," said Mary, "Pulse is one sixty and BP is seventy over thirty."

"Shit," said Stuart under his breath. "He's going into shock. Where are the parents?"

"I sent them down to the play room to wait," said Mary, "I'm giving them updates."

"Thanks. Smart move."

The pediatric resident looked up and took the earpieces out of his ears.

"His lungs are filling up. He's not moving much air."

"Do you want to transfer him to ICU?" asked Mary.

"I'm afraid there is no time for that," said the chief resident. "By the way, Dr. Stuart, I'm Nick Birnbaum, chief resident in pediatrics."

"Ray Stuart. Orthopedics."

"This your patient?"

"He is right now. How can I help?"

"Do you want help?" Mary asked. "Do you want me to call a code?"

"No. Just stat page respiratory therapy to this room and bring the crash cart," said Birnbaum. "Other than RT we have everyone we need here."

Stuart removed his coat and rolled up his sleeves. Birnbaum was in charge now. Nobody in the hospital was as experienced at the critical saving of children's lives as he was. The respiratory therapist arrived and the chief resident directed her to intubate Gregory.

With calm skill the respiratory therapist inserted a breathing tube into Gregory's airway. Birnbaum listened as the RT pushed air into the lungs with a breathing bag.

"Got air moving on both sides," said Birnbaum. "Suction him out."

The respiratory therapist ran a flexible tube down the breathing tube and turned on an electric suction machine. A large amount of bloody mucus came out of the machine.

"Shit," said Birnbaum.

"Blood pressure is falling," said Mary. "Fifty over ten."

"We need more fluids," said Birnbaum. "Can we get a second IV?"

"His veins are all collapsed," said Stuart. "Mary, is there an IO catheter set on the crash cart?"

"Yes, sir." Mary handed the trocar and catheter to Stuart. She prepared another bag of IV fluid and tubing. Stuart noticed a slight trembling in her hands.

Stuart pulled the covers off Gregory's legs. With an iodine solution he cleansed the skin over the left leg. On the shin, where the skin sits right atop the bone, Stuart took a stout needle and drilled right through the bone into the marrow. Stuart noticed that Gregory did not react when he drilled into the bone. That was not a good sign. Stuart attached a plastic catheter and the IV tubing that Mary handed him. The IO, or intra-osseous line was as good as an IV to get more fluid in. It was often a life-saver in cases of shock when a regular IV could not be started.

Other nurses came to assist in the resuscitation effort. Mary went to brief Leroy and Suzanne. Returning to Gregory's room, she encountered the charge nurse for the evening shift.

"Mary, your shift is over," said the charge nurse. "Go home. We'll take over."

"No," said Mary. "I can't leave."

Birnbaum. Stuart, Mary and the others worked as hard as they could for five more hours. Everything they could think of they tried. Despite Dr. Chin's instruction to stay the course, they added another antibiotic aimed at MRSA. Stuart watched Birnbaum struggle to remember all the medical knowledge he had in his efforts to save Gregory. Stuart saw the hope fade from the eyes of the chief pediatric resident, the efforts to stifle emotion, to hold back the urge to just scream out of desperation. Mary had tears streaming down her face, which she had to wipe away from time to time with her sleeve, but she refused to leave Gregory's side. She didn't miss a step in the frenzied resuscitation effort.

Stuart held himself together. He was a surgeon, after all. He had been in critical, life-or-death situations before. He knew that the time for personal feelings had to come later.

In the end, Gregory Burris was cold and blue. His little heart stopped at about midnight.

Someone turned off the heart monitor. The medical team stood for a minute in silence. One of the nurses began to sob. Mary made no effort to hide the flow of her tears. Birnbaum collapsed into a chair, holding his head in his hands.

"I'll tell the family," said Stuart quietly.

"I'll go with you," said Birnbaum, rising from the chair and composing himself.

"I'll go too," said Mary. She wiped the tears away, took a deep breath, and tried to look brave.

There is no good way to tell parents that their baby has died. One just has to come out with it. Leroy tried to be strong as he held his wife closely. Suzanne nearly collapsed.

"We did all we could," said Mary.

"Come on," said Stuart, putting his arm around Mary and guiding her away. "They know that."

Back at the nurses' station, Mary lost control and began to cry again. Stuart held her and comforted her.

"We tried, Dr. Stuart," she sobbed. "Those poor people."

"I know, Mary," he said, "This time we got beat."

Deep inside himself, Stuart was hurting. He was conditioned not to show his feelings, to be strong for others. He hated losing a child. That part of medicine never got easier, no matter how long he was in practice. In addition to his sadness and sense of helplessness, another emotion was stirring. He thought about the string of deliberate MRSA infections in the hospital and he felt a growing sense of anger.

SIXTEEN

Dr. Anthony Green entered the hospital board room. When the board was not meeting, the room could be used for some of the most important meetings of the medical or administrative staff of the hospital.

"I think you know why you're here, Dr. Green," said Richard Phillips.

The expressions on the faces of the seven doctors seated around the ornate board table were solemn. The Medical Executive Committee met in seclusion. The members could not discuss the agenda or the workings of the MEC. In these meetings, the doctors practicing at the hospital can look critically at the performance of each other. It is the essence of peer review. It really takes other doctors to judge the quality of patient care provided by doctors. No-one else is as qualified to judge, because no-one else has the education and the appreciation for the realities of the job of practicing medicine. There is no smoke and mirrors. No bullshit or theatrics. The MEC is the conscience of the medical staff.

Each doctor had a small stack of paper and a blank legal pad. Some fiddled with pens. None spoke. Most looked directly at Green.

The work of the MEC was serious. The mood of everyone at the table reflected the gravity of the topics before them. Words would be chosen carefully and spoken with formality.

Green took his seat. Nobody liked being summoned to meet with the Medical Executive Committee. It meant that the quality of one's own performance was being questioned. Most doctors think that they are practicing excellent medicine, even when they are not. Surgeons especially have large and fragile egos. They do not want to hear anyone suggest that their performance may be substandard.

"You're talking about the MRSA infections, I presume," said Green.

"Not just that, Dr. Green," said Dr. Nancy Helms, chief of pediatrics. "We also have the issue of a surgical death on the operating table without an explanation."

"And, there is the problem with Mr. Davenport, the hospital board member, and his surgical complication," added Dr. Marvin Thompson, an internist specializing in endocrinology.

"Now, just a minute," said Green. "My surgeons never put a knife to the skin of that lady who died on the table and Davenport's complication was a nursing error."

"A little defensive, aren't we, Anthony?" asked Phillips. "I thought you surgeons were very protective of your status as captains of the ship when it came to your patients. You certainly behave as though everyone else exists just to follow your orders. Now, when something goes wrong, you don't want to take responsibility. Well, captain, what happens on your watch is ultimately your responsibility."

Green thought that Phillips was probably loving this. The men were not friends. He thought that Phillips had an agenda that went beyond the quality of medical care in the hospital.

Green took three deep breaths and tried to compose himself. The slowly growing crescendo of a headache told him his blood pressure was rising.

"Our department is conducting an extensive investigation of the infected arthroscopic surgical cases," he said, "and I will, of course, inform this committee when we have identified the cause, or causes, of these regrettable complications. As for the death of the hip fracture patient, the autopsy failed to reveal a cause of death. I'm not sure how that case could be blamed on the surgeon."

"Perhaps a more thorough pre-operative work-up would have revealed some co-morbidity or underlying problem, which, had it been treated prior to rushing off to the operating room, might have prevented the death of the patient," said Helms.

"Perhaps," conceded Green, "but I must point out that the scientific literature is quite clear that elderly patients with hip fractures should be treated surgically promptly so that they can be mobilized. These individuals do not do well when confined to bed and in pain. They get blood clots, pneumonia, bed sores, and other problems. They're better off altogether if we promptly stabilize their fractures. We can get them out of bed and moving around with less pain. There really isn't time to do exhaustive work-ups."

"Well, there's a large study out of Boston which strongly suggests that the literature to which you refer is out of date," said Phillips. "The studies you are talking about were done before we had made many important advances in internal medicine. I believe that with modern medicine we can keep these patients quite healthy before their surgery. There are some who suggest that surgery may not be necessary at all for some hip fracture patients."

Bullshit, thought Green, this asshole has no idea what he is talking about.

Green wondered whether Phillips, should he break a hip, would want it fixed the same day or would he prefer to be confined to bed in agonizing pain while pseudo-intellectual internists like Phillips himself engaged in mental masturbation over which medications to prescribe. With enormous effort, he held his tongue. The pounding in his head was getting louder.

"And about Mr. Davenport," asked Thompson. "Are you convinced that one of your residents didn't give the insulin dose? We all know that the orthopedic residents are, well, tend to be, well, former athletes. Rather than scholars, I mean."

"Dr. Thompson," said Green between clenched teeth, "need I remind you that it was one of my residents, a former intercollegiate athlete, who saved Davenport's life with his quick diagnosis and treatment? And besides, the nursing service itself has admitted that one of the staff nurses made an error and has fired the nurse in question."

Green looked at the hospital CEO, Helen Crawford. He knew that she was attending the meeting by invitation of Phillips, chief of staff. She and the medical staff office manager, who took minutes and prepared the agenda, were the only non-physicians in attendance. They were there to assure smooth running of the meeting. Helen could answer questions from the hospital point of view. The non-physician members could be excused if the chief of staff decided to take the MEC into executive session.

"It is true that the nursing service has dismissed the nurse who was assigned to Mr. Davenport," said Helen.

"So, there," said Green.

"But isn't it also true that the hospital administration might, to protect the reputation of the hospital and its doctors, might have promptly fired the nurse?" asked Thompson. "Quick action makes the hospital look good. And the reputation of the institution is at risk, particularly with a high-profile patient like Mr. Davenport."

Helen smiled slightly, but said nothing.

"The action and motivation of hospital administration are not part of the purview of this committee. Our job concerns the quality of care provided by the medical staff. Right now, we are concerned about the problems with the quality of patient care which we are seeing in the orthopedic department," said Phillips. "I'm going to appoint a select committee to conduct a quiet, but thorough investigation of your department, Dr. Green. Of course, nothing will be said publicly until the investigation is complete. But you will be visiting this committee again, Dr. Green."

Green knew that Phillips was enjoying his victory. The pompous ass. His head was about to explode.

Green gritted his teeth. He needed a couple aspirin and a double Scotch.

◆ ◆ ◆

"Mary, you have a message. You're to call Dr. Stuart," said the clerk as Mary arrived for work.

She dialed the number of Stuart's office.

"How are you doing after the night before last?" Stuart asked.

"I'm trying," she said.

"Can I buy you lunch?"

"Yes. I get my lunch break right at noon."

"I'll meet you in the cafeteria at noon," said Stuart.

Mary always felt a bit in awe of Stuart, but after the Gregory Burris case, there was an even closer bond between them. They sat at a table for two off to the side of the cafeteria, offering some shred of privacy.

"We don't win them all, Mary," said Stuart. "We do the best we can with the knowledge that we have, but sometimes we lose."

"It still hurts, Dr. Stuart. I want so much to tell the Burris family that we did our best."

"They know that, Mary, if they think about it. It won't help them for us to tell them that we tried our best. They just lost their son. Whether we tried to save him or not is unimportant to them. They just know that he died. When we tell a family that we did our best, maybe we just want to say that for our own consolation."

"You're probably right," she said. "I really want to reassure myself that we didn't fail them, but the fact that the child died means that we did. We failed."

Stuart could not tell her about his suspicions. Mary and Dr. Birnbaum practiced the most knowledgeable, scientific medicine possible. However, Stuart was convinced that Gregory Burris had not died from a routine septic hip.

"Yes," said Stuart, "and in modern times, the public expects us to succeed every time. In previous centuries, doctors and nurses couldn't cure much of anything. We didn't have safe anesthesia or safe surgery. Women died in childbirth routinely. Before we had antibiotics people died of infections that are just considered nuisances now. Have you ever seen the famous painting of the old doctor at the bedside of a dying little girl? All he can do is hold her hand. All he can give is himself, his presence, his concern. That's the way things used to be. That's why medicine and nursing are a calling, Mary. Our professions are a calling to give ourselves to our patients. If we're really good, we feel with our patients. When they cry and hurt, so do we. You're like that, Mary. I can tell.

"Nowadays, we have vaccines to prevent all sorts of plagues, like smallpox, that used to kill thousands of people," Stuart went on. "We have operations to relieve pain and cure diseases. Antibiotics control most infections. We can reconstruct bodies ravaged by disease or injury and restore function to normal in most cases. Doctors and nurses aren't used to losing patients, except old people ravaged by cancer or dementia. We've gotten so used to happy outcomes that we've lost the ability to really suffer with our patients. What happened with Gregory Burris is rare. It's hard for you and me to accept.

And normal people don't understand. Modern medicine has become so successful that the public thinks that each failure is a result of either incompetence or indifference. So maybe it's best to leave the Burris family alone to grieve the loss of their child."

"I guess I think we should have done better," she said. "I hate it when one of my patients dies. I expect it when a child has cancer or horrible trauma, but when a child dies from something that I've seen get better so many times, well, it's hard to take."

"In a way, I'm glad that you feel that way. It means that you care, that you still love the patients. That's why you went into nursing. That's why I went into medicine. Are you talking about the Burris case with someone?"

"What do you mean?"

"I mean, are you sharing your thoughts and feelings with someone? Getting your emotions out there. Talking it out and crying it out. It's not healthy to keep this sort of thing bottled up inside."

"Yes, Dr. Stuart. I talk about this sort of thing with my mother. We're very close. She doesn't know anything about medicine or nursing, except what I tell her. But she knows me better than anybody. And she's watched me cry and comforted me my whole life."

"Good," said Stuart. "That's healthy. Have you talked to Keith about it?"

"Yes, I have," she replied. "Keith's a big help. He's lost patients, too. He understands."

"I'm glad for that. I was going to suggest you talk it out with Keith."

"How do you react to something like this, Dr. Stuart?" she asked.

"In my heart, Mary, I'm a surgeon. I'm a fighter and I hate to lose. I'm determined to learn the truth, to learn from this failure, so that I can prevent it from happening again."

Stuart had enough self-awareness to know that he had no-one in the world that he could talk to, no-one to share with. He would hold his emotions in check, suppressed. His medical knowledge told him that this was not healthy, but he was help-less to change his situation.

"Do you know what went wrong with Gregory?" Mary asked.

"I'm going to find out."

♦ ♦ ♦

Mary and Keith were curled up on the sofa in Keith's apartment. Supper was over and the kitchen was clean. It was time for cuddling and conversation.

"I had lunch with Dr. Stuart today," said Mary.

"Really?" asked Keith. "Why?"

"He was asking how I was doing after we lost the Burris baby," she said. "He and I fought hard for that baby. He knows it was devastating to me. Dr. Stuart is a very kind man. He just wanted to know that I was handling it."

"And you told him what?" asked Keith.

"I told him that I had talked it out with you and with my mother," she said. "And that I was doing okay. Keith, I had that sense again that Dr. Stuart carries a burden of sadness himself. I hope that he has someone he can talk to, someone to share his feelings with."

"Dr. Stuart is invincible," Keith replied.

Mary doubted that. She changed the subject.

"I also had a cup of coffee with Carol Ramirez after work today," she said.

"That's your Filipino cousin, right?" asked Keith.

"Yes. She's having a hard time finding a new job. She can't get a recommendation from Sutro State. It's tough for her. Carol feels really bad that Mr. Davenport had such a scary and dangerous complication, but she insists that she never injected him with insulin. She didn't have any diabetic patients that evening, so she wouldn't have been handling insulin. And there's no way she would make a mistake like that."

"Are you sure you're not just defending her because she's your friend?" asked Keith.

Mary wriggled around and stared into his eyes. Her expression revealed annoyance.

"No, I'm not. I think it stinks. Nursing administration doesn't bother to find out what went wrong. There's no effort to look for systemic problems that might pose a risk to other patients. No, just fire the innocent and defenseless staff nurse and continue on with business as usual. It's not just because Carol is my friend. I don't like how the nursing service is handling this and I'm mad."

"I thought they did an investigation," said Keith.

"Yeah, right," said Mary. "Ms. Roberts asked which staff nurse was assigned to Mr. Davenport and she fired that nurse. That was the investigation. And the fact is that she was right there on the orthopedic unit that night herself. Even visited Mr. Davenport."

"What?" asked Keith. This was news to him. "She was on the orthopedic unit? I didn't see her. Who told you that?"

"Carol told me over coffee. She didn't say anything that night because she was so busy helping you with Mr. Davenport. She didn't think it was important."

"I spoke with Duane today," said Keith. "He interviewed Ms. Roberts about the shooting at the gym. And he told me that he followed up on your observation that Roberts was present at the shooting and also the hospital the night Davenport got the bad insulin injection. Duane said that Roberts told him she was in her office and didn't visit Davenport that evening."

"Well, Carol says she did. She said Ms. Roberts went into Mr. Davenport's room, but came right back out, saying that he was sleeping and she didn't want to disturb him. Then she left the unit."

"Why wouldn't she tell Duane?" asked Keith.

"Because she's a bitch," declared Mary. "I don't trust her and I don't like her."

"You're just jealous because she flirts with me," teased Keith.

She jabbed him lightly on the shoulder.

"You like her, you can have her," she said.

"No way," said Keith. "I want you, bad temper and all."

"You know, I'm going to investigate this myself," said Mary. "I'm going to look into this whole Mr. Davenport thing and clear Carol's name. It's the right thing to do and the least I can do for my cousin."

"How are you going to do that? You work in pediatrics."

"I'll figure that out. I'll talk to people who were there that night. I'll find out what other patients were on the unit. And I'll find out if anybody besides Carol saw Ms. Roberts visit Mr. Davenport."

"You might get in trouble."

"You're not the only tough guy around here, Mr. Football Star. I'm pretty tough myself."

"You could get fired."

"You mean like Carol."

"Exactly."

"That's even more reason why I have to do this," said Mary. "Firing people because they do the right thing is one of the policies in nursing that needs to change."

Keith made the sign of the cross.

"God have mercy on Patricia Roberts."

♦ ♦ ♦

Stuart entered Matt's office in Pathology. "Dr. Harrison, you did the autopsy on Gregory Burris."

"Yes, I did," said Matt. "Very sad case."

"The cause of death?" asked Stuart.

231

"Sepsis. Overwhelming infection everywhere that blood flows. He had necrotizing pneumonitis, where the bacteria destroyed and killed off his lung tissues. The poor kid had no chance."

"Necrotizing pneumonitis?" said Stuart. "From ordinary Staph aureus?"

"Nothing ordinary about this bug, Dr. Stuart," said Matt. "This was a nasty strain of MRSA. It's not uncommon to see this kind of overwhelming infection with MRSA."

"MRSA?" asked Stuart, "Where the hell did that come from?"

Stuart had a strong suspicion of where the MRSA had come from. But the Gregory Burris case was different. This was not an arthroscopy.

"His hip, I guess," said Matt.

"No, the bacteria grown from his hip was ordinary common *Staphylococcus*. Sensitive to methicillin."

"Are you sure?" asked Matt.

"Positive. I checked the cultures sent from the operating room myself. Are you sure that he had MRSA in his lungs?"

"Lungs, blood, everywhere," said Matt. "MRSA. For certain. If he had ordinary Staph in his hip, where did the MRSA come from?"

"From the hospital, Dr. Harrison. From the hospital."

SEVENTEEN

A MESSAGE WAS waiting for Keith when he got out of surgery. It read "Call Dr. Stuart."

"Are you making any more progress on your infected arthroscopy cases?" Stuart asked.

"Not really," said Keith. "It's hard for me to believe that someone would be getting these patients infected on purpose."

"Yet nothing else explains the facts. It turns out that the Burris baby that Mary and I worked so hard to save also died from the same strain of MRSA."

"Really?" asked Keith. "That doesn't fit the pattern. All the other cases were arthroscopies. The Burris baby was a septic hip."

"There is a connection," said Stuart. "I talked at length with Dr. Howard and Dr. Travers, who did the operation on the baby's hip. It turns out that they opened the arthroscopy tray which was set out for the first case the next morning. They wanted to get a basket forceps to retrieve some debris from the hip. I'm certain that the arthroscopy instruments were contaminated with MRSA. Whoever is doing this intended to cause another infected sports medicine case. The cultures that were taken of the baby's hip were drawn before Howard and Travers began to irrigate and clean up the hip. They grew out ordinary *Staph. aureus.* The MRSA was introduced after the operative cultures were drawn. Nobody suspected. Except maybe Mary and me as the child was dying right before our eyes. The autopsy clearly showed that the baby died of overwhelming infection with MRSA."

"My God," said Keith. "That's murder."

"Yes, it is," said Stuart. "And I don't think it is the first murder we've had around here lately."

"Should we bring the police into this?" asked Keith.

"There's a risk in that. If the person responsible, who must be someone at the hospital, probably a doctor or a nurse, learns that the police are nosing around, they may disappear. The police are not known for their tact and discretion."

"Well, I know one who might be discreet," said Keith. "He's a good friend of mine. But he's tied up with two other cases that are proving hard to solve. Ironically, they also involve the hospital, sort of. One is the murder of the wife of one of the hospital board members. She was poisoned, but nobody knows who did it or why. The other is the shooting death of the hospital CFO at the gym."

"I've heard both of those stories," said Dr. Stuart. "There are no secrets in hospitals. Tell me a little more about those cases."

"Well, according to Duane Wilson, my friend the detective, Mrs. Patterson was a fairly harmless old alcoholic with a fondness for cream sherry. Somebody slipped cyanide into one of the bottles and killed her. Duane says she was a likable old drunk and nobody seemed to have much of a motive to kill her. The other cops think her husband did it, but Duane doesn't buy that. He's met the husband and is convinced that he actually loved his wife."

"And the other case?"

"Well, everybody knows about the mass shooting outside the gym where I work out. Most people, the media, the cops, think that it was a crazy person or a terrorist. Duane is on that case, too. He says that the shooter was very methodical, picked up the shell casings, didn't empty the whole clip from the weapon, carefully planned the shooting. Nobody has claimed responsibility for it, which argues against a terrorist. And Duane thinks that it's all too well planned for a nut case. He thinks that the shooter intended to kill Bill Henderson, then shot the other people to make the cops think it was random. Once again, no suspects, and no motive."

"Do you trust this fellow Duane?"

"Totally. He's a good friend."

"How do you know him?"

Keith hesitated. He decided that, if anyone in the world could be trusted, it had to be Raymond Stuart.

"Duane is the partner of my best friend from medical school, Dr. Matt Harrison. Because he's a cop, it's a little awkward for he and Matt to be totally out. But they're best friends of mine and Mary's."

"I know Matt Harrison," said Stuart. "He did the autopsy on the Burris baby."

"I know," said Keith. "Matt told me. It was awful."

"Can you set up an opportunity for me to meet with Duane? Privately, and away from the police station would be best," said Dr. Stuart.

"Sure. I think so. But Duane is pretty stressed with his other cases."

"I've been doing a little discreet snooping around the hospital," said Stuart. "There's a lot of talk here in orthopedics about the infections. Not so much about the woman who died on the table with the hip fracture. They signed her out as a death due to hypoxia, you know. Your friend Dr. Harrison again, I'm afraid. And they shipped her body back to Alabama. Case closed.

"Well," Stuart continued, "I looked at all the data about her case as well. The orthopedic resident did a very good health workup on her before they took her up to the operating room. He even got one of the internal medicine residents to see her and they did a very thorough evaluation. Nobody could have done a better job under the circumstances. There was absolutely nothing in her history, medications, physical exam, or preliminary lab work that would suggest that she would have a fatal complication. Likewise, the anesthesia resident did an excellent job in his pre-op assessment and with the anesthetic itself."

"So?"

"Do you remember when you were in medical school and they were teaching you about how to make a diagnosis of disease?" Stuart asked, "The faculty spent two years teaching you about various odd and unusual diseases, strange and exotic things from other lands. And then they sent you up to the wards to see real patients. And all the young students are thinking about dengue fever and pheochromocytoma when most of the patients had colds and essential hypertension."

Keith laughed.

"Yeah, I was one of those students."

"Then, on the wards, they taught you that when you hear hoofbeats, think of horses, not zebras," said Dr. Stuart.

"I remember that very well," said Keith.

"Well, sometimes the hoofbeats really are zebras," said Dr. Stuart. "And we can't make the mistake of thinking that all hoofbeats come from horses. I'm beginning to suspect that your patient with the hip fracture may have died as a result of foul play. And I want to talk to your detective friend about that case as well."

"Holy shit," exclaimed Keith, "Oh, sorry, sir."

"It's okay. Under the circumstances, that's exactly the right reaction. Think about it, Keith, there are now seven instances associated with the same hospital wherein people have been killed or injured in the span of two months. All seven are unexplainable. No motives, no suspects. Doesn't that strike you as a remarkable coincidence?"

"Do you think that all these things are related?"

"I think that as good diagnosticians we need to find out."

♦ ♦ ♦

"Keith, are you still working on those MRSA cases?" asked Matt as they carried their coffee to a table in the cafeteria.

"Yeah, kinda," said Keith, "I'm not having much luck. The only things that they all seem to have in common is that they are all first cases and they were all done by Dr. Warren. And, of course, all by the same strain of MRSA. And now Dr. Stuart tells me that there is another case, this time a fatality. A little baby with a septic hip. And that was the same strain of MRSA?"

"Yes, the infecting bacteria were all identical." Matt looked intently at his friend. "This is really scary, man."

"I think it's creepy. I mean, who would do this sort of thing in a hospital? I'm beginning to distrust every person I meet at work these days. Is somebody here a psychopathic killer?"

"It makes my dungeon down in Pathology seem like a safe refuge," said Matt. "I sure as shit don't want to have orthopedic surgery in this hospital right now."

Keith sipped his coffee and shook his head.

Matt said, "There may be one more interesting fact from the pathology department. As I told you, the hospital takes MRSA so seriously that the lab routinely does type testing on all MRSA and even phage typing. Well, maybe because I'm partners with a detective, I decided to do a little investigative work of my own. I thought that it couldn't just be a coincidence that all your arthroscopy infections and the baby were caused by the identical MRSA bug. And, since the lab tests all MRSA cases, I thought that I'd look at the other cases in the hospital to see if I could find any other infections caused by the same type and phage type of bacterium."

"Good thinking. Gosh, maybe Dr. Green should have assigned this project to you and Mary instead of me. Did you find any other cases?"

"Just one. Not long before your first infected arthroscopy. It was from a nasty skin ulcer on a homeless guy who was admitted here on the internal medicine service. And, before you ask, there was no orthopedic consultation, no visits to the operating room, no connection to your department or Warren at all. He was an inpatient for three days and sent home. Never came back to clinic for follow-up."

"No surprise there," said Keith. "The homeless tend not to come to clinic unless they feel sick or they really want something. In orthopedics, that may well mean that they want their cast off."

"There is one more very interesting thing," said Matt. "The homeless guy's cultures are missing from the lab. All of the other MRSA cases cultures are accounted for. They're either still there, for open cases, or have been destroyed. But this guy's culture went missing. It just disappeared from the lab."

"Did somebody throw it away?"

"I don't know," said Matt. "The lab staff is supposed to record what they did with it, especially with a bug as dangerous as MRSA. But this one went missing, right before your infections started."

"Are you suggesting that someone stole the damn MRSA culture from this homeless guy and is now deliberately infecting arthroscopy cases?" asked Keith.

"I think that it deserves consideration," said Matt.

♦ ♦ ♦

Matt shared his discovery of the MRSA culture from the homeless man with Duane that evening over supper.

"How often does this sort of thing go on in hospitals?" asked Duane. "Here you have a series of infections that have harmed people and killed an innocent kid. You tell me that they're all caused by the same germ. And you have a bunch of total amateurs looking into the problem. You and Keith, for God's sake. And some old surgeon with one eye. You may be very good doctors, but you don't know jack about being detectives. Is this normal for the hospital?"

"Well, yeah, kind of. We take care of sick people, and things are bound to go wrong. And nothing in medicine works all the time. Doctors are trying to help patients get well. They're not criminals. There's no criminal motivation. And, whether we doctors do the right thing or not, the trial lawyers are circling like sharks waiting to sue us."

"But you could have crimes committed right under your noses and never suspect it. Why not call in the police? That kind of thing is what we're trained to investigate."

"Because the police don't understand medicine. Seriously, Duane, would you know a Staph infection from a gunshot wound? Would a cop know which medication should have been administered to a patient with a heart attack? Or which operation should have been performed? You cops wouldn't have any idea where to start. And your whole mentality is wrong. You're out to catch the bad guys. Always looking for bad guys. People with malicious intent. That's not how things work in hospitals, Duane. We're good guys. But we're human. Mistakes happen. We investigate to find out ways to prevent future mistakes. It's a totally different mindset. Also, if the cops were called in for every medical complication, there would be no way to control publicity. Things would leak out and there would be more lawsuits."

"That's bullshit and you know it. If a police investigation found no criminal culpability, there would be fewer lawsuits, not more."

"You ought to know that's not true. Criminal guilt is not required to instigate a civil lawsuit. The burden of proof is totally different. No way that police involvement would reduce the number of lawsuits," said Matt. "Don't even start to go there about the cops reducing lawsuits. You don't know what you're talking about. Let's talk about something you do understand. How are your investigations going?"

"Not well," admitted Duane. "I still think that the mass shooting was an assassination with additional shootings as distractions, but I don't have much support at SFPD. The poisoning of old Mrs. Patterson is clearly a homicide. Mr. Patterson is still our best suspect, but we sure don't have enough evidence to indict him. And there are some things that just don't fit. I mean, whoever wanted to kill Mrs. Patterson knew to put the cyanide in the cream sherry. She was the only one in the household who drank that shit. And whoever poisoned the bottle did so in the few days prior to her death. Hell, she drank at least a bottle a day, so a fresh one in her house had a life expectancy of less than 48 hours.

"From all that I can tell," Duane went on, "there's a limited number of people who visited the Patterson house in the few days before the murder. There was a party for the members of the hospital board the night before she died. Mr. Patterson was helpful and gave me the whole guest list. Nobody remembers seeing anyone bring in a gift of a bottle of cream sherry specifically, but lots of guests brought liquor. And the thing is that I can't find any one of the guests who had the slightest motive to kill old Mrs. Patterson. As far as I can tell, she was a harmless, cheery sort of old lush."

"Sounds like you need a little help," said Matt. "Maybe you should call in some doctors."

EIGHTEEN

"**Is this seat** taken?" asked Mary, approaching a table for four in the hospital cafeteria. Three orthopedic nurses were just sitting down for their supper break. This was not a random encounter.

"Help yourself," said one of the nurses. "I'm Brenda. This is Kathy and Eva. We're from orthopedics. And you are?"

"Mary DeGuzman. I work in pediatrics. And I knew that you were orthopedic nurses. My boyfriend is Keith Grant, the orthopedic chief resident. I thought I'd check out the competition." Mary laughed and blushed.

"Wow, Keith Grant," said Eva. "You won the big prize there, girl. How did you snare that guy? He's a dream."

"Echo that," said Kathy. "Hot and sweet at the same time. You're a lucky girl."

"And don't forget smart," added Brenda. "He's not just your typical orthopedic jock. The guy has brains. How'd you meet him?"

"In truth, we met over a little kid with a nasty elbow fracture," said Mary, "Keith operated on the child and he was worried about the swelling. I was working nights. Keith stayed up all night checking on the little kid. We had a lot of time together to talk. The child did fine and Keith asked me out the next morning. Maybe a reward for bringing him good luck."

"If you ask me, you're the one with the good luck," said Brenda. "He's one hell of a guy and one hell of a doctor. You know, he saved the life of this grouchy old lawyer a couple of days ago. The old bastard started seizing for no apparent reason. Dr. Grant just happened to be coming by. He went in and diagnosed hypoglycemia. Ran in some D 50 and, boom, the old guy came out of it. If there had been five more minutes of delay, I'm sure that the old fart would have died."

"Yeah, I was on that evening," said Eva. "How many doctors would have made that diagnosis? Not many. And no orthopedic resident I ever saw. You have an impressive boy-friend, Mary."

"If you get tired of him, tell him I'm available," added Kathy.

"I'll remember that," said Mary with a grin. "But I think I want to hang on to him myself. You said you were on duty the night Keith saved Mr. Davenport's life, Eva. My cousin Carol Ramirez was Mr. Davenport's nurse. I just can't understand how she could have made a medication error that bad. Did she get him mixed up with some other patient?"

"No way," said Eva. "Carol got screwed by nursing admin-istration. She's a good nurse. She was always careful and metic-ulous. Way more than most of us, to be honest. There were no diabetic patients on the unit that evening. She could never have given him another patient's insulin."

"That's right," added Brenda, "and now that we have the new pharmacy system, we don't even stock insulin except on the crash cart. The pharmacy sends up each patient's medications to the unit. We don't keep things like insulin just lying around. We have some for emergencies on the crash cart, but none was missing from the cart. I know because I was working that evening too and I brought the cart to help Dr. Grant. I had to do the medication count after Mr. Davenport was transferred to ICU. No insulin was missing."

"So how could Carol have given the patient that medicine?" asked Mary.

"She couldn't," said Kathy. "Impossible. But nursing administration needed a scapegoat, somebody they could quickly fire and tell the CEO and the medical staff that they solved the problem."

"And nobody said anything?"

"You haven't worked here very long, have you, Mary? The wise nurse who wants to keep her job never, ever questions Queen Patricia's decisions. Your skinny little ass will be out on the bricks so fast it would make your head spin if you question her judgment. And if you complain to the union, you'll never work in San Francisco again."

"So if you want to complain about Ms. Roberts and get yourself fired, be my guest. That way I'd have a better shot at getting noticed by your Dr. Grant," added Kathy.

They all shared a laugh. Mary returned to the subject of her friend losing her job.

"Wasn't there some kind of investigation?" Mary asked.

"Hell, no," said Eva. "Why should they bother? After all, Ms. Roberts herself was on the unit just minutes before the whole thing happened. She doesn't care who was to blame."

So, Carol was right, thought Mary. Roberts was on orthopedics that evening. Why did she lie to Duane? Mary was more determined than ever to look deeper into this.

◆ ◆ ◆

As he drove down Highway 1 along the Pacific Ocean, Duane thought that this was not the first time that he had wasted his time on the advice of a friend. He did not want to do this, but he promised Keith that he would make the trip.

Raymond Stuart lived in a house on the bluff overlooking the ocean south of San Francisco and just north of Half Moon Bay. It was a small older house, beaten by years of ocean winds and fog. When the skies were clear, which was rare, the house afforded a spectacular view of the ocean. There was a rough path made of dirt, railroad ties, and large stones, crudely fashioned into a kind of stairway so that Stuart could easily walk down onto the beach. Duane found the place without difficulty. He had agreed to meet with Stuart at his home, away from the hospital and the police station. Stuart did not want anyone seeing them together. Duane felt that this was a little too paranoid and a little too dramatic, but he acceded out of respect for Keith.

Inside the house was impeccably neat and clean. The furniture was heavy and made all of wood. Several paintings of seascapes hung on the wall, of good quality, Duane thought. Everything about the house was masculine. Duane knew that

Stuart lived alone, that the house had never experienced a woman's touch.

Stuart got straight to the point. He laid out the information on the infected arthroscopic operations and his conclusion that the infections were deliberate. He explained that the surgeons operating on Gregory Burris had opened the instruments which had been intended for the first arthroscopy case the next day. That was the way that the MRSA had been introduced into the baby. Stuart knew about Matt's discovery of the stolen MRSA cultures, which confirmed his opinion of malicious intent.

"Yes," said Duane, "I know about the stolen cultures and about this case. Matt told me as well. It does sound like these cases are purposeful. If your theory is correct, the death of the baby is a homicide. The other cases are assaults. All of these are serious felonies. I promise that the police will look at these cases, now that you've informed me. I'm not sure that I'll investigate this personally, since my case load is impossibly heavy right now. Matt and Keith have no idea why anyone would deliberately infect these patients. Keith says that they have nothing in common. Who would benefit from getting these cases infected? Is this just some sort of medical psycho who gets a kick out of hurting patients? Do you have a theory about the motive?"

"I do have a thought, Detective," said Stuart. "I believe that the patients were never the target of these assaults at all. I believe that the infections were caused to discredit Dr. Warren, or, more likely, the orthopedic department as a whole."

"Who would want to do that?" asked Duane. "Why discredit orthopedics?"

"I'm not sure," said Stuart, "but there may be a similar motive in the Patterson murder that you are investigating."

"What? And how do you know about the Patterson case?"

"There are rumors all over the hospital. Also, Keith told me about the Patterson case and the shooting at the gym when he was explaining that you were too busy to get involved with hospital infections. Have you considered the possibility that Mrs. Patterson was killed in order to get at her husband? It's the same sort of thing, you know. The death or illness of the victims creates problems for the real target. In the case of the orthopedic infections, the department gets into trouble with the hospital infection control people and the peer review within the medical staff. With the Pattersons, the murder of Mrs. Patterson brings bad publicity and police suspicion on Mr. Patterson. His reputation is forever tarnished and, who knows, he might even go to prison if he's convicted of his wife's murder."

Duane was now very interested in what Stuart was saying. The possibility that Mrs. Patterson was killed to get at her husband was a very long shot. He thought out loud.

"Why would anyone want to hurt Mr. Patterson?"

"Perhaps a business competitor?"

"Wow," said Duane, "that's cold. Capitalism in action. Kill the wife of your business rival, get the cops to treat him like a murderer, wreck his reputation, and take his supermarket customers. I've heard of dirty tricks in business, but this seems a little extreme."

"Yes, it does. However, I doubt that Mrs. Patterson was killed by a business rival of her husband. I think that it has something to do with his work on the hospital board. And I think that it may have something to do with the orthopedic department."

'Why?" asked Duane. "What does Mr. Patterson have to do with orthopedics? I know he's on the board, but what is special about orthopedics?"

"We have regular faculty meetings in the orthopedic department, Duane. We get reports on all the services and the strategic plans for the department. Patterson was the board member assigned to review a very large proposal from our department. If the board approves, a special orthopedic institute will be built as part of the Sutro State University Hospital complex. The project will cost millions, but the potential profits, particularly for the orthopedic surgeons, could be monumental. Suppose that someone wanted to postpone or delay the board action on the proposed institute. We're talking millions of dollars here, so there's plenty of motive. Patterson was a major advocate for the institute. Now, if he was out of the picture, the project would lack an effective voice at the board."

"Who would want to stop the orthopedic project badly enough to commit murder?" asked Duane.

"I don't know that, yet. Perhaps some rival department that wants the hospital money for their own lucrative project. Perhaps the owners of the land where the proposed institute will be built. Perhaps someone else who wants to purchase that land."

Duane sat and thought. This old doctor with the eye patch was pretty sharp, just like Keith said.

"So, you think that both the infected surgical cases and the murder of Mrs. Patterson were indirect ways to hurt the real targets," said Duane.

"And they've been effective," said Stuart. "The orthopedic department is in trouble with the Medical Executive Committee over the infections. Mr. Patterson has stepped down from the board. If someone is out to hurt the orthopedic department, they may well be using a kind of criminal misdirection play to mislead anyone doing an investigation. And, if the infections are misdirections and the Patterson murder is a misdirection, it could represent a tactic that appeals to the perpetrator."

"Now you suggest that the same person is responsible for both the infections and the Patterson murder?"

"I think it's possible. And I think that maybe there's another murder as well, one that's harder to prove. Did Matt tell you about the elderly woman with the hip fracture who died on the operating table for no apparent reason?"

"No."

"Well, Keith told me about this case as well. It was an overweight old woman from Alabama who was visiting San Francisco. She fell out of a tour bus and broke her hip. She came to Sutro State for surgery and died before the orthopedic team could do her surgery. That case is also being investigated by the Medical Executive Committee. I think, but can't yet prove, that this may be a homicide, again intended to discredit orthopedics."

"Jesus," said Duane, "Sutro State is starting to sound like Murder General Hospital. If you're right, you have some kind of lunatic running around over there."

"Not a lunatic," said Stuart. "Whoever is doing this is very, very smart. Probably a doctor or a nurse. And very calculating."

"Not a crazy person, but smart and calculating," mused Duane. "That sounds like…"

"I know. It sounds like your theory of the mass shooting at the gym. A variation on a misdirection. Multiple gunshot victims to distract the police from the intended victim, the first one shot and the only one targeted."

"Holy shit," said Duane.

♦ ♦ ♦

"This is not at all good for the hospital," said Mr. Wright, striding into Helen Crawford's office and slapping a copy of the San Francisco *Mercury* on the large conference table. "Have you seen this, Helen?"

"Yes, I'm afraid I have," she replied. "This sort of thing is supposed to be highly confidential, even privileged. It should never have gotten out to the media."

"Then it's true? The hospital Medical Executive Committee is investigating the whole damn orthopedic department for substandard care? Jesus Christ!"

"It is just an investigation, John. Hospitals do this sort of thing all the time. It's part of what we call peer review and quality control. No charges have been filed. The MEC is just getting started. We've seen quite a few complications with patients treated by orthopedics recently. One of those is Jim Davenport."

"Jim is certain that someone tried to kill him," said Wright. "Are you saying that he is right? Did one of the orthopedic surgeons try to kill him? Jesus Christ!"

"Nobody is saying that, John. Calm down."

"Why was I not informed of the incompetence in orthopedics? I'm the chairman of the board. If these clowns are hurting patients and trying to kill board members, I should be informed."

"You are not informed as a matter of law," Helen explained. "The workings of the Medical Executive Committee are confidential and privileged. Nobody outside the members of the committee is supposed to know what goes on in their meetings."

"Did you know?"

"Yes. As CEO of the hospital I'm usually invited to sit in on the meetings of the MEC. But I, too, am bound to confidentiality about the activities of the committee."

"You should have told me. I have a right to know."

"No, you don't, John. You may be chairman of the board, but you're not a doctor. You don't know the difference between a random complication and a deliberate act of malice. Most of the time, neither do I. I'm not a physician. I don't attend the MEC to provide a professional opinion. I can't do that. And neither can you. I go to the meetings because the business they conduct is intertwined with the running of the hospital. I provide information that they don't have. As an example, with Jim

Davenport, I can tell them that Patricia Roberts investigated and decided that the nurse made a medication error. And that the nurse in question has been fired. But I'm not qualified to judge the quality of medical care. I'm there by necessity. I'm sworn to respect the confidentiality of that meeting. There is no reason for you to attend that meeting or to know what goes on there."

"Then how in hell did it appear in the *Mercury*? Now the whole damn city knows about it. And there are details as well. Some tourist from Alabama or Mississippi gets killed while having surgery here. Perfectly healthy young people get horrible infections from our sports medicine doctor. And an innocent baby with a routine infection is killed by the orthopedic surgeons. Nobody in their right mind will want to come to Sutro State University Hospital for care with news items like this. How did the newspaper find out about this and what the hell are we going to do about it?"

"The truth is that I don't know how this got leaked to the newspaper," Helen said, "but you can be sure that I'm going to find out. And someone will be severely punished. As for what we're doing about it, well, I'm having a press conference this afternoon. I'll explain that we're just being diligent in our hospital management. We've noticed a slight uptick in complications, particularly with infections, and we're doing everything we can to find the source and correct any problems. Part of our long-standing commitment to quality patient care. We have the highest standards and we're always looking to improve. The quality of care provided to our patients is now and has always been the most important thing here at the university hospital."

"Will they buy that?"

"Yes," said Helen. "And this story will fade away in a few days, like most things in the media. The public attention will shift to something else and this will be forgotten. That's part of our whole society. A couple of weeks ago, everyone in the city was running around in a panic because there was a terrorist or a madman on the loose. You might remember the shootings at the gym not too far from here. Is there anything at all about those shootings in today's *Mercury*? Of course not. American society has a very short attention span for news stories. I think we learned it from watching Sesame Street on TV as kids. A big interesting thing for a minute and a half, then off to something else. This leak to the press about the MEC investigating the orthopedic department will be old news next week. Ninety-nine percent of people won't even remember it. And things will return to normal. Business will return. Patients will continue to come. Insurance companies will pay. We won't suffer any long term harm from this story."

"You make me feel better, Helen," said Wright. "You have a great knack for that. But, as chairman of the board, I will say this. Any proposal to expand services by orthopedics will be rejected. They can stick their orthopedic institute up their incompetent asses. We are not going to reward their malpractice with a multimillion dollar new institute."

"Now, John, don't make hasty decisions until all the facts are in."

"My mind is made up on this one, Helen. I don't care what the facts turn out to be. There will be no goddam orthopedic institute at Sutro State University Hospital. And that is final."

Wright turned and left the administrator's office.

He did not see the little smile on Helen's face.

NINETEEN

KEITH WATCHED THE encounter with amusement.

"Do you think that Baby will rub beaks with me?" asked Mary.

She was inching closer to the parakeet, leading with her nose. Baby was watching her approach with interest, but not retreating.

"No," said Keith. "She only rubs beaks with me. It's a special bond we have. Only me. And besides, you don't have a beak. Just a short little Filipino nose."

Mary ignored him and got right up next to the bird. She made a soft clucking noise. Baby cocked her head, made a low muttering sound, and gently pecked at Mary's nose. Mary slowly rotated from side to side a few degrees. Baby followed the motion, rubbing her beak against Mary's nose and pecking affectionately.

"Wee-ooh-weet," whistled Mary quietly.

"Wee-ooh-weet," answered Baby, followed by some more muttering.

"See, you're not so special," teased Mary. "Baby loves me just as much as she loves you. You're conceited. Like all you surgeons, you think you're better than everybody else. But Baby knows. And I know."

"Why don't you leave that bird alone and rub beaks with me?" Keith replied.

She giggled and they rubbed noses in what they called an Eskimo kiss. Keith loved the feel of Mary's petite body close to his, the smell of her hair, the softness of her lips against his. They had romantic times. They had fun together. She was one of the few people in the world who had ever seen him cry. Keith realized that he and Mary were beginning to share life together. Mary was a keeper.

"I had lunch with a couple of orthopedic nurses today," Mary announced while she was still nestled in his arms. "They think I'm a pretty lucky girl."

"You are."

"They don't know about your surgical god complex the way I do."

"Yeah, they do. I'm the doctor who gives them orders. Just like I give orders to you, Nurse DeGuzman."

"Maybe at the hospital, but not here, Doctor," said Mary, pinching him on the flank.

He let go and they laughed. That was one of the best parts of their relationship, Keith thought. They did a lot of laughing when they were together. He had never been quite as happy as when he was with Mary. Outside of the hospital, they behaved as equals. Not only did Keith love her, but he respected her.

Mary was at least as smart as he was. She had good ideas and her opinions had value.

"What the ortho nurses also said proves that Ms. Roberts lied to Duane about being on the ortho unit the evening that Mr. Davenport had his troubles. They saw her there, just like Carol Ramirez said. They also said that there were no diabetic patients on the unit, nobody was supposed to be taking insulin injections, and there was actually no insulin on the unit outside of the crash cart. And, after you made your mess of the crash cart saving Mr. Davenport's life, they had to count all the meds on it. And there was no insulin missing from the crash cart."

"So?"

"So, it looks suspicious to me," said Mary, "They fired my cousin to cover something up, I think. And I think that Ms. Roberts is behind it all."

"Really? You suspect the Director of Nursing is covering something up?"

"You like Ms. Roberts, don't you?" Mary accused. "She flirts with you and you're attracted to her."

"Nonsense," said Keith. "The Cougar is definitely not my type. Cold and haughty and phony. Forget it. I go for miniature angels from faraway Pacific islands."

"I'm from Daly City. I'm not miniature and I'm definitely not an angel."

"Other than the Daly City part, which I will concede, the rest is a matter of opinion."

"Well," she announced, "I have tomorrow off and I'm going to investigate Ms. Almighty Cougar Roberts."

"Be careful."

$$\blacklozenge \; \blacklozenge \; \blacklozenge$$

The only occupant of the elevator when Richard Phillips got on was John Wright, chairman of the hospital board.

"Ride with me, if you will, Dr. Phillips," said Wright, inviting the doctor to his office on the tenth floor.

"Certainly, Mr. Wright," Phillips replied.

In the comfortable office of the board chair, Wright motioned for Phillips to take a seat.

"Wayne Patterson said that you had spoken to him about a proposal to build a new medical library," Wright said.

"Yes, sir, I think that our old library is out of date," said Phillips, warming to the subject. "Modern medical libraries need to be digital, with full internet access. Instead of books and journals, we need DVDs and interactive software. We need to keep up with how young people learn today."

"Do you have the proposal in writing?" asked Wright.

"Not yet," said Phillips, "but I can have it ready in just a few days."

"Please prepare a proposal and give it to Mr. Clay Ross of the board. Clay is taking over the chair of the Planning Committee. I have officially disapproved the proposal for the orthopedic institute. The opportune time for the board to hear your idea is right now."

"I'll have it in Mr. Ross's hands before the end of the week," said Phillips.

Things were looking up for Richard Phillips.

♦ ♦ ♦

"You got a minute, lieutenant?" asked Duane, sticking his head past the open door into the office of Police Lieutenant Kevin O'Hara. O'Hara was not just his superior officer, but something of a mentor. Duane knew that if he wanted to talk, O'Hara would listen.

"Sure, Duane, come on in," replied the beefy veteran.

"I need another opinion, maybe a little help," said Duane. "On this Patterson case, well, it just doesn't make sense to me. The other guys are sure that the husband poisoned the old broad, but the evidence just isn't there. I don't think we have enough on him to indict. To be honest, my gut tells me that the husband just didn't do it. I mean he really seems to have loved his wife, despite her drinking problems. He has no motive that I can find. And he really seems broken up over her death. Besides, if he wanted to poison her cream sherry, why not put the poison in a bottle of the stuff she regularly drank, rather than another label. A label, by the way, that isn't carried in any of his stores."

"You got any other suspects?"

"That's the problem. There are others who had the opportunity and the means, but nobody seems to have a motive. The late Mrs. Patterson seems to have been something of a harmless drunk. I can't find anything about her that would inspire murder. Basically every member of the hospital board visited the house within a couple of days of the murder, plus Helen Crawford, the hospital CEO, and Dr. Richard Phillips, the chief of the medical staff."

"Helen Crawford?" asked O'Hara. "Was she married to Phil Crawford?"

"I don't think she's married now. Who's Phil Crawford?"

"Who *was* Phil Crawford? That's the right question," said O'Hara. "Phil Crawford was an ATF agent of sorts. He died about three years ago. Big, fat guy. Drank way, way too much. And a lot of us thought he was crooked. Seemed like every time we made a bust with the ATF and Phil was around, some of the evidence went missing. Guns, cash, that sort of thing. Lots of booze disappeared between the bust and the evidence lockers. There was a rumor that Phil was diverting evidence and selling it on the black market. We asked the feds to investigate him, since we didn't have jurisdiction. I don't know if they ever looked into it or not. Probably not. Then he died and the whole thing became moot. I think his wife was named Helen and as I recall she did something in health care."

"How did he die?"

"Heart attack, the doctors said. Makes sense. He weighed well over 350 and his cholesterol was probably higher than the Dow Jones. His wife found him dead one morning in his big old La Z-Boy chair with a nearly empty fifth of Jack Daniels on the table beside him."

"Are you telling me this because you think that Helen Crawford could be involved?" asked Duane.

"Hell, no. Just struck me as interesting that the widow of a dirty federal agent was a guest in the house where a murder occurred. I'm sure it's just a coincidence, Duane. But you know how cops feel about coincidences. Still, it's probably nothing."

"Maybe and maybe not," said Duane. "Can I tell you some things that are bothering me? It's really unclear and I don't have a theory yet, but can I share a few things?"

"Sure. I'm your supervisor. And advisor. And I'm your friend. Share away. Usually two minds are better than one."

Duane summarized his concerns about the mass shooting and his suspicion that it was a deliberate assassination rather than an act of lunacy or terror. He mentioned that Mr. Patterson and Bill Henderson both had connections worked at Sutro State University Hospital. O'Hara probed for a few details, then scowled and shook his head.

"There's more," Duane said.

"More what?"

"More things going on at the hospital," said Duane. "One of my friends introduced me to a Dr. Stuart. My friend uses this doctor as a kind of advisor and confidant."

"Is that Raymond Stuart?" asked O'Hara.

"Yeah. Do you know him?"

"In a way. He's pretty famous in San Francisco," said O'Hara. "He's a damn good doctor. He's operated on the kids of a lot of cops in this city. How the hell is Stuart involved with this?"

"It's a little complicated," said Duane, "And it has to do with the other things going on at the hospital that I was starting to tell you about. First, a patient from out of town died on the operating table before the surgeons even got started. They can't figure out why. My friend was supposed to help with the surgery and he was really upset about the woman dying. He told Stuart about it. Then, a whole bunch of perfectly healthy patients having simple operations are getting infected. And a little baby comes in to the hospital with an infection in his hip. The doctors treat the infection, but the baby dies with an infection caused by a different germ. It is the same germ that infected the patients having the simple surgeries. I mean the identical germ. And my friends say that's very unusual. One of them was asked by his department to investigate the cases. He got stuck and couldn't solve the problem, so he asked Stuart for help. And Stuart thinks that all these cases are linked."

"Do you think that all these cases may be tied together? Related?" asked O'Hara.

"I hate coincidences, Kevin."

"Are there any things that the cases have in common? Any personnel at the hospital involved with all of them? Any motive? This seems a little crazy to me."

"So far, nothing ties any of the cases together. Except that all the cases inside the hospital involve patients receiving orthopedic surgery," said Duane.

"Not the Patterson case or the shooting," said O'Hara, "which, I might remind you, are the cases that you're supposed to be working on."

"Well, there may be a connection there as well," said Duane, "Mr. Patterson was on the hospital board and was a big advocate for the orthopedic department."

"I think that you have more work to do," said O'Hara. "If this was any thinner, you could see through it. Take the cases one at a time. And let the hospital deal with its own issues. As long as nobody from the hospital asks us to investigate, stay out of it. You have enough problems with the cases you've been assigned.

"Right. Yes, sir. And thank you, Kevin. By the way, did old agent Phil Crawford ever steal an AR-15?"

"Several," said O'Hara.

◆ ◆ ◆

Mary knocked softly on the doorframe of Stuart's office. Wearing his eyepatch, Stuart was engrossed in a video of a child with cerebral palsy struggling to walk.

"Excuse me," said Mary, "Dr. Stuart?"

He turned around in his chair.

"Mary DeGuzman, nice to see you," he said, "come on in."

"I don't mean to interrupt. I could come another time. Maybe make an appointment."

"Now is fine, Mary. What's on your mind?"

"Well, I'd like some advice," she said, taking a seat. "You see, my cousin Carol Ramirez, one of the orthopedic nurses, was fired and I think it's unfair."

"I know Carol Ramirez," said Stuart. "She's a good nurse. I didn't know that she was your cousin."

Mary laughed.

"As far as I know, we're not blood relatives, Dr. Stuart," she said. "It's a Filipino thing. Everybody is a cousin or aunt or uncle. All Filipinos, anyway. I keep forgetting that other cultures don't understand that."

Stuart grinned.

"It's rather charming, I think. I like it. And, when we're not around patients or parents, you can call me Ray."

"Oh, Dr. Stuart, I could never do that," she said. "It would be very disrespectful. My parents would be very disappointed if I called you by your first name."

"Dr. Stuart sounds so formal."

"How about we compromise? I could call you Dr. Ray."

"That has a nice ring. It sounds like one of the children made it up. Dr. Ray it is. So Carol Ramirez was fired? What happened?"

"She was taking care of Mr. Davenport, a member of the hospital board," Mary said.

"I know about Mr. Davenport and his complication. I didn't know that Carol was the nurse involved," he said.

"There was no investigation, no due process. Carol is devastated. She's having trouble finding a new job."

"Did Carol make a medication error?"

"No! Mr. Davenport wasn't on insulin. And neither was any other patient on the orthopedic unit that night. Carol couldn't have injected insulin into Mr. Davenport's IV."

"I know Jim Davenport. He's a good sized man. In a man his size without diabetes, it would take quite a high dose of insulin, even IV, to precipitate a seizure. Why was there no investigation?"

"That's just the way Ms. Roberts runs the nursing service," said Mary. "Just fire some innocent staff nurse. It makes everybody anxious. You never know who might be the next one fired. And she herself was there on the orthopedic unit that night. Just before Mr. Davenport had his seizure. And then she lied about it to the police. Said she wasn't on orthopedics, just working in her office. She told this to a police detective who is a friend of mine."

"Duane Wilson."

"Yes. How do you know Duane?"

"We've talked about a couple of other cases. So Ms. Roberts was actually on the orthopedic unit the night Davenport had his problem, but she told Detective Wilson that she wasn't? How do you know that she was there?"

"I dropped Keith at the hospital so he could see his patients and I saw Ms. Roberts in the parking lot. She was leaving. So, I know she was at the hospital. And she didn't exit the hospital from the doors near administration. She came from the other side of the hospital, from the exit beneath the patient units. Carol told me that she had been on the unit and a couple of the orthopedic nurses confirmed it. They said she went to see Mr. Davenport but came right back out, saying that he was sleeping. Carol said the same thing."

"And you think that Patricia Roberts is involved with injecting Davenport with insulin?"

"Well, maybe," said Mary.

"She's your boss, Mary. She's in charge of the whole nursing service. I think that maybe you don't like her. How well do you know her?"

"You're right, Dr. Ray. I don't like her. She's cold and mean and arbitrary. But I really don't know her very well. I mean, I know what she looks like and what people say about her, but I can't say that I personally ever talked to her."

Mary was too embarrassed to tell Stuart that Patricia flirted with Keith.

"Do you suspect that she's involved in some sort of foul play? Some sort of criminal activity?"

"Well, Dr. Ray, maybe she is," she said.

"That's a serious concern," he said, "and one that should not be lightly turned into an accusation. So why did you come to me?"

"Well, I don't know. I respect you and it seems like everybody in the hospital respects you. And you're powerful, more powerful than I am, anyway. I think that this whole episode deserves an unbiased investigation. So far there has been no investigation at all. And an innocent person has been made to suffer."

"So, you would like me to investigate what happened to Davenport?"

"I thought maybe you could tell me how to investigate it myself," she said. "Maybe work with me to find out the truth."

"Mary, I'll look into this," Stuart said. "I have contacts and I can learn things that you can't. I don't want you poking around asking questions. You could get yourself into a lot of trouble and you might make someone who is responsible go to ground and we'll never find the truth."

"But I feel like I need to do something," said Mary. "For Carol and for my own sense of justice."

"Please stay out of this, Mary," said Stuart. "I'll let you know if I learn anything."

TWENTY

THINGS WERE GETTING out of control. Helen hated when things got out of control.

"Helen, I feel awful," said Patricia Roberts as she carefully closed the door to Helen Crawford's office. "A baby died. An innocent little baby. That wasn't supposed to happen."

Tears began to form in Patricia's eyes.

"Stop it," said Helen. "It's just what the military calls collateral damage. You knew there were risks to this."

"But."

"But nothing," said Helen. "Forget it. Shit happens, Patricia. We get over it and move on. Think about what's really important here."

Emotional reactions like this were just the sort of thing that prevented Patricia from really succeeding in this world, Helen thought. Leaders need to be strong. It is important to keep one's eyes on the objective. Always.

"Pull yourself together," said Helen. "We've come too far to turn back. And we're very close to reaching our goals."

"I think we may have another problem," said Patricia, regaining her self-control.

"How so?" asked Helen.

"There's a resident in pathology, Dr. Matt Harrison," said Patricia. "He's been snooping around the microbiology laboratory a lot, asking a lot of questions. He's even pulled a few culture organisms for some pretty sophisticated typing and testing. He knows that all the orthopedic infections are from the same identical strain of MRSA. He's even narrowed it down to the culture we got from the skin ulcer in the old wino. And he knows that the culture went missing from the lab."

"Does he suspect that the orthopedic infections are linked and deliberate?" Helen was very serious.

"Yes, he does. But he has no idea of the motive," said Patricia.

"Does he know who took the culture out of the lab?" asked Helen.

"No. Not yet."

"Is there any way to trace the culture to you?"

"I don't think so, Helen, but I never thought that anyone would link all the infections to a single organism, let alone trace it to our specimen."

Helen tapped the fingertips of her hands together and said nothing for a few moments. Patricia lacked the attention to detail that would make her a truly equal collaborator. It was possible that Patricia had been sloppy when she took the culture out of the lab. Helen would have to act decisively to prevent her plan from completely falling apart.

"We're done with the orthopedic infections," said Helen. "The board chairman has completely cancelled all plans for the orthopedic institute. That threat is over. The infections and the other little problems we've created have succeeded in totally discrediting the orthopedic department. And your little phone call to the *Mercury* got it all out there in the public eye. Well done, Patricia. You make a great anonymous tipper. The board is livid. Mr. Wright was in my office and is fit to be tied. Richard Phillips hates Tony Green and he has the MEC out for blood. I think it's certain that the good Dr. Green is finished as chairman of orthopedics. Now that the orthopedic institute is toast, I think that I can persuade the board that there's no need for a full financial audit. Which means that nobody is going to look too closely at the financial figures until the regularly scheduled audit in a year and a half."

"We should be happily drinking Mai Tais on a beach in the Caymans before then. Our most stressful activity should be counting our money." Patricia had recovered her composure.

"Yes," said Helen, "all that beautiful money. No more arrogant doctors. No more old asshole board members. Just sunshine and all the boy toys that money can buy. It's a dream life."

Helen had plans for the Caymans, for certain. Patricia might not be part of those plans.

"That's all good," said Patricia, "but to bring us back to earth, what about Dr. Harrison?"

"First of all, Patricia, get rid of the culture. Do you still have it at home?"

"Of course. I keep it in the refrigerator. Are you sure we don't need it anymore?"

"I'm sure," said Helen. "Get rid of it. Put it in a canvas bag with a bunch of bricks and throw it in the Bay. Do something so it will never be found."

"Consider it done," said Patricia. "I'll get rid of it this evening after work. But what about Harrison?"

"Can he trace the culture to you?"

"I don't think anybody was in the microbiology lab when I took the culture, but I can't be sure. One of the nursing managers on orthopedics told me that Harrison and Dr. Grant were roommates in medical school and are the best of friends. Grant is the orthopedic chief resident and has been assigned to investigate the series of infections by the orthopedic department."

"Yes," said Helen, "Grant has already appeared on my radar. He's becoming something of a pest. Do you know if Harrison talked to Grant about this?"

"We must assume that he has. They're good friends and see each other often. In fact, I wouldn't be surprised if Grant asked Harrison to help him with his investigation. It would make sense that Harrison got nosey because Grant asked for his help."

"That's too bad," said Helen, tapping her fingertips again. Helen disliked surprises. She prided herself on her careful planning. She had complex plans to deal with every possible scenario. This would require some thought and preparation.

"Patricia, this could be a serious problem. We may need to advance our timetable and plan an earlier move to the Caymans than we'd planned. We probably have a few weeks at least, but you might want to ship some of your valuables to the

Caymans in the next week or so. I think we can probably get plane tickets up until the last minute."

"I had hoped we might get a little more money," said Patricia.

"And I had hoped to make a little more by selling my car and subletting my apartment here in San Francisco," said Helen. "But we have plenty stashed away. We mustn't get too greedy. We have enough to live very comfortably for a very long time."

Especially, Helen thought, if Patricia never got her share of the money.

"I'll start packing," said Patricia as she exited the office.

Too bad that I threw the AR-15 in the bay, Helen thought. It would have been perfect for the good Doctor Harrison.

In her mind, she reviewed the inventory of weapons that her late husband had stashed in the storage locker. Phil had been a drunk and a lousy lover, but the fat old crook had been useful. The storage locker was the best part of the estate that Helen had inherited from him. Of all the remaining weapons in the locker she selected a Hechler & Koch G3SG/1 sniper's rifle. That should do the trick. She vaguely remembered that it was rather heavy when she fired it at the gun club with Phil. But her father had taught her how to shoot very well and she was confident that she could handle any weapon with skill.

As Patricia left the office, Helen turned to her hospital computer to look up Matt's home address.

♦ ♦ ♦

Mary could not get the situation with Carol Ramirez out of her head. Despite Keith's warnings and Stuart's admonitions, she just had to do something. She had the day off and decided to follow Patricia around the hospital. Dressed in scrubs with her hospital nametag and a stethoscope slung around her neck, Mary was invisible. Patricia had no idea that Mary was watching her. There was nothing suspicious. It really was pretty boring. Patricia made a visit to a medical nursing unit, then returned to her office area. Meetings, meetings, meetings.

Mary decided that she was wasting her time and took a bus to the Marina district. The apartment building in which Patricia lived was small, perhaps six units. There was no doorman or security cameras that Mary could see from the street.

She stood across the street staring at the building for a long time. Mary was frustrated and angry and desperate. She wanted so much to do something, to take action.

The idea came to her slowly. At first she could not believe that she was even having such thoughts. On impulse, she reached into her purse. She easily found what her fingers sought. She crossed the street. The lock was easy to pick.

Mary had no idea what she expected to find in Patricia Roberts' apartment. There was no reason for her to be inside the apartment at all. But she was angry and wanted to hurt Patricia. The bitch got her friend fired, was lying to everybody, and was trying to put the moves on her boyfriend. A break-in was a way for Mary to make a statement to herself, to violate Patricia. It was a sin and it made no sense and she could go to jail, but it was exciting. God, what am I doing? She could wind up in prison just like her brother Alex. She shuddered at the thought of herself going to prison and hoped that she had done a better job than Alex.

The apartment was furnished in elegant style. Very high end furniture and art, everything gleaming and in perfect order. A rack of very expensive wines. King-size bed. In case Patricia gets lucky at the gym, Mary thought. Odd that Patricia had such a simple lock when there were so many valuable things in the apartment. Mary was wearing vinyl exam gloves that she had brought from the hospital so that she wouldn't leave fingerprints. She had picked the lock skillfully and Patricia would have to look closely to see that it had been tampered with.

Aimlessly Mary opened the door to the refrigerator. On a shelf was a bottle of fast-acting insulin. Wow, thought Mary. But then another object on the shelf caught her eye. A plastic dish three or four inches in diameter. In the dish was a kind of red gel with dozens of little yellow dots on top. Mary knew immediately that she was looking at a bacterial culture of the sort found in hospital microbiology laboratories. Mary figured that the culture was important. Thinking quickly, she took three photos with her cell phone, then a couple of shots of the apartment.

Mary stared at the bacterial culture again. She was tempted to grab it and head straight for the hospital to find Keith or Matt. But she couldn't take it out of the refrigerator. Surely Patricia would notice. But she could not just leave it either. She had to know what was growing, which bacteria were represented by the little yellow dots. She needed to improvise a temporary bacterial culture. Trying to remember the techniques she learned in microbiology class as a student, she knew she had to scrape some of the bacteria from the agar dish in the refrigerator and plant them on another substance that the bacteria could eat. And it had to be moist, she thought. Mary looked in the dishwasher and found a butter knife in the rack, little bits of Patricia's breakfast toast and jam still on the blade.

Mary took a little hand soap and rinsed the knife under hot water.

That should clean it up pretty well, she thought.

She went to the refrigerator and sliced a pat of butter from the stick in the door shelf and put it on a spare vinyl glove. Finally she opened the culture dish and carefully scraped two of the little yellow dots off, taking a tiny bit of the red agar with each. She put these on the pat of butter, turned the glove inside out, and slipped it into her pocket. She rinsed off the knife and returned it to the dishwasher.

Just as Mary was closing the door to the dishwasher she heard the key in the door. There was nowhere to run and no time. Her heart racing, she looked for somewhere to hide. A sliding glass door led to a balcony, but it was locked and she was on the third floor of the apartment building. No good. There was only one bedroom and one bathroom. Surely that was where Patricia would go first, so no hope there. At last she spotted what looked like a pantry. She opened the cabinet door and was relieved to see that it was a broom closet. Not much room, but Mary did not need much room. With her tiny frame, Mary slipped easily in beside the mop and broom and vacuum cleaner. Mary eased the door closed just as Patricia entered in the living room.

Mary tried not to breathe as Patricia walked deliberately into the kitchen. Her heart was beating so hard and so fast that she feared that Patricia would hear it. The door to the broom closet allowed only a sliver of light, but Mary could hear the footsteps and picture in her mind exactly where Patricia was.

"Oh, God," she prayed, "I hope she didn't see me come in this closet."

Patricia went straight to the refrigerator and opened the door. It only took a second but Mary was sure that Patricia had removed the culture dish. Mary heard the refrigerator door close, then Patricia walking into the bedroom. Carefully, Mary opened the closet door a crack. She didn't think that anyone would notice unless they stared right at the closet door. And so far, at least, Mary didn't think that Patricia knew she was there. Patricia went straight into the bedroom, not stopping at the bathroom or even to remove her jacket. In a few moments Patricia emerged from the bedroom with two duffel bags, one fancy designer bag bulging with what Mary thought might be her sneakers, towel, and gym clothes. The other was a cheap bag with the logo of some pharmaceutical company and looked empty. Without looking around, Patricia opened the door and stepped out. Mary heard the door lock behind Patricia.

Mary waited in the broom closet for perhaps ten minutes. To her it seemed like ten hours. She took her own pulse and estimated it at about 120. Finally she opened the door. No one was in the apartment. Mary exited the closet. The insulin was still there but the bacterial culture was gone. Mary slipped out of the apartment, using her picks to re-lock the door. She ran down the stairs and caught a bus to Keith's apartment. She sat in the back of the bus, glancing furtively at every passenger that boarded. She folded her arms over each other and hugged herself. She fought hard not to cry.

There was no need to pick the lock to Keith's apartment. Mary had a key. When she entered, Baby chirped from her favorite perch high on the curtain rod.

"Wee-oo-weet!"

The familiar greeting comforted Mary. But just a little. Mary did not turn on any lights. Baby flew to the top of her cage.

"Wee-oo-weet! Wee-oo-weet!" chirped Baby, waiting impatiently for a response.

"Wee-oo-weet," Mary whistled softly. She drew her face close to the little bird and the two of them rubbed noses. Baby was satisfied that the greeting ritual was properly completed. But even the little parakeet could sense that Mary was not okay.

Carefully, she removed the vinyl glove with the bacteria smeared on the butter and placed it in the refrigerator.

Mary shuddered with fear. She was terrified after her burglary experience and having nearly gotten caught. She went into Keith's bedroom, knowing exactly what she wanted. Mary found the little stuffed rabbit that Keith still had, an old friend from his earliest childhood years. Mary hugged the rabbit and returned to the living room. She sat down on the sofa next to the birdcage, drawing her knees up to her chin. She needed to think and to calm down. She checked her pulse again. About 100. Not good, but getting better, she thought.

Mary was certain that the culture in Patricia Roberts' refrigerator was connected to all the orthopedic infections. She knew that it was Patricia who was responsible for the death of little Gregory Burris. Patricia was not just an arrogant liar. Patricia was a murderer. If she had gotten caught, Mary knew that she would not have been fired. She would have been killed.

Mary needed to get her bacteria sample to Matt in pathology so he could test it. She knew what the tests would show. So Patricia was killing and hurting patients, but why? Mary had started to investigate Patricia because of the complication with Mr. Davenport and the firing of Carol Ramirez, not the infections that Keith was investigating. She wondered if the insulin bottle in the refrigerator was connected to Davenport's so-called medication error. Or was Patricia diabetic and the insulin rightfully her own? Mary doubted that the insulin was for Patricia's own use. This was the insulin that was injected into Mr. Davenport. So, Patricia was complicit in both the infections and Davenport's insulin overdose. The biggest question remained. Why?

Mary called Keith's cell phone, but her call went straight to voice mail. She looked at her watch. A little after six. Keith was not on call, so he probably left his phone in the locker at the gym. If he was still at the hospital and not in surgery, he would have answered. Trying to sound calm, Mary left a message to call her. It was important, she said.

Mary sat on the sofa, hugging the stuffed rabbit and occasionally exchanging soft whistles with Baby, who remained on top of her cage, looking at Mary. Baby muttered from time to time. Mary looked at the bird. She had the notion that maybe the little bird wanted to help. For a minute, she considered telling Baby the whole story. But Baby was just a bird. Who used a parakeet as a confidant?

In about an hour, Keith called.

"Hey, what's up, love?" he asked.

"Are you at the gym?" she responded.

"Yeah. Just finished my workout."

"Is Ms. Roberts there?"

"Er, well, yeah, she's here."

"Did you see her come in? How many duffel bags did she bring?" Mary was very worried. Was Patricia going to infect all the people in the gym?

"Jeez, Mary. I don't know," said Keith. "I don't pay attention."

Mary told Keith the whole story of her break-in at Patricia's apartment. She said that she had a sample of the bacteria from the refrigerator on a pat of butter. She explained that Patricia had taken the culture and two duffel bags out of the apartment.

"Please come home, Keith," she said. "I'm scared. Really scared."

◆ ◆ ◆

As Keith was starting his Harley to go home, he saw Patricia exit the gym. One duffel bag, the fancy designer model.

Keith found Mary still on the sofa, sitting with her knees against her face, hugging the rabbit. She rose when he came into the apartment and wrapped her arms around his neck. She was shaking and sobbing. He held her tenderly until the trembling stopped.

"Maybe I'm not as tough as I thought," she said.

Mary showed him the butter with the bacteria on the exam glove in the refrigerator.

"Butter, eh?" he said. "Maybe not the best culture medium for MRSA. May have other bugs in it as well."

"I didn't have a lot of options," said Mary.

"You did fine, my love." Keith kissed her on the forehead.

They called Matt and agreed to meet at the hospital in the pathology lab. Matt would see that the cultures were planted so that he could identify the bacterium. It would take a couple of days before they would know if this was the strain of MRSA that had caused the orthopedic joint infections.

TWENTY-ONE

TWO DAYS LATER Keith was busy in the outpatient clinic. He was irritated when his cell phone rang.

"Grant, Jim Davenport here."

The voice was so loud that Keith had to hold the phone away from his ear. Even with the bedlam racket of the chief residents' clinic, Davenport's abrasive vocals were painful to listen to.

"Sir?"

"Do you have a car or just that goddam motorcycle?" demanded Davenport.

"Er, well, just the motorcycle, sir."

"Shit. Can you even drive a goddam car?"

"Yes, sir. I can drive a car."

"Well, then get over here and we'll take my car," said Davenport. "I need you to take me to the hospital. And I am sure as hell not riding on that goddam motorcycle. And this goddam knee hurts so bad that I can't drive myself. What the hell did you and Green do to me in there anyway? Did you botch something up? This knee operation was supposed to relieve my pain, not make it worse, goddam it."

"Are you having some problem with the knee, sir?" asked Keith. "Do you need me to take you to Emergency?"

"No, goddam it," said Davenport, "I need to use the computer in John Wright's office. It turns out that he has access to all the hospital data except patient medical records. Comes with the job of board chairman. God knows what John would do with a computer, though. I doubt that he can even turn the goddam thing on. John said that I can use it. I didn't tell him that I was going to research this Five South thing. So get over here and pick me up. Drive me in my car to the hospital."

"Mr. Davenport, sir," said Keith, "I'm still in the clinic seeing patients."

"Get someone to cover for you, Grant. Jesus Christ, do I have to think of everything?"

Davenport really was a world class jerk, Keith thought. In addition to Keith there were two very good junior residents in the clinic. It was the chief residents' clinic, so most of the patients were follow-ups of fractures from the Emergency room, a lot of minor aches and pains, and the sad ravages of poverty, homelessness, and bad habits. Essentially all of the patients were uninsured or on MediCal, people that nobody else wanted. The clinic was busy, but the junior residents could handle it while he took an hour or so to retrieve Davenport.

"I'll be there as soon as I can, sir."

"Hey, who are you talking to?" asked Ray Stuart with a smile.

"Dr. Stuart, what are you doing here?" asked Keith.

"Just passing through, looking at the x-rays," said Stuart. "Checking up on you and your junior residents, I guess. Looking for interesting cases, wondering if you could use any help."

"Wow! You may be a gift from God," said Keith. "I need to go over to Mr. Davenport's house and bring him to the hospital. Would you supervise the junior residents for a while? It would be a big help."

"Jim Davenport? The lawyer?"

"You actually know him?"

"Yes, we go back quite a few years," said Stuart. "You might even say that we're friends, or as close to friends as Jim Davenport gets. Why are you talking to Jim?"

"Well, it has to do with the multiple shooting case that my friend Duane Wilson is working on," said Keith. "Bill Henderson, had a bunch of hospital documents and computer printouts with him when he died. Duane had the documents as evidence in the shooting case, but couldn't make sense of them. I showed them to Mr. Davenport, thinking he might help. He got kind of excited when he looked at the documents, but I really don't understand stuff like that. Now he wants me to bring him here so he can look at the hospital computer."

"Does he think that the documents are related to the shooting?"

"I'm not sure. Maybe. He's pretty worked up about them."

"Keith, how about if I drive over and pick up Jim Davenport?" said Stuart. "You can stay here with this clinic.

It looks like it is going to be hell on wheels here today. Leave Davenport to me."

"You can have him, Dr. Stuart. Thanks a lot."

♦ ♦ ♦

Duane was playing a hunch. When he was summarizing his thoughts on the Patterson murder with Lieutenant O'Hara, he pointed out that the brand of cream sherry was not even stocked by Mr. Patterson's chain of supermarkets. It was a lead that had not been followed. The sherry that contained the poison that killed Mrs. Patterson was fifty dollars a bottle and imported from Spain. Only three stores in San Francisco carried that brand. Duane was on the second store.

"I see you carry a cream sherry from Andalucía, Spain," Duane said to the store clerk, pointing to a bottle inside a glass case.

"Oh, you have exquisite taste, sir," replied the clerk. "How many bottles would you like?"

"Actually, it's a little pricy for my taste," said Duane, showing his badge. "How much of this do you sell?"

"Not much, to be honest, sir. While sherry is becoming more popular with up-and-coming millennials, most of our sherry-drinking customers are still, well, wealthy senior citizens. We might sell one bottle of this Andalucía brand a month, at the very most."

"Did you sell a bottle to this woman?" Duane showed the clerk a hospital public relations photo of Helen Crawford.

"I'm not sure. Maybe. She looks familiar, like maybe she's been in the store sometime."

"I see you have security cameras. How far back do you keep the video?"

"Six weeks," said the clerk. "There are no customers right now. Would you like me to pull the footage?"

"That would be great," said Duane.

Duane spent half an hour looking at boring security video. The clerk hung over his shoulder for much of the time, only twice stopping to serve a customer.

"There she is!" exclaimed the clerk as Helen appeared on the screen. "See, very elegantly dressed, corporate-looking. There I am talking to her. I remember her now. Totally certain about the brand that she wanted. Didn't even want to look at a less expensive bottle. There we go over to the case. I need a key to open it. There I am taking out the bottle."

"Did you get her name?" asked Duane. "Did she use a credit card?"

"No, sir. She paid cash. I guess you would have to have a special taste to spend that much on a bottle of sherry."

"Or buy it for a very, very special occasion," said Duane. "I need to keep this security footage."

"No problem," said the clerk. "I'm sure the owner of the store will be happy to assist SFPD."

"Thank you. You've been a big help."

Now Duane had a suspect in Mrs. Patterson's murder. But what was the motive? Unless Stuart was right and the killer was trying to hurt Mr. Patterson by killing his wife. Now, why would Helen Crawford want to hurt Patterson?

◆ ◆ ◆

Davenport's unpleasant housekeeper scowled at Stuart when she opened the door. She seemed shocked at the eye patch.

"Who might you be?" she asked.

"I'm Dr. Raymond Stuart."

"Is Mr. Davenport expecting you?"

"Not exactly."

"Well, then, wait here," she said, closing the door. Ray heard the deadbolt turn. In a few minutes, the house-keeper returned.

"Mr. Davenport will see you. He's in the library."

"I know where that is," said Stuart. "Thank you."

"Ray, you son of a bitch," said Davenport. "What the hell are you doing here? Did you come over here to see me suffer? Your colleagues have butchered my knee and I am going to sue them for every penny they have."

"Good afternoon to you, too, Jim. Too bad they just replaced your knee and not your personality."

"They also tried to kill me, goddam it. If it hadn't been for young Dr. Grant, they would have succeeded. What the hell are you people doing up there at the hospital, anyway?"

Davenport proceeded to tell the whole story of his post-operative misadventure with the insulin overdose, Keith's timely rescue, and the firing of the nurse who had been taking care of him that night. He remained steadfast in his conviction that the incident was really a case of attempted murder. Stuart listened attentively.

"You know, you may be right, Jim," said Stuart. "Now tell me what you're up to with the hospital records that Bill Henderson had when he died."

"How the hell do you know about those?"

"Keith Grant told me."

"Whatever happened to doctor-patient confidentiality? And where the hell is he? I told him to pick me up."

"Those records are not covered by doctor-patient confidentiality and you know it. He's busy doing his job in the clinic, not that you would care, you selfish old bastard. I'm here to pick you up and take you to the hospital."

"You?" asked Davenport. "You don't think I am getting into a car with you. Shit, you only have one eye and last I heard you wrapped your car around a tree and damn near killed yourself. Hell, I'll call a taxi. I don't feel at all safe in the car with you."

"You felt pretty safe when you trusted me with your grand-daughter's clubfoot deformity."

Davenport's scowl relaxed a little and his voice became quieter.

"And I'll be forever grateful for that, Ray. Each time I see her running around, a normal little girl, I'm grateful for that. What you did for my grand-daughter is the whole reason that I serve on the hospital board."

"So, get in the car and we'll go over to the hospital," said Stuart. "You can fill me in on these papers and printouts on the way over."

"Hell. Get my briefcase, for Chrissake. I need both hands on this goddam walker."

Rolling his eyes, Ray Stuart picked up Davenport's over-stuffed briefcase.

"What do you have in here, Jim? Your bowling ball and half the law library?"

"Just a few essentials," said Davenport. "What the hell are you driving, Ray? Did you buy another sports car after you trashed the red one?"

"I have a Jeep, now," said Stuart.

"How the hell did you get into that accident, anyway?" asked Davenport. "I never learned the details, just that you wrapped the sports car around a tree on Highway 1. Were you drunk?"

"Shut up, Jim," said Stuart.

♦ ♦ ♦

Davenport grumbled in pain with every step as he pushed the walker across the expensive carpeting leading to the hospital wing reserved for the board. Stuart lugged the briefcase, walking behind the lawyer and ignoring the complaints.

Davenport stopped in front of the door to the spacious office of the chairman of the board, located adjacent to the board room on the tenth floor of the Sutro State University Hospital. He fumbled for a key and opened the door. Rarely used, the office offered a spectacular view of the ocean. There was nothing on the cherry wood desk except a desktop computer terminal. Davenport methodically made himself at home, directing Stuart to deposit the briefcase on the desk.

Davenport removed Bill Henderson's files from the briefcase, along with a large stack of his own notes, a handful of pencils, a calculator, and four fresh pads of yellow legal paper. He seated himself in the great leather throne behind the desk and directed Stuart to pull one of the lesser armchairs around beside himself so that both could see the computer monitor. He took a small piece of paper from his shirt pocket with the chairman's password into the hospital information system. Putting on his reading glasses, Davenport logged in.

"Henderson was an accountant, Ray," said the lawyer, gesturing to the stack of files. "Not at all imaginative. He was always fiddling with the numbers, making sure that he was prepared to answer any questions that his boss or some outside authority might ask about the hospital finances. For some reason, he was looking at the hospital billing to MediCal and noticed a large spike in the billing on the last Monday of each month. To make sure that it wasn't just a coincidence, the looked back over time and found that the spike had been recurring on the last Monday of the month for two years."

"Henderson's curiosity must have been aroused by this phenomenon. He seems to have been looking at the nature of the billings with other computer searches. He found that a high percentage of the patients for whom bills were sent on the last Monday were inpatients housed on nursing unit Five South. He must have been going home to work more on the data when he was killed."

"Five South?" asked Stuart. "That nursing unit's been closed for, well, about two years. There are no patients on Five South. It's just used for storage of old beds and equipment. In fact, I think the doors to it have been padlocked."

"Yes, I know that now," said Davenport. "Although I suspect that Henderson didn't know that. Grant told me that his girlfriend, Mary DeGuzman, was the first to notice this. Prior to that, I certainly didn't know. My guess is that Henderson wanted to look more carefully at the whole business of what was going on with Five South. Something smells rotten to me. So I'm going to use John Wright's computer and access to the hospital information system to get the answers to the questions that I think were bothering Bill Henderson. I should be able to get almost anything except the patient medical records."

"I can get that with my computer access, Jim, as a member of the medical staff, but I don't have access to the administrative or financial data."

Davenport raised an eyebrow and smiled conspiratorially. "Isn't it illegal for you to look at patient records if you're not the treating physician? Something about federal patient privacy laws?"

"Yes. You going to turn me in?"

"You could be sued, you know, for violating patient privacy."

"It wouldn't be the first time I've been sued, counselor. Look, we're trying to stop somebody from assaulting and killing patients. If that gets me sued or in trouble with the feds, bring it on."

"Well, if you get into trouble, I'll represent you."

"That's a comfort."

"Well, it's a lovely partnership," said Davenport. "Between the two of us, we should be able to get to the bottom of this."

Davenport began to type furiously on the keypad.

"Say, Ray," he said, "we're going to be here a while. Would you mind going down to the cafeteria and getting us some coffee? I like mine with two sugars and just a dash of cream."

When Stuart returned with the coffee, Davenport had nearly filled one legal pad with scribbled notes.

"This is very interesting, Ray," he said. "I can't find any records of any patient being admitted to Five South whose bill was not submitted to MediCal on the last Monday of the month. Nor is there any patient admitted to Five South with any insurance other than MediCal. No private insurance. No uninsured patients. Interestingly, I can't find any patient admitted to Five South whose bill was submitted on any day other than the last Monday of the month. And, each patient who was admitted to Five South was a repeat admission, that is, somebody who had been in the hospital before."

"Really?" asked Stuart. "Can you get the medical record numbers of these patients?"

"Sure, it's on the billing information."

"Let's write them down," said Stuart, "then, while you work on the financial stuff up here, I'll go to my office and log on to the hospital information system and see if I can learn something about the medical cases of the patients."

"Sounds good. Grab a pencil and a legal pad and start taking down numbers."

It was noon when Stuart returned. In addition to a pad filled with handwritten notes, he brought two more cups of coffee and a paper bag with sandwiches.

"Time for a lunch break."

Davenport stood up and stretched.

"God, this knee hurts," he said. "You surgeons certainly know how to inflict pain. Good, you brought more coffee. Did you remember the two sugars and the dash of cream? What's in the bag?"

"Screw you," said Stuart. "Drink your coffee. There are turkey sandwiches in the bag. Help yourself."

"I would've preferred a ham sandwich."

"So don't eat it. I don't care."

"Fuck you, Ray. What did you find while you were gone all goddam morning?"

Stuart didn't look at his notes. He sat in a chair, sipped his coffee, and unwrapped a sandwich.

"You know, it took a while for me to figure out what I was looking at. These records are incredibly believable frauds. The patients and their medical records look so realistic. Whoever put this scheme together is very, very smart and very sophisticated. As you know, each patient is a MediCal client. Each had at least one previous admission to the hospital, in most cases two or three. And that's really important. The previous admissions provide information on the physical examination of the patient, the previous history, medications and medication allergies, all the stuff that is essential to build the record. The previous admissions, the ones that were not to Five South, show how the patient responded to treatment. There is even information about dietary preferences and you can get a sense of how the patients interacted with the hospital staff. When the patient was supposedly readmitted to Five South, the diagnosis for the admission reflects the same disease process that was identified on a previous admission. The records are cleverly concocted pieces of fiction. The Five South admission hospital records are incredibly complete, with history and physical exam, daily progress notes by the doctors and nurses, lab reports, you name it. None of the admissions reflect surgeries. All of the medical records have been cobbled together from old medical records. Somebody used a computer to highlight parts of the record, copy and paste them together to make a new record. The whole thing, if you looked at it for the first time and didn't compare it to previous records, looks totally authentic. Each patient is a real patient and the medications prescribed are precisely correct and in the right dosage. Interestingly, several of the patients admitted to Five South were actually dead at the time of the admission. They had died on a previous admission. Overall, it's brilliant. It's nasty and evil and brilliant. I've never seen anything like it."

"The billing is equally brilliant, considering it's felonious," said Davenport, munching on his turkey sandwich with enthusiasm. "It's all there, everything charged for. Lab tests, x-rays and CT scans, dietary and housekeeping, supplies and medications. Nothing is left out. Even the fucking bedpans and toilet paper. These are perfect hospital bills. Whoever is behind it not only knows how the hospital works and how to send bills, but also how MediCal works. It's a big, stupid government agency. It's staffed by bored government employees who are really only interested in collecting their salaries. Bills are submitted and receive only a superficial, cursory examination. If things look okay on the surface, the government clerk authorizes payment. As long as nothing stands out, nothing looks outrageous, the bill just works its way through the system and is paid. Nothing in these bills is unusual, so nothing draws attention."

Davenport let out a belch and digressed from his report. "You know the problem with most crooks who commit fraud is that they get greedy. In a situation like we're looking at, I'd expect some big, expensive procedure, a heart operation, something with a big price tag, so the crooks would make a big killing. That's the sort of thing that the MediCal auditors are looking for. But whoever dreamed this up is disciplined, restrained. Our crook is content with a steady stream of uninteresting charges."

"You know," said Stuart, "you could use the same term to describe the records. They're ordinary, uninteresting. It's amazing to me how careful our crooks have been."

Davenport resumed his narrative. "The clerks at MediCal have just been approving everything without question and cutting the checks. And here is where we find another example of brilliance. The checks are going to a different account number at the same bank where MediCal normally pays Sutro State University Hospital. It's a different fucking account number. But who looks at account numbers? Nobody. So the money goes into a separate account that nobody pays attention to. Our crooks who own the phony account get rich. My bet is that the crooks clean out the account from time to time and transfer it to another account, probably in an untraceable offshore bank.

It's a fantastic fraud. The best I've ever heard of. You know, Ray, I actually admire these guys."

"Maybe you can hire them for your law firm when they get out of prison," said Stuart.

Davenport ignored the comment. He looked at the computer screen and typed a few more characters, stared at the screen some more.

"Which brings me to my most recent discovery," he said. "Simply fantastic. Look at this, Ray. Not only is somebody making a fortune in MediCal fraud, but there's also a totally different income stream out of the hospital revenues. In the human resources and payroll sections of the hospital information system, there's a complete staff for the nursing unit called Five South. We have nurse managers, staff nurses, nurses' aides, ward clerks, even dietary and housekeeping staff. All on the payroll. All with personnel files. They get promotions, go on vacations, take maternity leave, even get fired. Each employee has direct deposit of his or her paycheck into a banking account. My guess is that the balance in these personal accounts is periodically swept into offshore banks just like the phony hospital account."

"What?" asked Stuart. "How can there be fictitious personnel?"

"When the nursing unit at Five South was closed, the staff were transferred to other units or laid off, but there remained personnel files," explained Davenport. "It wasn't difficult to duplicate the personnel files, change the Social Security numbers and the account numbers for direct deposit of the paychecks and, presto, you have a new employee working on Five

South. Other employees who never worked on the real Five South have fictitious doubles on the payroll. Let's take, for example, Grant's girlfriend Mary DeGuzman, RN. She works on pediatrics. She might be surprised to know that there is another Mary DeGuzman, RN, same age and address as hers, but a different Social Security number and different bank account, working night shift on Five South."

"Holy smoke. Who would even think of that? I mean, a lot of people try to rip off Medicare and MediCal, but this is a kind of double dip. They're ripping off the hospital, too. Isn't it risky to use the same names as real employees?"

"Hell, no," said Davenport. "As you've said, the bureaucracy in the hospital is such that nobody from payroll ever checks human resource files. If they did, they would look up, for example, Mary DeGuzman, RN and there it would be, a personnel file in perfect order. It's safe and secure. And nobody in either human resources or payroll could pick the real Mary DeGuzman out of a police lineup. There is simply no contact between the clinical staff of the hospital and the business staff. Whoever is behind this knows this and is turning that knowledge into profit. In a way it's almost funny. Somebody is taking advantage of the way health care works in this country. The business side of a hospital lives in a parallel universe to the clinical side. It's a setup for mischief."

"So, we've found evidence of massive fraud at the hospital," said Stuart. "Someone is creating fictional medical records and fictional bills for real MediCal patients, then inventing hospital admissions to a nursing unit that no longer exists and is staffed by imaginary nurses. The mastermind behind this collects the money from MediCal and also the payroll checks of the imaginary staff."

"That's pretty much what we know now. I can only think of one person with the power, the access, and the knowledge of the health care system to pull this off."

"Helen Crawford," said Stuart. "It has to be her."

"Can we prove it?"

"I doubt it. But, the good news is that we don't have to," said Davenport. "The only way to prove it all and catch her and any possible accomplices would be to trace the money into the offshore accounts. And we won't be able to do that from the hospital computers. But the police or the FBI should have forensic accountants and they might be able to do it. MediCal is part of the federal MedicAid program and if the money is going offshore, those would be federal offenses. The police will ask the FBI for help. The feds have pretty good computer crime solving resources and very good forensic accountants. Our job is done. We just need to give this to the cops."

"How much money do you think that we're talking about, Jim?"

"My guess is between fifteen and twenty million dollars, but there's no way you and I can tell for certain."

"That's plenty of money to be a motive for murder," said Stuart. "I think we know why Bill Henderson was killed. He inadvertently lifted the lid on a huge can of worms. And he was about to open it more."

"God damn," said Davenport. "Do you think the same people tried to kill me?"

"You didn't know about Bill Henderson's files when you were given an insulin overdose," said Stuart. "So what happened to you wasn't because of what Henderson was about to discover. But, did you and Mr. Patterson have anything in common? On the hospital board, I mean."

"Wayne Patterson is a preening, arrogant nitwit," said Davenport. "I'm not sure we ever agreed on anything. It's too bad about his wife and all, but the old broad was drinking herself to death anyway. But, let me think."

Stuart reflected on the idea that Jim Davenport could think of something offensive to say about anybody, living or dead.

"Patterson was heading a committee to look at building the big orthopedic institute," said Davenport. "A multi-million-dollar boondoggle so you orthopedic surgeons can make a fortune inflicting pain on unsuspecting innocent patients. Like Grant and his evil boss, Green did to me. Our illustrious hospital administrator suggested that the hospital might not have enough money to build the institute. Patterson suggested a full audit of the hospital finances. I supported the idea of an audit, not because I give a good goddam about the orthopedic institute, but because I don't trust Helen Crawford and her gaggle of sycophants. Other than that, I don't think that Wayne Patterson and I could agree on the smell of fresh shit."

Stuart sat silently thinking for a few minutes.

"It does come together," said Stuart. "The threat to Helen Crawford and her accomplices, assuming she has one or more, is the hospital audit. An audit would have discovered what Bill Henderson was about to stumble upon. You and Patterson were the advocates for the audit because of the proposal for the orthopedic institute. To stop the audit, Crawford had to stop the orthopedic institute. So, she arranged all the complications to discredit the orthopedic department and cause it to lose favor with the board. She tried to knock you and Patterson off the board, because you two were the big advocates for the audit. And poor Bill Henderson, well, he just bumbled into something. Something fatal."

"God damn," said Davenport. "For a guy with only one eye, you certainly see things that everybody else has missed. We need to talk to the police."

TWENTY-TWO

HELEN SMILED AS she walked through the Castro district. She was dressed to fit right in with the neighborhood. Baggy trousers, hiking boots, plaid shirt. Her hair was hidden under a fedora, eyes concealed by sunglasses. No makeup, of course. The neighborhood was perfect for her purpose.

The streets were crowded with all sorts of people. Male couples holding hands and strolling. Black and white and Asian all mixed. Female couples kissing right on the streets. A kaleidoscope of clothing and costumes. Stores advertising elegant designer outfits which could be worn fashionably by literally anyone. There were rainbow banners hanging from lampposts and signs everywhere proclaiming the freedom and joy of the LGBT lifestyle.

Perfect, thought Helen. This was the perfect neighborhood to kill a man.

She had selected the rooftop of an apartment building across the street from the building where Matt Harrison lived. Access was easy through an unlocked roof door at the top of a stairwell. Harrison had an apartment on the third floor. Helen had checked it four times. As far as she could tell, he lived alone.

Because of the neighborhood, Helen assumed that Harrison was gay. That meant nothing to her. Harrison was a problem, gay or straight, and she had plans to solve that problem.

The Hechler & Koch sniper's rifle was tucked into a guitar case. No-one would suspect. At nearly ten pounds, the rifle weighed quite a bit more than a guitar, but Helen handled the case with ease. Nobody noticed her enter the building and climb the stairs to the roof.

She found the spot with the best view of Harrison's building and set up. There was a nice little wall on which she could rest the rifle while she waited.

Waiting gave her time to think about her late husband. Philip seemed like a good man when she married him. Great in bed, at the time, unconstrained by any particular moral or religious scruples. His job as an ATF agent meant access to lots of high grade booze, occasional recreational drugs, and plenty of money to supplement their incomes. They had a lot of fun at first. While her father was the one who taught Helen how to shoot, she and Philip had many happy hours together on the rifle range. She was a natural marksman with any sort of weapon, long gun or handgun. Helen had loved it. Philip was able to bring home all sorts of weapons from big ATF busts. They had quite a collection in the storage locker.

Too bad he criminals had a taste for the military weapons, she thought. This job of taking out Harrison would have been perfect for a deer rifle with a high-powered scope. And a deer rifle would have been a lot lighter. But Philip never brought one of those home. Philip had sold all the AR-15s and AK-47s except the one she used on Bill and the others at the gym. And that one, of course, was at the bottom of the bay. Oh, well.

Eventually, Philip developed more of an appetite for food and drink than he had for Helen. He ballooned up into a grossly obese drunk. The sex life totally disappeared. He never hit her or anything. He just became useless and rather disgusting. Helen never once regretted slipping a hefty dose of digitalis into his fourth or fifth Jack Daniels. When she claimed to have discovered his body in the Lay-Z-Boy chair the next morning, nobody thought anything of it. Just another fat alcoholic who had a heart attack.

She could see Harrison in the window of his apartment. He was just leaving. In a moment, he would come out the front door and onto the street. Just where Helen wanted him. Here he comes, she thought. It's show time.

Right behind Harrison was that black police detective. Helen was shocked. What was the cop doing there? It was the same detective that had interviewed her in her office. Suddenly it dawned on her. The cop lived here. With Harrison. These men were obviously a couple. She really did not want to shoot a cop. Nor did she want to make her shot in front of the cops. This was the one thing that Helen hated, surprises. She did not have time to recalculate her plan. She had to act now. Her hands began to tremble slightly. Helen did not do well when things did not go according to her plan. The little trembling in her hands made Helen flinch just as she was pulling the trigger.

◆ ◆ ◆

Duane heard Matt scream in the same instant that his lover collapsed. Blood was spurting out of Matt's leg, which was twisted into a grotesque position.

Duane's first instinct was to protect Matt. He covered his body with his own, using his bare hands in a futile attempt to stop the gushing blood. Duane waited for a second shot. Nothing. Just Matt's groaning, and the awful bleeding.

No more gunshots, so Duane had to act to save Matt. He removed his belt and made a crude tourniquet around Matt's thigh. That seemed to slow or stop the bleeding. Drenched in blood, Duane dragged Matt off the front porch into some bushes. Duane's head and eyes looked in all directions for signs of the shooter.

Duane's priority had to be to his lover. The bleeding was slowing, maybe stopped for now. Matt continued to groan, mumbling an occasional word. He was clearly conscious. Duane felt that, for the time being, Matt was safe and probably stable. Now he could concentrate on being a good cop. He took out his pistol and looked across the street. The single shot had to have come from one of the rooftops. In his heart, Duane knew that he would see no sign of the assailant. The sniper had missed and was surely long gone by now. There was no reason to leave Matt's side. Just keep the pistol out and call for help.

♦ ♦ ♦

Helen's fingers were shaking as she tossed the fedora, sunglasses and guitar case into the trunk of her car. The impossible had just happened. She had to do something. She had to act quickly. As the BMW pulled away from the scene of the shooting, Helen called Patricia.

"I missed," she said.

"What? You never miss. What happened?"

Helen regained control. Her nerves calmed down and her hands stopped shaking. "Shut up and listen. They're taking Harrison to our hospital. You have to do something. Maybe what you did with the fat lady from Alabama."

"What are his injuries?" asked Patricia, her words clear and under control. Helen was glad that Patricia seemed able to focus on the problem at hand.

"I shot him in the thigh. From the look of his leg, it's probably broken. He's lost a lot of blood. I think his partner may be that black cop. The cop was there and I think he'll ride in the ambulance with Harrison to the hospital. Be careful. And don't fuck this up like you did the Davenport thing."

"I'll take care of it. Make sure you get out of there. And don't forget to toss the rifle in the bay."

♦ ♦ ♦

When the junior resident called from the emergency room, Keith was already in surgery, finishing up plating a fracture of the forearm.

"Keith," said the junior resident, "Dr. Harrison from pathology is in the ER. He's been shot. Femur's shattered to hell. I think it got the femoral artery as well. Fortunately a cop put a tourniquet on. We're bringing him straight up to surgery. Vascular surgery has been called and they're on the way. Of course, we need to stabilize the fracture before they can do their vascular repair."

"Matt Harrison?" Keith's heart felt like it stopped and he could not get a breath in. His best friend had been shot. It took a few seconds for Keith to calm himself, but he knew he had to give his best for his friend.

"How bad is the femur?"

"Like a box of cornflakes," said the junior resident.

"I'll have the nurses pull the locking plates," said Keith. "We'll stabilize the fracture quickly so they can fix the vascular injury. See you in O.R. 10."

◆ ◆ ◆

Mary caught a glimpse of Patricia Roberts running down the hall toward the stairwell. It was a remarkable sight. Staff was repeatedly taught not to run in the halls. So, seeing the Director of Nursing sprinting in a fancy dress and spike heels got Mary's attention.

For a moment, Mary wondered how anyone could run in those shoes. Patricia's regular gym activity must be paying off. Then Mary asked herself the more important question. Why was Patricia running down the hall?

Mary decided to follow her. Quickly, but silently she entered the stairwell. The clicking of high heels was above Mary, on the fourth floor, the door opened and the clicking stopped. Mary followed. As she opened the door to look, she saw Patricia entering the female locker room for the surgery suite, still moving quickly. Mary decided to enter the surgical suite by the front door and pass the front desk. The desk was not staffed. Everyone must be in the operating rooms. Mary found a paper cap and a surgical mask, which she donned, leaving only her eyes visible. Mary was already in scrubs, since that was her uniform while working. She grabbed a clipboard with some forms on it from the front desk. Then she found a cabinet in the hallway with a good view of the door to the female locker room. Squatting on the floor, she pretended to inspect and re-arrange some bottles in the cabinet.

Soon Patricia emerged from the locker room, dressed in scrubs, sneakers, cap, and mask. Walking briskly and purposefully, she headed down the hall to a corridor which went behind the operating rooms. This corridor had little traffic, it was used mostly by housekeeping and maintenance or for circulating nurses who needed to get special equipment that was not stored in the operating room itself. Mary peeked around a corner and saw Patricia enter Operating Room 10 from the back door.

OR 10 was for orthopedics, Mary knew. The corridor was now clear, so she silently opened the back door into which Patricia had disappeared. Patricia was kneeling behind the anesthesia machine, a wrench in her hand. The tubing from the oxygen tank to the machine was dangling loose. Patricia was about to apply the wrench to the tubing carrying the nitrous oxide.

"Hey!" shouted Mary, "what the hell are you doing?"

Patricia startled, then jumped to her feet. With amazing speed she threw the wrench straight at Mary's head.

Mary could not completely get out of the way. The wrench struck her behind the right ear, a glancing blow but enough to knock her down. Mary saw sparking lights, then darkness. It only lasted a few seconds. Then Mary was foggy, but aware.

Patricia raced past Mary, who struggled to her feet and followed. Mary did not even think about what she might do if she caught up to Patricia, who had six inches in height and thirty pounds in weight over her. Patricia was also in excellent physical condition. Mary just had to catch her, to stop her. At that moment, it didn't occur to Mary that she was in pursuit of a killer.

Back into the stairwell and up one flight of steps. Patricia produced her master key and opened the doors to the old Five South nursing unit. All was dark inside.

Mary managed to get two fingers around the door to Five South just as it was swinging shut. No light and no sound. For a minute, Mary stood beside the door and listened. The only sounds she heard were the pounding of her own heart and her rapid breathing. She tried to hold her breath, but could not. She tried to breathe slowly and deeply, making as little sound as possible. This failed. Mary was scared. She felt along the wall until she found the overhead light switch.

The fluorescent bulbs in the light above the nurses' desk sputtered and flashed as they came on. Mary's eyes had not adjusted when Patricia came flying at her, wielding the top half of an IV pole like a broadsword and screaming like a demon out of hell.

Mary managed to duck and the metal pole swished above her head. Patricia's momentum carried her past Mary, which allowed Mary to scamper behind the nurses' desk. Frantically she looked around for something she could use as a weapon to defend herself. Dusty old gurneys and wheelchairs were everywhere, along with patient bedside cabinets.

Wham! The IV pole slammed straight down onto the nurses' desk, missing Mary by inches. She retreated behind the desk. Patricia was between her and the door, so there was no hope of escape. She would have to stand and fight. Patricia came around the desk toward her, whirling the IV pole in the air above her head. The look on Patricia's face was pure hate. Mary continued to back up, groping for anything she could grab.

Suddenly Patricia struck again, screaming in rage. Mary ducked to avoid the blow, down onto her knees. She groped desperately for a weapon. Then her hand contacted a small round stool on wheels. Desperately, Mary shoved the little stool with all her might toward Patricia. Patricia was charging at Mary, ready to bring the IV pole down on her head. The little stool hit Patricia in the right knee. Her left foot was in the air, almost leaping toward Mary. The little stool had enough impact to cause Patricia to lose her balance. It was a perfect shot.

Patricia lost her balance and fell down flat on her face, dropping the IV pole. This was Mary's chance. She looked frantically for something to use. Patricia was up on her hands, coming to her feet. Mary grabbed a dusty four-year-old copy of the Physicians' Desk Reference from the old nurses' desk. Using both hands and all the strength she could bring to bear, Mary brought the heavy book down on Patricia's head.

Patricia went down like a stone, hitting her forehead on the tile floor. Mary stood and looked, holding the book. Patricia was breathing, but not moving. Fumbling through the drawers at the nurses' desk, Mary found a roll of two inch adhesive tape, the old-fashioned cloth tape that was strong as hell and took all the hair off a person when it was removed. With the skill of an experienced staff nurse, Mary wrapped the tape around Patricia's wrists, binding them together. She repeated the tape binding at Patricia's ankles. As Mary was finishing, Patricia began to stir.

Patricia hissed and cursed like a trapped she-devil, writhing like a serpent with her wrists and ankles bound.

"You goddam, fucking Filipino bitch. I'll kill you. I'll cut your eyes out. I'll carve out your heart and eat it for lunch. Goddam you! You're fired!"

"One of us is going to lose her job," said Mary, "but I don't think it will be me."

Mary had won. She was safe. But she didn't feel like a victor. Fear and relief welled up in her and spilled out of her eyes.

Mary took a deep breath and dialed 911.

TWENTY-THREE

WHEN KEITH AND the anesthesia resident entered OR 10, the anesthesiologist saw the wrench on the floor of the operating room and the disconnected oxygen tube. Muttering curses, he hooked up the anesthesia machine properly and made sure that everything was working normally.

It broke Keith's heart to see Matt so badly injured. Dr. Romano, head of the orthopedic trauma service, happened to be in the hospital and was called in. Keith and Romano made an excellent, fast team. The big locking plate that they applied to the side of Matt's femur maintained the length of the bone as well as the alignment. With the strong, rigid plate, the section of bone that had been shattered into tiny fragments by the bullet was bypassed. The big incision and the rigid plate allowed excellent access for the vascular surgeons to repair Matt's artery. While it took nearly four hours altogether, the surgery was a success. While the recovery would be lengthy, Matt would be fine.

There were several messages from Mary on Keith's cell phone when he got out of surgery. He called and she said they needed to talk immediately. Mary and Duane were in the hospital cafeteria, sipping coffee and waiting for word about Matt. Duane was still covered in dried blood. Mary's scrubs were filthy from her scuffles with Patricia.

"Matt will be fine," said Keith when he joined them. "He needed a few units of blood and he's going to be hell in the airport metal detector from all the hardware we put in him. But he'll be fine. He'll be whining and griping, I'm sure. And he'll complain that I gave him an ugly scar."

"Did you give him an ugly scar?" asked Duane. "I'm the one who has to live with him, you know."

"Matt will consider any scar ugly," said Keith, "and we'll really enjoy listening to his moaning, because he'll be alive to torment us all for a really long time."

The three of them laughed a little. A few tears formed in Duane's eyes.

Mary told them about catching Patricia trying to switch the oxygen and the nitrous oxide tubes on the anesthesia machine in the orthopedic room, the chase up to Five South and the ensuing fight.

"Ms. Roberts was going to finish the job that the bullet failed to complete," said Duane. "Why try to kill Matt, though?"

Keith knew the answer.

"Matt was helping me look at the series of nasty infections on routine orthopedic cases and one fatal infection in an innocent baby," he said. "They were all caused by the same identical germ. It turned out to be a germ that was stolen from the hospital laboratory. Mary found the germ growing in a culture in Patricia Roberts' refrigerator. She stole some of it and

Matt was testing it in the lab. Matt called me this afternoon and told me that the germ that Mary brought him was the one that caused the infections."

"So Patricia was deliberately infecting the orthopedic patients with MRSA," said Mary.

"How did you get the germ out of Ms. Roberts' refrigerator, Mary?" asked Duane.

Mary blushed and looked at the floor.

"Well, I kind of broke in to her apartment."

"Oh, Mary," Duane said, "I'm impressed. But that's a crime, you know. And the evidence you stole isn't admissible in court."

"But we have plenty of evidence that is admissible," said Stuart, who had entered the cafeteria.

Nodding to Duane he said, "I was told that I could find you here, Detective. I heard about Dr. Harrison. I'm sorry. But Jim Davenport and I have, I think, unraveled this mess. And it may be time for you to make some arrests."

"I know what killed Mabel Osborne, the lady from Alabama," said Keith. "Patricia Roberts switched the gas lines on the anesthesia machine. She was trying to do the same thing and kill Matt tonight. Until Mary interrupted her. Mary, you probably saved Matt's life. Patricia somehow learned that Matt was onto her with the MRSA and she decided to silence him forever."

"Not just Ms. Roberts," said Duane. "She couldn't have pulled the trigger in the Castro district and gotten back to the hospital. She's in this with someone else. Someone who called ahead and ordered her to finish the job."

"The person who shot Matt," said Keith.

"Yes," said Stuart, "and certainly the person who killed Bill Henderson and shot all those other people. An expert marksman."

"Why?" asked Mary. "So much harm. So many people hurt. Why?"

"To prevent a hospital audit that would expose the fraud and theft of millions of dollars," said Stuart. "Jim Davenport and I have been working on this all day. Patricia Roberts and Helen Crawford stole fifteen or twenty million dollars, Mary. Maybe more. Jim Davenport and Wayne Patterson were two members of the hospital board who were demanding a complete audit of the hospital finances. They wanted to make sure that the hospital could afford to spend money on a new orthopedic institute. The audit might expose the fraud. Crawford and Roberts knew that if they could undermine the orthopedic department and get the orthopedic institute project cancelled, there would be no reason to do the audit. Also, they wanted to get rid of Davenport and Patterson. Crawford poisoned Patterson's wife so that the police would suspect him. The combination of the loss of his wife and him being a murder suspect would get Patterson off the board. Then they tried to get rid of Davenport, the other supporter of the audit."

"So somebody really did try to kill that old bastard Davenport?" asked Keith. "He wasn't just paranoid?"

"Oh, my God," exclaimed Mary. "I forgot in my excitement about the bacterial culture. There was a bottle of insulin in Patricia Roberts' refrigerator."

"Jesus," said Keith, "she tried to kill Davenport, then blamed it as a medication error on your friend."

"Is the insulin still there, Mary?" asked Duane.

"I think so," she said. "Patricia took the culture out and put it in an old duffel bag. I saw that. But I didn't see her take the insulin. In fact, now that I think about it, the insulin was still in the refrigerator. I looked before I left the apartment. I took pictures in the apartment with my phone, including some that show the insulin bottle in the refrigerator."

"Very resourceful, Mary, but your phone pictures aren't admissible in court either. They were taken during the commission of a crime."

Mary and Keith looked at each other. Mary had done something very brave, very daring, but also something very illegal. She did not want to follow her brother Alex into prison.

"Where is Ms. Roberts now?" asked Duane.

"At Sunset police station," answered Mary. "When I called the police, that's where they took her. I'm not sure that they believed my version of what happened. She was spewing curses and lies as they hauled her out of Five South. I think they were going to hold on to her until they talked to you, Duane."

"I've got to get over there," said Duane. "It's all unraveling now. Dr. Stuart and Mr. Davenport helped discover the fraud. Mary found the bacteria and the insulin. And Mary caught her trying to kill Matt. That's a serious load of facts. When I confront her with that, I should be able to get her to confess. We can cut her a deal if she gives up Helen Crawford. I need better evidence against Helen Crawford."

"Now I know what Helen Crawford did," said Keith, "and I don't need any more evidence."

Keith was furious now. He had maintained his focus and his composure while he operated on his best friend. Now he knew who shot Matt and who shot Bill Henderson and the innocent people at the gym. Keith felt only rage.

♦ ♦ ♦

Helen Crawford's first stop had to be her apartment on Nob Hill. The clothes she wore to shoot Harrison had to go into a trash bag. A bunch of do-gooders in the building had a collection bin for Goodwill. Helen planned to drop the trash bag full of clothes into that bin.

She called Patricia on her cell phone. It went straight to voice mail. Changing into business clothes, Helen poured herself a double Johnnie Walker Blue. She needed the warm reassurance that the whiskey gave her. She scolded herself for missing with the sniper rifle today.

Not good, she thought. The damn thing was too heavy.

She much preferred the AR-15 that she had used to kill Bill Henderson. But that was at the bottom of the bay, as the Hechler and Koch would be in an hour or so.

Damn rifle. And damn her dead husband. Why the hell did he sell all the AR-15s?

She would never admit that it was her fault that she blew the shot.

After her drink, Helen took the car out of the garage. It was a short drive to the marina at South Beach Harbor, near AT&T Park. Nobody noticed when she parked the car and removed the guitar case from the trunk. Just another artistic San Franciscan on an evening stroll by the bay. There was no one around when she stepped out onto a pier and slung the guitar case, weighted down by a sniper rifle, into San Francisco Bay. Helen smiled as she watched the bubbles from the sinking case.

She tried Patricia on her cell again. Once more, it went straight to voice mail.

Soon after getting back to her apartment, her second double Scotch in hand, her cell phone rang.

"Patricia?"

"Ms. Crawford, this is Daniel Silverman, the administrator on call at the hospital."

Helen had instituted a program of having one of the middle managers on call at all times. It looked good to the board and the medical staff, but was mostly just a gesture, creating the illusion that administration was always available to help. Or that administration actually gave a shit. Administrative call was only for second-tier executives. Top-ranked administrators, like Patricia, the CFO, the COO, and, of course, Helen herself were simply too important to be bothered by nuisance calls from nurses or patients. Helen told the board when she created the program that the administrator on call could get in touch with her at all times. However, to be called personally by some obsequious flunky was unprecedented.

"Yes."

"Well, ma'am, I just thought that you should know. The police are all over the hospital. One of the doctors has been shot. And there is some sort of fuss in the operating room. And the police just arrested Ms. Roberts. It is all very embarrassing. The front of the hospital is full of squad cars."

Helen had to think to breathe.

"Thank you, um, Mister…."

"Silverman, ma'am."

"Yes, of course. Mr. Silverman. I'll be on my way in to the hospital immediately."

Don't panic, thought Helen. You've been planning your exit from San Francisco for months. You didn't plan to have to make an emergency exit, but you know what has to be done. First, the airlines. Get your ticket. You can do that online. Pack the suitcase. Put the bank account information in your purse. Clean out the little safe in your home office. Stick the little .25 caliber automatic in your purse. No, wait. Do you need the pistol? If there are cops all over the hospital, someone may come looking for you. Maybe a solitary cop. It won't hurt to have it. Don't try to take it through security at the airport, though. Ditch it in the lady's room before you get to the security checkpoint.

There was a plane at 2:00 AM for Houston. She bought a first-class ticket on the internet and printed her boarding pass. From Houston she could easily get a flight to the Cayman Islands. She had ten million dollars in a bank account in the

Caymans. Helen had little doubt that she could get Patricia's ten million as well, with a little work at the bank. Assuming that Patricia would not be joining her. Not likely if the cops had her. Helen wondered if Patricia had been arrested before or after she killed Harrison. Hopefully after.

Helen took her time packing the suitcase with everything she could fit in that was of value. Before she left the apartment, she turned off her cell phone, resolving to toss it out the window on the 101 freeway. One last glance at the apartment and she was off to the airport.

♦ ♦ ♦

It took Keith only a short time to learn the hospital CEO's home address. Keith had only seen her a few times. Usually when Ms. Crawford was giving a hospital tour to some real or potential big donor. She never spoke to him, of course, or even made eye contact. But Keith was sure that he could recognize her. And he was mad as hell. Keith did not need to be bothered with warrants and evidence and the sorts of things that Duane needed to act. Keith was going to bring this bitch in himself and let Duane take it from there. And Keith was going to do it now.

The roar of the Harley-Davidson echoed on the streets of San Francisco. There was not much traffic, for a change, and he made good time to Nob Hill. As he arrived at Helen Crawford's building, he saw a woman driving a silver BMW x6 luxury sedan pull out of the underground parking. Keith knew it was Helen Crawford.

Keith was not trained in police surveillance and had no idea how he was supposed to follow a car without being spotted. The throaty rumble of his Harley-Davidson V-twin was hardly subtle in any event. Keith just stayed behind the BMW. When Helen got on the 101 freeway headed south toward the airport, Keith learned what the BMW commercials on TV were really all about. The TwinPower Turbo engines kicked in and the BMW took off like a rocket. Keith pushed the Harley as hard as he ever had, up to 100 miles an hour. He had never taken the bike that fast and he was scared to death. The Heritage Softail was a touring bike, a street hog, not some crotch rocket racer. Neither the Harley nor Keith were built for this kind of riding. He kept a vice-like grip on the handlebar, throttle wide open, knowing in his heart that if he dropped the bike at this speed, it would be his last ride. All the time, his eyes were fixed on the tail lights of the BMW. It swerved and changed lanes with the agility of a gazelle. Keith kept her in sight but could not keep up with the BMW. She was almost half a mile ahead when he saw her get off the Bayshore freeway.

♦ ♦ ♦

Helen had to slow down for the airport exit. She had a lead on the motorcycle, enough time to slip into the parking garage and grab her suitcase. With a confirmed first-class ticket and a boarding pass, Helen simply checked her suitcase at the American Airlines desk and headed toward the TSA security checkpoint. She was nearly home free.

♦ ♦ ♦

Keith had acquired a few police cars chasing him down the 101. Weaving the Harley around the gate arm, he entered the parking garage. The sirens told him that the police had followed. He spotted the BMW in a slot near the exit that led toward the American Airlines departure area. He parked the Harley in a reserved handicap spot, tossed his helmet onto the handlebar, and took off at a run into the terminal.

Glancing right and left, Keith thought he saw Helen heading left toward the security checkpoint. That was fine with Keith. Between the TSA agents and the cops on his tail, there should be plenty of representation from law enforcement. He ran to his left.

♦ ♦ ♦

Glancing around, Helen saw Keith behind her coming at a run. There weren't very many people in the terminal at this hour, but enough of a crowd that she could get lost. She did not see any San Francisco police or airport security nearby. They would come quickly, she knew, but she had time. If she did this right, the police would not know who to look for. Dressed in a professional business suit, she would be the last person that the cops would suspect.

She carefully removed the .25 automatic from her purse. She figured that she could shoot the orthopedic resident, then scream and run for the nearest ladies' room. She knew that the gunshots would incite panic and people would be running in all directions. No-one would suspect a nicely dressed woman. She could kill Grant and drop the pistol in the trash in the bathroom, then board her plane.

♦ ♦ ♦

Stuart gripped Helen's arm firmly.

"Drop the gun, Helen," Stuart said. "You've done enough shooting for the day."

He tightened his grip and the pistol slipped from her hand. She turned to face Stuart, her face a mask of rage.

"I'm afraid that you're going to miss your plane," said Stuart.

Keith arrived, followed by two out-of-breath Highway Patrol officers and two more uniformed SFPD officers.

"Officers, take this woman into custody," Stuart said. "She's wanted for attempted murder and is attempting to flee the country. Contact Detective Duane Wilson of SFPD to confirm what I just said.

One of the CHP officers was grabbing Keith and applying handcuffs. The others looked at Stuart and Helen and the pistol on the floor in confusion.

"Who the hell are you?" an SFPD officer asked Stuart.

"I'm Dr. Raymond Stuart and this young man is Dr. Keith Grant. We were in pursuit of this woman, Helen Crawford. Please call Detective Wilson. You'll see we're telling the truth."

"They're lying," said Helen, "I was just going to catch a plane to Houston to visit my mother. This man with one eye attacked me with that gun."

The SFPD officer drew his pistol and motioned to Stuart and Helen. "You're all coming with me to our airport office and we'll get this sorted out. Consider yourselves all under arrest."

One of the CHP officers picked up the pistol. The other tightened the handcuffs on Keith. Stuart was the only one smiling as they marched off to the police office.

"Dr. Stuart, thanks for coming," said Keith, still handcuffed. "How did you get here so fast?"

"Modern technology," Stuart replied. "I figured that Crawford would run when her plans were falling apart. So I headed for the airport. While you were chasing her, I was on the cell phone with Duane and Mary. Great technology, this Bluetooth. Even works in my Jeep. Duane was able to tell me about Crawford's reservations on American Airlines. He also alerted the SFPD at the airport. As for the Highway Patrol, well, you brought them along."

TWENTY-FOUR

THE FOG WAS just beginning to appear on the western horizon when Stuart got down the steps to the beach. He carried his jacket, knowing that the temperature would fall rapidly as the fog arrived onshore. He was alone and wore the eye patch.

Helen Crawford and Patricia Roberts were locked up. The business side of health care had, in a way, reached a pinnacle in those two. For them, it was all about money. People were just there to be manipulated, discarded, or eliminated. For most of his career he had believed that health care was above that sort of thinking. All of us, doctors, nurses, administrators, therapists, even housekeepers and building engineers were supposed to be in this field to help other people. All of us should have some form of altruism. Caring for the sick was supposed to be a calling. What Crawford and Roberts had done was a kind of a betrayal. He felt hurt and very sad.

Raymond found this time of day to be particularly peaceful. He needed peace right how. He needed to heal. So he sat on his favorite rock and stared out at the ocean. A handful of brown pelicans dove like dive bombers into the water in search of fish. An occasional seagull squawked. Otherwise, there was just the rhythmic sound of the waves, the declining sun, and the approaching fog. He would sit there silently until the fog enfolded him, caressing him in its cold, silent embrace.

♦ ♦ ♦

The four young friends gathered at Matt and Duane's apartment, so that Matt would not have to bear the discomfort of travel. Mary brought the food, sparing them all the ordeal of Duane's cooking. Keith was very proud of her. Mary, in his view, could do it all.

"There is nothing at all sexy about crutches," complained Matt, hobbling around in the apartment after supper.

"Quit your whining," said Duane with a grin.

"I deliberately chose a career in pathology to stay away from all the action and excitement," said Matt. "Lots of money and almost no risk. Supervise the lab techs who do all the work. Sign the bills and collect the cash. Look at microscope slides while I drink coffee. The occasional stinky autopsy, but overall this is supposed to be a great gig. And who the hell gets shot? Me. The lab rat. The ghoul who lives in the autopsy room. I'm not supposed to see daylight, let alone get shot."

"You got shot in the evening," said Duane. "The sun was set, so you were fair game. Even for ghouls."

"For lunatics," said Matt, "or zombies or werewolves."

"Don't forget vampires," added Mary. "Vampires are my favorites."

"Since I was a witness at the time of your specialty selection, as you call it," said Keith, "let me set the record straight.

You didn't choose pathology because it was easy money and little risk, although those things are true. You chose pathology because you couldn't do anything on living people. You couldn't find the exit door with an otoscope. You couldn't hear a Led Zeppelin concert with a stethoscope. You couldn't feel an abdominal tumor the size of a watermelon. To this day you don't know what the retina of the eye looks like because you could never visualize it. In surgery, you couldn't tie a square knot. You only had two choices. Pathology or psychiatry."

"Oh, God," said Duane, "Matt as a psychiatrist. Then we literally would have the crazies in charge of the asylum."

"You're lucky that you had such good surgeons to put you back together," said Keith. He grinned at his friend. Keith was incredibly grateful to see his friend alive and hobbling on crutches. He would never admit it to Matt, but the sound of Matt's voice, even griping and whining, warmed his heart.

"Who care nothing for my sexy legs," complained Matt. "Did you see these scars?"

"Yes," they all answered in unison. Nobody wanted to look at Matt's scars again.

"You know," said Duane, "despite being total sociopaths, Helen Crawford and Patricia Roberts were very, very smart. Their scheme nearly worked. I think that if Bill Henderson hadn't discovered the problem with the books, they would have gotten away with it."

"Unless the board members got the audit they were asking for," said Keith.

"You know, I think they would have succeeded in stopping the audit. The orthopedic department would have been so discredited by the infections and the operative deaths that the proposal for the orthopedic institute would have died," said Duane. "And without the proposal, there was no reason to conduct the audit. By the time the regular hospital audit came around in a year or so, Crawford and Roberts would have been safely ensconced on a beach in the Caymans. They were very smart criminals indeed. No, the plan unraveled because of Bill Henderson."

"Poor Bill," said Keith. "A geeky guy just trying to do his job well. Bill was an accountant, for God's sake."

"I think that Helen Crawford and Patricia Roberts are pure evil," said Mary.

Keith saw Mary's lip start to quiver and a slight tremor in her hands. He put his arm around her and pulled her close.

"Well, Mary, you must be living proof that good triumphs over evil," said Duane. "You must have given Patricia Roberts one hell of a whupping. I don't know what you did to her, but she could hardly wait to confess to everything. She was begging for a deal. I think you must have scared the hell out of her."

"That's hard to believe," said Mary. "I was so afraid of her. Looking into her eyes when she was trying to kill me, I thought that I was staring at a demon straight out of hell."

Keith felt her shiver again and tightened the grip of his hug.

"Are you going to charge me with burglary?" Mary asked.

"What burglary?" said Duane. "With Patricia Roberts' confession, the district attorney doesn't need any of the evidence you uncovered in her apartment. She'll take a plea, get thirty to life with the possibility of parole. There won't be a trial for Ms. Roberts. She attested that Helen Crawford dreamed up the plan to infect the orthopedic patients and kill Mr. Davenport. Roberts was just the assassin for those things. We don't need the cultures or the insulin to convict Helen Crawford. Besides, the defense lawyer would argue that finding the germs and insulin in Patricia Roberts' refrigerator doesn't establish a link to Crawford. Even if the evidence was admissible it wouldn't be helpful. So, I repeat, what burglary?"

"Thank you, Duane," she said.

Keith alone heard her sigh and felt some of her tension relax.

"Thank you, Mary," said Duane. "You were the smartest detective on this case."

"Don't let that go to your head, Mary," said Keith. "You do need to discuss your burglary with Father Flynn in the confessional."

"Yeah, I know," she said, "and he'll give me a really big penance for this one."

"Well," said Duane, "I need to add to that penance. I'd like to confiscate the lock picking tools in your purse."

"Oooh, they have sentimental value," she said. "My brother gave them to me."

"Yeah, I know about your brother. He's not all that good with his own lock picking. If he was good, he wouldn't be a guest of the California Department of Corrections and Rehabilitation. And he has no business trying to teach lock picking to others since he's not very good himself. Get over it, Mary and hand them over."

Reluctantly, Mary gave Duane the little package of lock picks. Keith knew that parting with them was not as painful as she pretended. Mary was the one person in her family that Alex trusted with his secrets. Keith was certain that Mary knew where Alex had hidden his own set of lock picks.

"Maybe now we can get back to the business of medicine," said Matt.

"Like finding out new ways to raise the fees on routine lab tests," teased Duane.

"Or working on my investment portfolio," Matt added. "That BMW that Helen Crawford was driving is a sweet ride. I need to get one of those."

"Or maybe studying for my written board exams," said Keith. "Gotta get through that before I start my fellowship in pediatric orthopedics."

Keith looked right at Mary and was delighted with her expression of surprise and joy.

"Pediatrics!"

"Really, Keith, there's no money in that at all," said Matt. "Why did you pick pediatrics? Bunches of screaming kids with boogers and poopy diapers and broken arms. What are you, a masochist or a martyr?"

Keith looked deeply into Mary's black sparkling eyes. All he saw was love.

"Money isn't everything."

Later, Keith and Mary returned to Keith's apartment. Baby was perched on top of her cage. The mandatory exchange of greeting whistles and chirps was accomplished according to ritual. Noses and beaks were rubbed.

"Sit with me a minute," Keith gestured to the sofa. Mary sat down next to him. Baby moved to the edge of the cage and stared down at them, watching intently.

"You know, we make a pretty good team together," said Keith.

"You mean as amateur detectives?"

"Well, that, but more," he replied. "We laugh together. We've cried together. Each of us has held the other when the world seemed to be out of control."

"Yes. We've seen each other at our best and at our most vulnerable. We have the same values."

Keith slipped off the sofa and knelt on one knee.

"I love you with all my heart. I think that life with you really would be a sacrament. Mary, would you consider making our partnership complete and permanent?"

She stared at him. Her eyes began to tear up.

"Yes, Mary, this is a proposal," he said. "Will you marry me?"

Mary's face lit up with a radiant smile and tears of joy ran down her cheeks.

"Yes. Yes. Oh, yes."

They embraced and kissed. They held each other tenderly, saying nothing, for several minutes. Then Mary pulled away. With the usual sparkle in her eyes, she smiled at Keith.

"If Baby approves, of course. What do you say, Baby?"

"Wee-oo-weet."